'A slim volume rich in nuance and filled with deep passion for folklore and myths. In this spooky and eerie debut Matt Wesolowski introduces a very interesting contemporary concept of narrative structure which keeps the readers on their toes' Crime Review

'This gripping and slightly intense tale is one of the most unique and original plot-driven stories I have ever read' Postcard Reviews

'Wesolowski has taken a unique structure and used it to create a brilliantly written, enigmatic novel that draws the reader into the mystery of this story' Segnalibro

'The ending … well I didn't see THAT coming…' It's Book Talk

'Matt Wesolowski has shown that there are still new ways to excavate mystery within the crime-fiction genre' Bolo Books

'Outstanding. Five stars from me' Mrs Bloggs' Books

'What a creepily fantastic book! And man, that curve-ball thrown at the very end, WOW!' The Pages in Between

'Fantastic storytelling in a unique style' Steph's Book Blog

'It crosses multiple genres with Matt Wesolowski's background in writing horror seeping through the pages, with unexpected twists and truths unveiled' Swirl & Thread

'The most original book I have read in a long, long time' Reflections of a Reader

'A very creeping, slow-building and tantalisingly surprising read' Jen Meds Book Reviews

'Highly original and superbly executed, and makes for an absorbing and thrilling read' The Book Review Café

'A perfect choice for a Book Group' Never Imitate

'A great book: original, engaging and written by an author that is one to watch' The Book Whisperer

'The frightening descriptions make the setting of the crime absolutely creepy and turns a beautiful but dangerous place into an eerie and living location' Chocolate N Waffles

'Once the last interview is over, the book just ends and then the cogs in your brain start turning…' Keeper of Pages

'Atmospheric, chilling and compellingly written' From First Page to Last

'Unique, original, compelling' Girl vs Books

'Blowing between past and present, legends and reality twirl a deadly dance with one another in this haunting tale of ethereal darkness and mystery. I urge you to read this incredible book!' Ronnie Turner

'Fantastically plotted … with depth and fear!' Have Books Will Read

'Perfect, original and so unexpected' Varietats

'Brings past and present colliding together to reveal secrets that I could never have guessed' By the Letter Book Reviews

'Dark, creepily atmospheric and horrifically intense' My Chestnut Reading Tree

'*Six Stories* will be one of my books of 2017' Espresso Coco

'You want to get lost in a book? Wesolowski makes it easy' Clues & Reviews

'A creepy tale that keeps you guessing!' Crime Book Junkie

'Once started you will not put this book down. It is impossible' Last Word Book Reviews

'Brilliantly, cleverly executed and a highly immersive read' Novel Gossip

'I am keen to see what Wesolowski releases next. There is always a high expectation to release something as compelling as the debut, but I have a suspicion that I don't need to worry with Wesolowski' The P Turners Book Blog

'A clever, original and captivating debut from a gifted storyteller' The Curious Ginger Cat

'Compelling, atmospheric and spine-tingling, it's the unseen terrors that cause us the most fear – think *The Blair Witch Project* with bells on it! Read it and weep!' Chapter in my Life

'Beautifully written' A Lover of Books

'A tense, dark tale of destruction, delivered with innovative style and a devastating ending' Claire Thinking

'At times it did not feel like I was reading a book – more akin to listening to an old storyteller spinning a yarn for the crowd in a smoky tavern. If you want a richly rewarding reading experience then *Six Stories* is it' Grab This Book

'This novel just packs a punch and is such an original and refreshing read' Chillers, Killers & Thrillers

'One of those books you so wish you'd thought of first…' Crime Worm

'I'm not sure what else to say, other than READ THE BOOK!' The Suspense Is Thrilling Me

'Brilliantly modern and gripping take on the classic thriller' Misti Moo Book Review

'Ultimately this is an author who knows exactly how to create a chilling atmosphere and who is able to tell a chilling story in a most imaginative and yes, chilling, way!' Bibliomaniac

'It's definitely a unique read – for a debut book it's altogether something else. Podcasts wrapped up in intrigue, a web of lies and some of the most complex characters you'll ever meet. Tell you something, those Northumberland woods will never look the same again…' The Book Trail

'The novel is essentially a crime thriller but it's Wesolowski's unique narrative structure that sets *Six Stories* apart' Words Shortlist

'A haunting and unsettling debut from an exciting new voice' The Owl on the Bookshelf

'The tension is on the verge of overwhelming … a truly unmissable read' Book Drunk

'This is a fantastic debut, incredibly assured' The Crime Novel Reader

'Seriously, seriously, SERIOUSLY good!' Page Turner's Nook

'A terrific mystery story, well written and full of suspense' Portobello Book Blog

'Utterly compelling and despite being entirely engrossed, I defy you not to be shocked by the ending. An original concept with skilled execution – totally unputdownable!' Elementary V Watson

'There was an addictive quality to the writing, tinged with just enough horror and unexplained phenomena to make you shudder and read on, peeking through your fingers' Finding Time To Write

'It flows so beautifully and sucks the reader in completely!' Lisa's Book Reviews

'Skillful writing that blindsides you with a twist you never see coming … masterful' Jena Brown Writes

'One of my top reads of this year, in great company with Hanya Yanhingara's *A Little Life* and Ali Land's *Good Me Bad Me*' I Loved Reading This

'Wesolowski has managed to combine literary brilliance with modern technology – what a fu*king achievement! Absolutely mind blowing!' Emma the Little Bookworm

'One of those stories that you know will get picked up by a TV production company and when they film it on location, it will be gritty, dark and down right grim – but some of the best television you will ever witness' The P Turners Book Blog

'If this was made into a radio drama it would be one of the best and darkest programmes out there…' The Library Door

'The haunting, chilling narrative draws to a clever and shocking conclusion that will leave your mind racing and have you questioning every detail you've read' Earl Grey and Cupcakes

'Unique, interesting, modern and unpredictable' Always Trust in Books

HYDRA

ABOUT THE AUTHOR

Matt Wesolowski is from Newcastle-Upon-Tyne in the UK. He is an English tutor for young people in care. Matt started his writing career in horror, and his short horror fiction has been published in numerous UK- and US-based anthologies such as *Midnight Movie Creature Feature*, *Selfies from the End of the World*, *Cold Iron* and many more. His novella, *The Black Land*, a horror set on the Northumberland coast, was published in 2013. Matt was a winner of the Pitch Perfect competition at Bloody Scotland Crime Writing Festival in 2015. His debut thriller, *Six Stories*, was an Amazon bestseller in the USA, Canada, the UK and Australia, and a WHSmith Fresh Talent pick, and film rights were sold to a major Hollywood studio.

Follow Matt on Twitter @ConcreteKraken and on his website: mjwesolowskiauthor.wordpress.com

Hydra

MATT WESOLOWSKI

ORENDA
BOOKS

Orenda Books
16 Carson Road
West Dulwich
London SE21 8HU
www.orendabooks.co.uk

First published in the United Kingdom by Orenda Books, 2018

ISBN 978-1-910633-97-7
eISBN 978-1-910633-98-4

Typeset in Garamond by MacGuru Ltd
Printed and bound by CPI Group (UK) Ltd, Croydon CR0 4YY

This is a work of fiction. Names, characters, places and incidents are either products of the author's imagination or are used fictitiously. Any resemblance to actual events, locales or persons, living or dead, is entirely coincidental.

SALES & DISTRIBUTION

In the UK and elsewhere in Europe:
Turnaround Publisher Services
Unit 3, Olympia Trading Estate
Coburg Road
Wood Green
London
N22 6TZ
www.turnaround-uk.com

In USA/Canada:
Trafalgar Square Publishing
Independent Publishers Group
814 North Franklin Street
Chicago, IL 60610
USA
www.ipgbook.com

In Australia/New Zealand:
Affirm Press
28 Thistlethwaite Street
South Melbourne VIC 3205
Australia
www.affirmpress.com.au

'Everyone lives in two worlds.'

Joe Hill, *NOS4R2*

'All life is only a set of pictures in the brain, among which there is no difference betwixt those born of real things and those born of inward dreamings, and no cause to value the one above the other.'

HP Lovecraft, 'The Silver Key' in *Weird Tales*

TorrentWraith – Audio (Music & Sounds)

Type	Name
Audio	**Arla Macleod Rec001 [320KBPS]** Uploaded **6 weeks** ago, Size 45.4 MiB. ULed by JBazzzzz666

I heard them at lunchtime, over the sound of the radio.
    They followed me here.
    After everything that's happened, they followed me…
    I don't know what they want.

❉❉

So, anyway, hi, hello, this is me. As you can see, I'm recording this in my room. Look, there's the window; it's sunny out today. If I zoom in – hang on … There; it's blurry cos of the window, but look, you can see how the sun falls on the fields, on those hills up in the distance, like a slice of yellow. Beautiful isn't it? I wonder if you stood up there and looked back here, would you see this place, in the shade? I wonder what it would look like from up there.

❉❉

You told me I had to record myself as soon as I saw one – or heard one – it's hard to remember which it is sometimes, everything's all … fuzzy … like I'm walking through treacle. I get distracted by smells: the smell of the floors in the corridor first thing – lemony. I breathe it in, take great gulps; I can almost taste it. That's what I imagine when I see the sun on the fields, that yellow, lemony smell.
    Sorry, yeah, so I heard one just before, at lunch. I'm recording this after lunch.
    I listen to the radio when I'm having my lunch: Radio 1, the lunchtime show. It's funny and I like the music – hum along while I'm eating. Imagine

telling fifteen-year-old me that I'd be humming along to the radio. Fifteen-year-old me would've snorted and called bullshit. Fifteen-year-old me would have flashed the band names scrawled in Tipp-Ex on her schoolbag and called present-day me a fat, brainwashed sellout.

Food, though. You can smell cooking everywhere here; it's like the whole place is breathing the smell of food. It's not that nasty, canteen smell either, like old, brown fat. You can smell potatoes roasting; you can smell meat cooking, pastry baking. It drives me crazy, makes my tummy rumble constantly. When I was a kid, my mam used to make soda bread. I used to help her, stirring it all together in a bowl – buttermilk and flour. Mam used to let me do the salt. I'll never forget the taste when it first came out of the oven. And the texture: hard and crispy on top, fluffy in the middle, like biting into a storm cloud.

At lunch we were having toad-in-the-hole, and I just sat staring down into it. They do it in a circle; it looks like a moon. Each portion's a circle of Yorkshire pudding with the two ends of the sausage sticking out like a sea monster. A sea monster in a muddy gravy puddle. My mouth was watering, like, so much, I was having to swallow it back or else it would have gone all over the table, joining that puddle of gravy. That would have been embarrassing. But luckily there wasn't anyone else here. I have my lunch in my room.

Sometimes we have cake for pudding. Fridays, usually. They're the best days. We have fish and chips in batter, the flesh so soft and fluffy it glides into sections on your tongue before you've even bitten down; the batter crispy, melt-in-the-mouth. Vinegar. I always ask for vinegar, loads of it, so my chips are soaking.

Denise always shakes her head but she doesn't really mind. 'What are Fridays for?' she always says, and that makes me smile. She levers the fish onto my plate, on top of the chips, and you can see the vinegar pooling around the pile of mushy peas.

Fish and chips; cake and custard for afters.

I need to stop talking about food. Really.

I used to have a thirty-inch waist, you know? You wouldn't believe it, would you? Look at that. Ugh. That's called *flab*. I reckon I'm forty inches now, at least.

Oh well…

But yeah, anyway. I'm going to talk about what I'm supposed to be talking about. Rather than food.

I heard it above the noise of all that – the knives and forks and eating, and the smells, and Radio 1.

I'd been doing so well, too.

It were crying. That's what the sound were: crying.

It were coming from outside. Through the window at first, like it were far away. Not as far as the fields. Just … away…

I didn't mind it at first, not until it started sounding like it were *in* the room. Right beside me, then behind me, then in front – you know how sounds do if you think about them for too long?

Crying.

Just this awful crying.

Mams and dads, they're programmed to react to stuff like that. Like, if they hear it, they can't help doing something about it. I think it's instinct.

Well, it must be like that for me too. Some instinct was pulling at me to react. I wonder what that instinct was? That's what you'll ask me in our next session.

Every part of me – every cell, every molecule of that cell – was telling me to go out there, to just push back my chair, climb over the table, smash the window and get out. I can't remember if the urge was to go *towards* the crying or get away from it. I can't remember.

I didn't though. I didn't. Not this time.

Well done me.

It started just as I sat down. My table faces the window and that's why I kept my head down. It were horrible. I very nearly looked up. That would have been bad. I could have called for someone; that would have been worse.

There were a load of options, a load of possibilities laid out in front of me, and I had the choice of what to do.

What I did was keep staring into that plate of toad-in-the-hole, proper staring at it like it was the most interesting thing I'd ever seen. After a little while the toad-in-the-hole became a face, the two ends of the sausage became the eyes, a crease in the batter became a mouth.

The crying kept on, louder and louder. It was like someone was tightening a screw in the side of my head, its tip pressing onto my brain, then bursting the side and going right in. Over and over, I could feel it in my veins, my nerves, my organs. Crying, crying.

I put my fork down gently, really gently, no slamming or crashing, and reached up for the little ticket thing you use to pull the blind down.

There was a moment then – a moment when I could have looked; I could have looked out. I know that view by heart: the lawn is stripy like a football pitch, the polytunnel like a big white caterpillar, the borders and two little circles of soil like eyes. We planted up the borders with bulbs last year, watched them sprout shoots – little green spears like there was an army of elves under the ground. Beyond that are the trees, which clump into a brown fuzz if I've not got my glasses on, and just disappear into the horizon with the hills all rising up … misty mountains.

They say if you see fairyland, if you look upon it, you'll never be able to go home. I've always known that. A part of me – an old, struggling part that hides under the meds – was pulling at me, biting at my heart, begging me to look.

The crying was coming from the lawn.

I could have seen what my mind was telling me was there.

When the crying began, they'd tried to make it sound like a cat. They did it to fool me, so I would look.

I'm not stupid though.

But they tried to make me look. They got louder with every cry, and I could hear breathing; rattling breath, lungs pulling in for another wail. I still held strong. The cries didn't have words – they said everything they needed to say. You know that saying, 'tugging on your heartstrings'? Well these were bell-ringers heaving up and down, relentless and desperate.

They were telling me to do what I shouldn't be doing; they were telling me to spoil everything, to break the window, feel the explosion of summer air over my face. It would smell like leaves and flowers and cut grass; underneath would be that sour tang of silage, manure, hot animal.

I would feel the grass under my feet, that rush in my chest as I ran. With all this extra weight I'd get a stitch. I wouldn't get far.

The thing is, though, I knew the crying had nothing to do with me leaving and running away across the fields; it was all about them.

About them coming in.

Then the crying turned into their voices. I've heard those voices before. They never cry, they just speak – on and on and on, the same questions. 'Why, why, why?' they ask, their questions curling round me, penetrating through everything like mist or fog. Over and over, their voices begging. But I don't answer.

Today, though … today they told me what I need to do.

How to stop them crying.

How to make them go away.

Episode 1: Black-Eyed Boy

—That knock. *Rat-a-tat-tat.* I could almost hear the ... the *smallness* of the finger. Not a knuckle but the joint, the index finger folded into a point. *Rat-a-tat-tat.* Against the wood.

I remember it sent this jolt of fear through me. Most knocks on the door do. Well, they did back then. I always thought that it was going to be someone coming to get me, to take me away. Yeah, I remember that anxiety from when I were young. It were always mixed with a little tug of ... what? Excitement? If someone were coming to take me away, where would we go?

Imagine thinking like that when you're a kid?

But hearing that knock then, that night, it were more than that; it were real. It were so real, it went through me. I felt that folded finger tapping against my bones. There were like a voice inside me, shouting at me, screaming at me – to stay put, not to answer the door.

If only I'd listened...

If only I'd listened.

The voice you've just heard – and please excuse the interference on the phone line – is that of Arla Macleod. Yes, that Arla Macleod. You've seen her face. Black-toothed, grinning like a ghoul on the front of T-shirts; staring from memes on the darker corners of the internet. Her name resonates through a whole generation.

I know there'll be a few of you who are already writing this podcast off as unethical and even callous, unkind. You'll say I'm taking advantage. A few of you are wondering why I've broken my usual protocol, stepped outside my comfort zone and investigated what seems to be a case that's at the other end of the spectrum from the cold graves I usually rake over.

Please, though, stick with me, hear me out. If only for a short while. Just hear why I'm prodding this sleeping bear.

You must forgive me for attempting to set up an interview with Arla Macleod. Practically every single journalist the world over has done the same, but I'm the only one that has succeeded. I didn't think she would even respond to my request and, to be perfectly honest, I had no idea what I wanted to ask her – I had no ideas prepared for this series, no story arc. But you can't pass these opportunities up.

You could even say that Arla chose me. Perhaps Arla is a fan of Six Stories. *Certainly,* Six Stories *will entice an influx of new listeners, as Arla has her own fans. For whatever reason, she agreed to speak to me. So I had no choice but to go ahead with the interview, did I?*

I should also say, before you press the 'stop' button, the unsubscribe button or make that nasty comment on iTunes, *that this interview was conducted with Arla's full cooperation. She was allowed to terminate it at any time and everything you hear in this opening episode has been approved by Arla herself.*

So rather than questioning the ethics of what we're about to do, or why Arla has become the unlikely poster child of a defiant generation, I'd say what you should be concerning yourself with instead is the question at the centre of Arla's case.

I've thought long and hard about this, I'm aware of the impact this series could potentially have and I've come to the conclusion that the crux of this can be found in what you're about to hear: in our first story; Arla's story. And the question at its centre is not about guilt or innocence. It's about whether what Arla is telling us is true.

—I thought, *they've found me.* After all these years, they'd finally tracked me down.

Maybe it was a relief? I think there was a small part of me that almost welcomed them, like I could stop running at last.

Welcome to Six Stories. *I'm Scott King.*
In the next six weeks, we will be looking back at what happened to

the Macleod family in 2014 – the incident more commonly known as 'the Macleod Massacre'. We'll be looking back from six different perspectives, seeing the events that unfolded through six pairs of eyes.

Then, my dear listeners, it'll be up to you. As you know by now, I'm not here to make judgements, draw conclusions, or speculate. I'm here to allow you to do that.

For newer listeners, I should make it clear that, as frustrating as it may be, this isn't an investigation that will reveal any new evidence – I am not a policeman, a forensic scientist or an FBI profiler. My podcast is more like a book group – a discussion about an old crime scene. We discuss things with the help of others, those who have agreed to look back on a tragedy.

We rake over old graves.

In this opening episode, we'll refresh ourselves with what we know – the so-called 'facts' about what happened to the Macleod family. We'll also allow Arla to have her say. And then we'll see where we go from there.

That OK? Good.

Welcome to episode one.

§§

—They asked me in court; they asked why I didn't close the door, why I didn't raise the alarm … why I said nowt to no one about them. And, it's like, for me that's just the most stupid question I've ever heard.

Arla's talking to me on the phone, a landline. The phone is the way we'll conduct our discussion. Unfortunately, Elmtree Manor will not allow me face-to-face access to its most notorious patient. They tell me about their reluctance in no uncertain terms: they fear a media firestorm, a feeding frenzy, like sharks around a school of sardines. I agree. That's why we've managed to keep this interview a secret until now.

Elmtree are aware of the questions they'll face when this series airs; they are aware of the spotlight that will shine on their facility. It won't help their patients, it won't help me and it certainly won't help Arla Macleod.

However, patients at Elmtree are entitled to make and receive phone calls, sometimes via video link. Where patients such as Arla are concerned, these are often monitored. Elmtree prefers that we do this rather than meeting personally – that we talk on the phone or via video.

I'm happy to respect that. As you know, I'm not interested in sharing my identity either. Who I am has no bearing on this, or indeed on any of my cases. What I do know is that my phone calls with Arla are conference calls and that, at any time, the medical professional who sits patiently beside her may advise whether our conversation can continue. Despite what she's done, Arla's welfare is paramount here. Wrong or right, that's the way it is.

But I digress. For now, let's lay out our intentions. Let's explain everything.

In this series of Six Stories, *we will look back on the events of November 2014. Through talking to Arla Macleod and others who knew her, we will try and formulate an opinion on a very complex and disturbing case.*

So what do we know about what occurred at 41 Redstart Road, Stanwel, England in the early hours of that winter morning?

Stanwel – with one 'l'; an apt symbol for the attitude of the town: stubborn, resistant to change – was once a thriving coal-mining community on the northwest coast of the United Kingdom. The Stanwel colliery was closed by the National Coal Board in 1965 – long before the miners' strikes of the 1980s. Some say that Stanwel itself closed then too. The town never recovered. The silent towers of the Stanwel coal-fired power station still stand along the coastline; bleak, monolithic reminders of a bygone age.

Stanwel is a hard place, crouched on the Fylde Coast, north of Blackpool. Betting shops have infected the town, bright in their unashamed opportunism. Men in ill-fitting suits stand under a gazebo on Stanwel High Street between the pound shop and the library, hawking cable television to passers-by. The older people of the community remember window ledges caked with soot, handkerchiefs with black stains and the grinding of the great wheel that brought the workers up from the coalface at the end of the day. To say Stanwel is depressing is a tired cliché about northern towns that have had their industry pulled from under their feet. But visiting the place as a diamond-bladed breeze cuts in from the Irish Sea and jangling electronic fairy music laced with the smell of old carpet wheezes from the door of yet another amusement arcade, one could be forgiven for using it.

—I don't know why anyone would want to stay there. When I was a teenager and that, me and my mates used to say that Stanwel's full of freaks and junkies. All we wanted to do were get out of there. Manchester or Liverpool, or up to Newcastle. Not too far but far enough.

Arla Macleod was not born in Stanwel. Her mother, Lucy, fled a life of poverty in Saltcoats, Ayrshire, on the west coast of Scotland when Arla was two years old and her sister Alice was a year younger. Arla's father, Conor Walsh, was a violent drunk and remained behind. Neither Arla nor Lucy was known to ever make contact with him again.

—I don't like to remember my real dad. I don't remember him, I think. I … dissociate. There are flashes. Like, sometimes, when people shout – men especially – I get this … this *tingling* feeling all over and I'm scared…

Lucy Walsh was accompanied south of the border by Stanley Macleod, who Lucy had befriended at her church group back in Scotland. Both of them spirited and hardworking, they persevered on their arrival in England, Stan taking a job as a refuse collector and Lucy working as a teaching assistant in a nursery. They married as soon as they could afford to. Like most in Stanwel, their life was modest. The Macleods did not stand out.

—I remember growing up down Redstart Road. It were a proper

nice childhood really. There were lots of other kids my age and the back gardens had this, like, interconnecting path at the bottom, with a great big fence where the train line was. Us kids used to play down there, for days it seemed. Out front was the road, and there was no reason for anyone who didn't live on Redstart to walk down there. Perfect really. Our mams and dads, they could just ... get on with stuff, I suppose.

The overriding thing I've noticed about Stanwel is its dignity. To look at, it's fairly run down, with its sagging high street, shops clinging on, tight rows of miners' cottages that open directly onto narrow pavements, and the largest road being the one leading out of town. But with the single 'l', the gardens fastidiously weeded and watered, the scrubbed wheelie bins, the trails of soap suds dribbling from driveways, it clearly has a stubborn pride.

Despite this, the 'grinding poverty' often affixed to descriptions of the town is clear for anyone to see. Jobs are rare – only to be found in call centres in the out-of-town industrial estates, or else accessed by long commutes to the region's larger cities. And drug addiction is a huge problem for the town – possibly its most obvious one. I'm alluding here to Arla's 'freaks and junkies' comment.

So, on the surface it appears that Stanwel has little going for it. Which begs the question, why did Stanley Macleod bring Lucy here? But Arla herself tells me how grateful her family was to get away from her real father. And, scratch beneath the surface and you find there's a lot more to this place than meets the eye. Stuff that might make it attractive for a family. Community allotments and a city farm nestle between the old slag heaps near the old colliery. The land around the abandoned power station is home to a few species of wading birds, and a small trust has been set up to protect them.

—Even when me and Alice were only little, Mam used to sit us down after Dad – Stan I mean when I say that – after Dad had one of his ... his little 'episodes', and she used to tell us what it were like living with my *real* dad; how he used to drag her round by the hair when she were pregnant. Alice used to get proper scared and she used to cuddle into me with her hands over her ears, like she couldn't bear to hear it. Mam said that sometimes she used to have to go out to the shop in sunglasses, grabbing onto the walls cos he'd battered her and her eyes were all swelled up. She said Stan's little episodes were nowt compared to that, and we should be grateful to him. We were.

The street Arla Macleod grew up on is a pleasant one: a row of cottages in what you might call a suburb of Stanwel. Many of the back gardens of Stanwel's houses are linked by paths like the one Arla describes, providing easy access to the neighbouring gardens. This small addition gives many of Stanwel's streets a sense of community; it's another of those hidden gems you find below the surface.

Later we'll learn more about what life was like for Arla in her younger years. For now, let's leave behind these peripheral observations and discuss what happened on that infamous night.

§§

Extract from North West Tonight, 10th February 2015
—Welcome to the programme. The headlines this Wednesday evening:

Stanwel family massacre: a woman has been sentenced to life in an institution for the killing of her parents and young sister. [*Fade out*]

[*Fade in*] Good evening. Twenty-one-year-old Arla Macleod of Stanwel was found guilty today of the manslaughter of her mother, stepfather and younger sister back in November of 2014. The judge gave the verdict of guilty with diminished responsibility… [*Fade out*]

[*Fade in*] It is considered particularly upsetting that twenty-year-old Alice Macleod's blossoming career as an athlete was cut short. Alice was undergoing trials to represent her country as a swimmer.

Arla Macleod, who bludgeoned her family to death with a hammer, was immediately taken to a secure hospital from Preston Crown Court, where she was convicted of manslaughter on the grounds of diminished responsibility. Macleod showed no emotion as her sentence was passed amid cheers from the public gallery and will now live out her life as a resident of Elmtree Manor Hospital, north Lancashire.

—That were made a big thing of, the fact that I showed 'no emotion'. They said it were because I were a psychopath, that I wasn't 'able' to feel things. Truth is I'd been medicated up to me eyeballs before the trial; I could barely even stay awake. The world was like … it was like I were wrapped up in cotton wool, like I were only half there, do you know what I mean? Like it weren't even me.

—Mr King? I need to let you know that's enough for today.

—*That's fine, thank you. And thank you, Arla, for talking to me.*

—A pleasure.

§§

I'm not sure what it was that stopped our interview; our agreed hour was far from up. Perhaps it was a test to see whether I would respect Elmtree Manor's wishes. These are tentative days, though, so I let it go. We'll hear from Arla again later.

For now, let's get some perspective.

Elmtree Manor, where Arla resides, is one of sixty medium-secure mental-health hospitals in England and Wales that house people deemed to be a danger either to themselves or others. At Elmtree, there are around two hundred residents – or patients, as they're known. The overwhelming majority have committed offences while mentally ill or else have been diagnosed with a mental illness while in prison. All are being held under the terms of the Mental Health Act. There are some who would say that Elmtree's patients, especially those like Arla Macleod, belong in higher-security institutions such as Broadmoor in Berkshire or Rampton in the East Midlands. Indeed, there are those who would say Elmtree is not punitive enough, especially for someone like Arla Macleod.

Elmtree is renowned for its modern design and for spearheading new therapeutic techniques. A state-of-the-art facility, it has been described by the columnists of the tabloids as 'better than a Premier Inn' and 'luxury slap-on-the-wrist with full board'.

The decidedly modern structure, which nestles near the Forest of Bowland, was once the imposing Fell Hospital, a towering Victorian asylum that blighted the picturesque countryside, its single, bat-haunted spire rising up into the sky amid the winding single-lane roads like Tolkien's tower of Orthanc.

All traces of those days are long gone now. It seems that even the screams and wails of its inhabitants have been fumigated out from between the cedar trees, neat lawns and working organic farm. What has rankled many a tabloid columnist is that, as Elmtree is 'medium secure', Arla Macleod and her ilk are free to wander the surrounding woodland, watch birds or help out on the small farm. Perhaps the fact that Arla's parents and sister will never again smell the grass and the tilled earth, or see the roll of thunderclouds cross the horizon, is what irks so many. However, unlike most medium-secure hospitals, Elmtree focuses on the maintenance of its patients' illnesses rather than their rehabilitation. This means its patients are rarely, if ever, discharged.

Arla, who will therefore see out the rest of her living days at Elmtree, never contested her guilt; the only questions were around the degree of her responsibility – whether she was aware of what she was doing at the time. I'm in no way qualified to comment on mental illness – I won't give any pop diagnosis; it would be an insult to the psychiatric profession for me to even try. All I can say is that Arla's guilt and her diminished responsibility were eventually decided in a court of law and her sentence was passed accordingly.

—Of course, it's too simplistic to explain what exactly is 'wrong' with Arla Macleod. We understand so much more about mental illness – and specifically the psychosis that the psychiatrists in court presented – that I think I'm safe in assuming her condition is a complex combination of things.

The voice you're hearing belongs to a doctor of criminal psychology, Dr Sarah White. Dr White has appeared on many television true-crime documentaries, most recently the three-part award-winning documentary on Robert Bonnet, The Quiet Ripper. *She talks to me via Skype.*

—I've never spoken to Arla Macleod, so I can't say with any true conviction what it is that's 'wrong' with her. I can only make a reserved judgement from what I know.

—*You can speculate though?*

—We can all speculate, but we can't give a diagnosis. That task is for her doctors at Elmtree, and I imagine that they're not at liberty to discuss their conclusions with you, right?

—*That's right. Hence I'm talking to you.*

—I'll take that as a compliment…

—*So what are your thoughts on Arla's condition?*

—Like I say, I can only speculate based on the evidence before us. From what we know about the case, I think I can say with some confidence that Arla Macleod was, and perhaps still is, suffering from psychosis. I strongly suspect she has been for a number of years.

—*Psychosis?*

—It's an umbrella term used to describe a range of different diagnoses, including schizophrenia.

—*So is it possible that Arla Macleod was or is schizophrenic?*

—Yes, that's entirely possible. However, each person's experience of psychosis is individual. Psychosis is characterised by the following symptoms: extreme paranoia, hearing voices, and hallucinations. From what I've read of the case and the therapy I know is practised at Elmtree Manor, I wouldn't be surprised if Arla is struggling with a degree of extreme psychosis.

—*What do you think made Arla that way? As far as I know, that sort of condition does not run in her family.*

—While we're getting closer to answering that age-old question of whether 'monsters', as they're called, are born or made, we still don't have a definitive answer. Arla's psychosis could be explained as a genetic predisposition, exacerbated by environmental factors.

—*And you? What do you think?*

—I think there's no straight answer. A person's childhood, their home life in their early years, can have a huge impact; but it can also aggravate underlying problems or conditions. It is also entirely possible that psychosis is simply chemical.

—*What do you mean?*

—People with psychosis produce too much dopamine in their brains. Dopamine is a chemical, produced naturally, that acts as a sort of filter, a buffer for the sensors. At normal levels, it helps the brain focus and choose between perceived and actual threats. So someone whose brain is producing too much dopamine struggles to decipher what is important in their immediate environment and what isn't. So, for example, the woman pushing the pram next to the busy road becomes as threatening as the busy road, as does the bird singing in the roadside tree, the music coming from inside the corner shop. Does that make sense?

—*It does – too much dopamine produces a sort of state of constant fear?*

—More or less. A constant state of hypervigilance.

—*And this, combined with hearing voices and hallucinations, could have caused Arla to do what she did?*

—Causation is a tricky one. I'm talking generally, and each sufferer of psychosis experiences things differently. As I say, I don't know enough about the case, but in short, yes, Arla Macleod's psychosis *could* have caused her to do what she did. But we don't know the full story, do we? Will we ever?

—*Is there any cure?*

—Not as far as we know. Arla will be treated with medication – antipsychotics, I imagine – which we know help block the action of dopamine when it's released in the brain, helping to make the paranoia and hallucinations subside. She will have complementary therapy; Elmtree Manor has an outstanding reputation for their therapeutic practice. A lot of it is new, but it seems to be having decent results.

I must apologise to those of you who are unfamiliar with the case – although I doubt there are many of you. I am yet to explain fully what Arla Macleod was charged with, what she is proved in a court of law to have done to her family. We will hear about it, I promise you. In this episode, we'll hear both the facts as they were presented and Arla's version of what happened on that cold night in 2014.

This is Six Stories *with me, Scott King.*

This is the story of Arla Macleod.

This is episode one.

§§

—I first saw them when I were about fourteen … fifteen … I can't remember really; it seems like a long time ago now. We were … we were away somewhere, on holiday.

After Arla agreed to talk to me, Elmtree Manor wrote to me at length – lists of things I could and couldn't talk about. Discussion of her medication and details of her therapy are prohibited. As are the condition of the hospital, Arla's room, the therapy sessions. I suppose because all of it is tabloid fodder. No one wants to learn about innovation and state-of-the-art therapy; they want to see Arla Macleod rotting in a cell.

But if Arla volunteers any information … well, we'll see.

—We stayed in this big white hotel. I don't remember much …

just the swimming pool and the cocktails. They did kids' ones with juice and fresh mint and that. I thought I was so cool, just sat there drinking them. A bit of me remembers doing that with Mam and Alice, taking photos of them on Mam's camera while the sun went down behind us. But maybe that's just rose-tinted glasses, I don't know.

Arla's holiday with her family took place around 2008, she thinks. It was summer and Arla was about fifteen, Alice, just a little younger. Arla can't remember the name or the location of the hotel, but tells me it was on the coast in Cornwall – an all-inclusive place: kids' clubs in the day, entertainment at night. From what I know of the Macleods, they would have saved for this holiday for a long time.

—In the basement of the hotel there were this games room. There was a pinball machine, I remember, and a few arcade games. We all went down there when we first arrived. Just to have a look. I remember begging Dad for coins to play pinball. I remember him getting cross, telling me it were pointless, saying you 'don't win nothing' and Mam putting her hand on his arm. 'We're on holiday, love,' she said.

It goes all blurry then. I can't remember properly. Mam and Dad and Alice, they weren't there anymore; it were just me. I ... I remember it were hot outside, really hot. And everything had that *smell*, like when you're abroad? Like sun cream and warm skin. But we weren't abroad. It were England. Down in that games room it were cool, the walls and the floors were marble, and there were those cheese plants everywhere. Big, thick, waxy leaves like green hands, waving.

I remember it were the last day and I wanted to be on my own. I remember walking to the very back of the games room where there were some fruit machines. I remember they had flashing lights but no sound, like someone had turned the volume down. It were well weird.

And that's ... that were the first time I knew that something ... something weren't right.

I'm sorry, I know – let Arla tell her tale. I will, but I need to make one thing clear: I have no way of corroborating what Arla is about to say next.

—I had my headphones in – those ear-bud ones. I had my music on dead loud, Skexxixx proper blasting my head. Alice hated that music. She were into all that Katy Perry and X-Factor rubbish. She had no idea. She agreed with Dad. He said it were 'satanic', that it would 'corrupt' me. I used to ask him what his ma thought of Elvis wiggling his hips – that were 'satanic' too, right? He would get all red then and so I would just walk away.

Anyway, down in the games room that day, I remember the music just stopped – just cut out – and this … this wall of silence *fell* around me.

Suddenly I knew I wasn't on my own anymore. I could *feel* that someone else was there, in that room. It were like I could *hear* them holding their breath.

—*There was more than one person?*

—Yeah. It were like they sort of *appeared*, like, sort of just slithered out from a crack in the wall or something.

—*Who did?*

—It were these kids … these little kids. They were all standing suddenly round one of the fruit machines, like they'd been there all along. It were horrible.

—*Do you remember what they did?*

—I remember being scared, frightened cos they were just … *silent* … all of them clustered around this fruit machine like an old photograph gone wrong.

—*Did they speak to you at all?*

—No and that was what was so weird. They were silent. There was a boy, a few years younger than me, and he started pushing the buttons on the machine, but all the while, his head was turned round towards me.

—*This sounds like a vivid memory.*

—It is, and now I'm saying it out loud it sounds so … it sounds so nothing-y. Like, maybe they were simply some people – another family that had just arrived that day and I hadn't seen them before. I were in a funny mood that day, I were feeling … lost. So at first I thought maybe I hadn't seen them, like it were a daydream or something. And back then, I were used to people staring, cos of the way I dressed and that. I were a proper little goth back then, in my Skexxixx T-shirt and all that black eyeliner. I were used to kids looking at me but…

—*But?*

—It was like … they didn't look right, just standing there, all of them together like that. Then it seemed like there were more of them – like there were suddenly five when before there'd been two, and they were all just silent, staring. It was as if … as if they'd been waiting for me…

Yeah, that's how it felt, like they'd been waiting.

For me.

In all the research I've done about Arla Macleod, I've never heard this story. It's a strange thing to make up – if indeed Arla has made it up. Going on from what Dr White has told me about psychosis, there could well have been a group of children at the hotel and Arla's condition caused her to distort the intentions behind an inquisitive gaze at a teenage girl. Looking at images of the musician Skexxixx and his fans, you can understand, as Arla alludes to herself, why someone might stare at her. Or, of course, the children may have not been there at all. Dr White also implied that this could have begun as a form of dissociation. Although why at this point, I'm not entirely sure. Arla continues.

—It were proper odd but maybe explainable – like, they were just some kids. Maybe they were shy, or scared, or just weird, right? Maybe they were just weird, like me?

—*It does sound like quite a strange thing to see.*

—But there were something else about them that just weren't right, that was just like … off.

—*Go on.*

—You see, however long I looked at them, I couldn't tell how many of them there were – one minute there was just two and then there was five.

But that wasn't the only thing. That wasn't what was so *off* about them. What freaked me out about those kids was their faces, their skin. They all had this really smooth skin, like … like those china figurines that Mam collected; like, Little Bo Peep, all innocent-looking with huge eyes and pouty lips. Their skin were immaculate, smooth, like it were made of plastic; their lips just these perfect little bows. But they weren't *happy*, they didn't smile at me. They just stared like they were … like they were *hungry*.

This is certainly a strange story … or is it? Arla's memory is almost certainly distorted. That's no slight, it happens to us all, it's natural. And I don't doubt for a moment that Arla encountered other children on that holiday. But this chance meeting with an idiosyncratic group of children on her last day, while it only lasted for a few moments, seems to have remained with Arla for a long time.

Arla continues.

—After that holiday in Cornwall, I saw them again … I saw them all the time.

—*Back up north?*

—Yeah.

—*In Stanwel?*

—That was the thing. Not in Stanwel. We could never afford big holidays like that one in Cornwall. That must have been a one-off; maybe Dad won the pools, I dunno. But we did go to a caravan in Cleethorpes a lot – it belonged to one of Dad's mates, and we often used it when he wasn't there.

—*Did you see them there?*

—Yeah but not *there*, if you know what I mean.

—*Go on…*

—Like, I'd see them when we were on a day out at the market, or in the town. Jesus, I remember seeing them once at the swimming baths – all of them again, and they looked so *wrong*. They were in one of the cubicles. The door sort of swung open as I went past, and they were there, all of them just staring at me.

—*Are you sure it was them? I mean those specific children. How can you be sure?*

—Yeah. And no. I mean, like, there was something inside me that just sort of knew, you know? I knew it was them somehow.

—*Did you tell anyone? Your parents?*

—No, never. I couldn't. I wouldn't have even known how to start. 'Mam, I'm being stalked by a bunch of kids.' She'd have thought I'd gone mad. What would folk have thought of us then? Mam would have lost it with me. And then Dad would have had an episode and … well, I couldn't be doing with all that praying and stuff…

We pause here. Discussing Arla's late family is a flash point that the staff of Elmtree Manor have warned me about, so I let Arla compose herself. When Arla comes back, the tears I can hear at the other end of the line sound genuine. During this break, I'll briefly discuss Arla's parents.

Both Lucy and Stan Macleod were staunchly religious. From what I understand, Stanley had 'saved' Lucy from her former husband and attributed his ability to do this to the power of God. Lucy was, I gather, a follower by nature, and often felt indebted to Stanley – a debt he apparently referred to whenever she disagreed with his views about how to raise the girls. The 'episodes' that Arla mentions earlier sound very much like fits of internalised rage Stanley experienced when he saw or heard something he didn't like or couldn't comprehend.

During our earlier discussions about family life, Arla describes one of these moments.

—His face used to get red and he'd clench his fists and start muttering. It were like a giant baby about to throw a tantrum. He used to shout all this Bible stuff and then we all had to hold hands and pray – like, right there and then, wherever we were. It were so embarrassing. We used to make sure he never saw, like, 'sinful' stuff; we made sure we never went anywhere good when Dad was there – the cinema, the fair, anything. Honestly, even the sight of a woman in a skirt could set him off. Mam just sort of let him get on with it; never told him he were being daft…

I'm not here to criticise anyone's religious beliefs but I do know Stanley McLeod's attitude was far from progressive. He was anti-abortion, he found the LGBT community 'abominable', and don't even start on his attitudes to music. I imagine that Arla's tastes and dress sense as a teenager were in direct opposition to this. It is interesting to note, though, that Alice Macleod didn't follow her sister; she never showed any resentment about her father's ways.

From a young age, both Arla and Alice were expected to pray, attend church and be fearful of their parents' God. Restrictions were in place for both children. While Alice put her head down and complied with her parents' wishes, Arla felt these restrictions tighten as she grew from a child into a woman.

Smoking, drinking and boyfriends were a big no-no for Arla. Her life was lived under the law her parents imposed. Could this have played a part in what happened? Undoubtedly, yes, though how significant that part was is difficult to gauge. It could be said that Arla had become disappointed in the reality her parents had carved out for her and the restrictions they imposed. But many parents are protective; and many are religious.

As we'll discover, Arla rejected her parents' values almost completely when she became a teenager. It's hardly a surprise, and I doubt Mr and Mrs Macleod had the nuance to realise that the more they tried to limit her, the more Arla would rail against them.

The media played up this aspect of the case to almost ridiculous excess. In a bizarre succession of headlines and articles, the tabloid press suggested that Arla's teenage rebellion was the most likely cause of what happened in 2014, conveniently forgetting the fact that by the age of twenty-one, Arla Macleod was very different from how she'd been as a teenager. The online community that holds Arla Macleod up as an icon certainly like to keep her perpetually frozen in this rebellious phase of her life. We'll look at this in more detail later in the series, when we start building a true picture of who Arla Macleod was and who she now is.

Anyway. When Arla is composed enough to continue, she does.

—Every time I saw them – those kids – I'd be frightened. They were always silent, always staring at me, through crowds of people, all of them just sat there on something – stairs, a picnic table. They never did anything, just stared. But afterwards, after I'd see them, I'd forget. Like, almost immediately, I'd forget I'd seen them.

Until I saw them again.

—*How many times do you think you saw the kids?*

—I don't know … loads when I was a teenager and then … then the last time. That was the last time I saw them and I knew it was them … I knew it was them…

We're all aware of what happened to the Macleods on the 21st of November 2014, so I'll be brief with the recap.

The police were called to 41 Redstart Road, Stanwel at 2.40 am on the 21st of November 2014. A neighbour had expressed concern about a commotion at around 2.00 am, then a screaming that did not stop. So scared was the neighbour, she didn't dare go and see if everything was OK, despite being on first-name terms with the Macleods.

Crucially, that neighbour stated she had not, to the best of her knowledge, seen anyone enter or leave the Macleod house that night, nor had she heard or seen anyone passing by. In fact, she stated that she had spent the whole of that evening in the living room in front of the television and had seen nothing unusual.

When the police officers arrived at the Macleod house, twenty-one-year-old Arla answered the door. She looked dishevelled and manic, her eyes wide and her hair tousled. She was wearing pyjamas that were streaked with blood and in her right hand she was holding a hammer, also covered in blood.

In the hallway lay the bodies of her stepfather, Stan Macleod, sister, Alice, and mother, Lucy. All of them were covered in blood. Twenty-year-old Alice had been beaten so badly, her face was unrecognisable and her skull was shattered. Stanley Macleod was crumpled at the bottom of the stairs in a foetal position, bruises and blunt-object trauma marks all over his right side; his skull also broken in several places. Lucy Macleod lay in the kitchen doorway; like her husband, she had sustained blunt-force trauma to her body and head.

Arla Macleod did not deny what she did to her family. She went willingly with the police and seemed unaware of what was going on around her, only repeating the words 'I let them in. I let them in'. Arla never gave an explanation as to what she meant by this.

—I knew it were them. Something inside me just *knew.* As soon as they knocked on the door. I knew it.

—*So let's hear your story Arla, tell us what happened that night.*

There's a long pause – it sounds like Arla's phone has been muted. She is, perhaps, discussing something with the staff. There's a part of me that thinks they might shut things down, that Arla's story, which has taken me so long to track down, might vanish before me, dissolve into the air like kettle steam.

When Arla comes back on the line, it takes everything I have not to cheer out loud.

—Thanks Mr King.

—*For what, Arla? To be honest I've done little but disrupt your routine. I'm the one who should be thanking you.*

—Maybe.

When Arla continues, her voice is different, lighter – dream-like almost. I wonder if in our short break she's been medicated. Who can say?

—*Take your time, Arla. Just tell me what happened.*
—OK, I will. So, well … where do I start?
—*Wherever you feel comfortable, I suppose. Why not start with that day. Had you been at college?*
—Umm … yeah, yes I had.

Arla was studying part-time at Edge Hill University in Ormskirk, an hour or so south of Stanwel. At the behest of her parents, she was completing an MBA in Business Administration. It's no secret that this was not Arla's choice of subject. Arla tells me she wanted to study performing arts but Stan Macleod dismissed that idea entirely.

—I always used to have a sleep when I got back from college. If I couldn't get a lift, I'd have to take two trains. I didn't mind when it was warm – it were a nice journey – but in the winter, it were horrible, sat frozen in one of those rickety little two-carriage jobs.
—*Did someone give you a lift on the 20th of November?*
—No. They was all going out straight after college. They were doing a super-hero bar crawl or something, getting dressed up and that.
—*Why didn't you go to that?*
—I just … I didn't fancy it, that's all. Not my sort of thing.

I find it strange that a twenty-one-year-old would not want to be part of a university social life. Yet it is worth bearing in mind that Arla was only part time at the university and was commuting from home. Maybe she never really felt part of the scene, or maybe her parents didn't want her attending such events.

I manage to track down a student on the same course as Arla: she wants to remain anonymous. She says she was not particularly close to Arla, but does remember her.

—Yeah, she was very … umm … like she would only be there to study, you know? She was on her own a lot of the time, like, she was always walking to class on her own or sometimes with one other person.

—*She had friends though, right?*

—I'm not sure if she had *friends*. There were people who Arla talked to but sometimes she would like ... she would eat lunch on her own. She reminded me of ... umm ... like me...

—*What do you mean?*

—Umm ... like ... my parents say I am not here for making friends, that I am here to do well at my studies and at work, you know? That is my reason to be here.

—*Do you think it was like that for Arla?*

—That was strange to me because Arla was ... umm ... when you talked to her, she was nice and happy, but she spent a lot of time by herself. She didn't look keen to hang around in the group, you know? When I spoke to her sometimes, she said it was her parents that wanted her to study here. To me it seemed like she ... she wanted to be somewhere else.

What can we read into this? Perhaps nothing. As I've mentioned already, Arla was not particularly interested in business administration; but isn't it the case for a lot of young people that their parents want to dictate what's best for them? However, Mr and Mrs Macleod also had a hand in dictating how Arla lived her life outside classes.

Is any of this a reason for what happened to Arla's parents? Did her psychosis in some way enable her to act out her resentment? But why take her younger sister too?

Let's go back to Arla's recollections of the night in question.

—I were tired and cold, and, like I said, I always had a nap first thing when I got back home. It were lovely, just snuggled up in my bed with the heating on. I always woke up to the smell of Mam cooking tea. She would leave it in the oven while they went to watch Alice at training.

—*So this was a night like any other?*

—It started off that way, a night just like any other.

Arla's second train in the journey from Ormskirk to Stanwel was delayed due to a fault of some sort. It would have been around four or five pm, already dark and freezing cold.

—So when you get near Stanwel station, there's always a wait. Loads of trains go past and don't stop; all the delayed ones going to London or the other way up to Scotland. Because you're on the piddly little one, they take priority. It's well annoying; you have to sit there for ages.

The station's high up on a hill so when you're waiting, you look down on Bull Road, watch all the cars driving out of Stanwel.

Bull Road's got woods and stuff on either side of it. The woods are thick and you can't really see much through the trees. In the spring and the summer it's gorgeous, all green and lush. The branches spread out and you can hear them clatter on the train windows like they're waving you off.

In the winter, though, it's horrible, just dark and spooky. That night, as we stopped and waited above the road, the wind had got going and the trees with their bare branches were crashing against the train windows. There were a few folk looked a bit scared. The train carriages only had these flimsy doors and the wind was screaming in through the gaps, making them shake. I was in my gloves and hat. I had my scarf wrapped up round my face.

Anyway, the train started moving again, but it went dead slow, like it does when the station's only one minute away. I'm looking out the window and...

Arla sighs at this point, takes a few deep breaths, and I'm worried she's going to stop. Or else whoever's supervising our call is going to tell me that it's time to finish. Luckily, however, Arla comes back on the line and carries on with no explanation for her pause.

—So we pass over the road and you could see it had started to rain, black specks all flying through the light of the street lamps that light the road. That's when I saw them.

—*Saw who?*

—Like … a little way on from the road there's a pedestrian crossing bit, but there's never anyone on it. It's a rambler's track that goes round the edge of the wooded bit then up to the old coalfield. There's just no *reason* for anyone to be there, especially not on a night like that.

But that night there was someone – more than *a* someone. There were two of them – two kids. They were stood on the coalfield side of the tracks, as if they'd come from that direction, through the bit of woods towards the town. Just the sight of them sent this chill through me. They were stood there, holding hands – no coats or owt – just staring up at the train.

—*No coats? These were young kids, right? Were they alone?*

—Yeah. Yeah they were. It were horrible. One of them – the smaller one – was a boy; he can't have been much older than six. I remember he was wearing a shirt: a dress shirt with a collar; it were soaked through. You could see his skin. There was an older one with him – his sister I suppose, maybe twelve. She were wearing a dress, like a frock thing, and that were soaked too. They proper freaked me out, gave me a right funny turn. They weren't even waving, you know, like kids do. They were just looking. It were … ugh … I'm getting goose bumps just thinking of it.

It's gonna sound stupid but it … It felt like I were being watched. Like, I doubted they could even see anyone on the train, we probably looked like black shapes from down there, but still it felt like … it felt like they were looking at me, like it were *me* they was staring at.

—*Did anyone else see them, do you know?*

—That was the thing, I just don't know. I wanted someone else to see them, to make a comment – some old biddy to say, 'Eee, look at them poor kiddies in the cold.' But the more I sat there, the more I stole glances at everyone, the more I thought no; no one else can see them. It's just me.

And I … I couldn't tear my eyes away from them. They were like a pair of twin shadows, hand in hand. The wind and the rain was coming down on them, and it was like they couldn't even feel it, like they were … oblivious.

It was them – those kids from all them years ago in the hotel. The ones I'd seen on other holidays, too.

—*Did you seriously believe it was them?*

—It … I … it's hard to explain. Like, I'd seen those kids a few more times, always when we were away: once when we went to Scarborough, then the last time was in Cleethorpes when I were seventeen…

Arla maintains she saw the kids from the hotel in Cornwall numerous times over the years, but never in Stanwel, not until that night in 2014 – until then she'd only seen them when her family were on holiday. She'd always seen them from a distance and there were always a varying number of them.

—*From that distance, and, of course with the weather conditions and the darkness, it must have been difficult, nigh on impossible to tell if it was definitely those exact kids, no?*

—Yeah … I mean, no, I couldn't be a hundred percent sure it was them. Even now when I try and remember what *those* kids looked like, I just … can't. These ones though, the ones by the train, they were … it's hard to explain … it was like there was something *wrong* with them … ah … it's hard to explain.

—*Was it just a feeling perhaps? The fact that these two sodden children were out of context?*

—Yeah, there is that I suppose. They could have just been some lost children maybe? Or else they were – what do you call them? – latchkey kids or something? Sometimes the gypsies … sorry, the travellers, they passed through Stanwel on their way to Appleby Horse Fair. So maybe it was a couple of them. Maybe it were nothing.

—You imagined them, you mean?

—Maybe. Maybe that's right, cos, as the train began picking up speed, a car started coming down Bull Road and its headlights passed over those children. I followed its movement, and when I glanced back, they were gone.

—Back into the woods?

—Dunno. Maybe…

If we think back to what Dr White said, and then compare it to the idea of these children, and to Arla's assertion about the kids that have pursued her throughout her life, we could be talking about a clear case of psychosis here – paranoid schizophrenia. But I'm no expert and totally unqualified to dish out such diagnoses.

—So later on that night, after you got home, did you see them again?

—It's not like I have a bad memory or anything. I remember loads of stuff – what happened in Cornwall, parts of my childhood – but those kids, they just seemed to have a strange effect on my brain. It were like they cracked open an egg, pulled a plaster off an old cut. It was like, as soon as they were gone, I forgot about them. I were left with only traces.

Our brains have a strange way of forgetting things more easily if they're not in a context we understand. Maybe this is why Arla has trouble with her immediate recollection of what she saw. Despite this, she remembers it now – quite vividly it seems.

—Let's move forwards a bit – until later that night, when you were at home.

—Mam had made fishcakes that night; the whole house smelled of them. Even though it were a dead strong smell, I kind of liked it: smoky and fresh, mixed with chopped-up parsley from the garden. Those fishcakes were lovely. We ate a lot of fish. Protein, for Alice's sake, protein.

—Had there been any ... disagreements between you and your parents that evening – arguments; anything like that?

—No. Not that I remember. It were a really normal evening. After tea they took Alice out to training. I washed up, cleaned the kitchen, then I went upstairs to study. Just a normal night like any other really.

It all ... the ... the bad stuff all happened later on...

I'm amazed how matter-of-fact Arla is when she talks to me about the night in question. It's as if she's recounting a trip to the seaside. Maybe it's the medication. Arla will be taking antipsychotics, among other things, I presume, and these may slow her down, or at least blunt her emotions.

—It were really coming down outside by bedtime – sleet, I think. I could still feel the chill. It had got right into my bones, you know? I had a bath that night to try and, like, warm my soul up. I don't usually have a bath. I haven't got the patience to lie there in the water.

—Was there anything about that evening that was out of the ordinary?

—Not unless you think me having a bath was! No, it was just a normal night. I went to sleep at around ten or eleven. It would have been around then cos I had to get up the next day at seven to get the train to uni.

—No lift?

—No. Everyone was going out that night, remember? I was a bit sad cos I knew I'd be pretty much on my own the next day. The others would all be too hungover to come to lectures and that.

—You never missed a lecture from being hungover?

—Oh my God, no. I mean, I couldn't *miss* stuff. What would people have thought of me?

—OK, don't worry about it, Arla. I'm sure you never did. Let's move on to later that night, when you woke up.

—I woke up and like – look, I don't sleepwalk; or if I do, no one's told me – but I sort of 'woke up' and I was stood downstairs in the kitchen, filling a glass with water.

I hadn't even put the lights on or nowt. I were just stood there, with the cold tap running on my hand. That's what woke me up, probably.

—*Did you usually get water from downstairs?*

—Yeah. The bathroom's upstairs but, you know, I don't like drinking water from the bathroom. It's just a thing I have, you know?

—*I think that's fairly common, Arla.*

—So I think it was the cold water flowing over my hand that properly woke me up. There was a dream though, still lingering in my head. That's even harder to remember, but I do know there was one.

—*What* can *you remember about it – the dream?*

—No images … just a *feeling*. Like a memory.

—*Do you remember what of?*

—I … no.

With every second that passes I realise that I'm treading on thinner and thinner ice. A sense of anxiety fills me. I know that the Elmtree Manor staff member is within their rights to terminate this call whenever they like, and I'm worried that's going to happen soon. At the same time, I don't want to push Arla too hard, nor ask any leading questions. What I want is Arla's version of that night.

—*What time did this happen, approximately?*

—Umm … it was pitch black outside. Our kitchen opens up onto the back garden and I couldn't see anything. So I reckon it was about 2 am, something like that. Everyone was asleep.

So I turned off the tap. I were a bit confused about being downstairs but … that's … it kind of made a strange sort of sense. So I turned off the tap and had a drink, and that's when I heard it.

—*Heard what?*

—The knock at the door.

What Arla describes next is the passage you heard at the beginning of the episode: about the knock made by what she describes as 'small hands'. It is important to note that Arla claims the knocking was at the back door of the Macleod house. Remember Arla's description of the back gardens being connected by that path?

Now, it is certainly possible that someone could access the back gardens of Redstart Road. All they would have to do is walk around the side of number one and unlatch the waist-high gate, which is almost obscured, even today, by an arch of privet.

The Macleods lived on the odd-numbered side of the street, roughly in the middle, so whoever was knocking in the middle of the night must have specifically targeted the Macleods. At least, that's the conclusion most people drew.

—*What happened when you answered the door?*

—It … You see I didn't at first. At first I went to the window. The sleet and rain were coming down and the wind was buffeting the place – you know when it comes in those great big gusts, almost flinging the water against the glass? There are switches on the kitchen wall, next to the key rack that Dad hung up – it's shaped like a sporran with little hooks where the tassles should be. Next to that there's the light switches. One … no, two for the kitchen and one for the porch light.

—*Was the light on in the kitchen?*

—No. But either my eyes were used to the dark by then or the light from the hall was on. Whatever it was, I couldn't really see outside, just my reflection in the window. It were double-glazed so I looked really weird, like an overexposed photo … like a ghost.

—*What happened next?*

—I had my fingers on the porch-light switch … I remember the feel of it under my nails. I were about to turn it on when I heard … I heard them speak.

—*Go on.*

—It were horrible. It were like they were in the house already.

—*What do you mean?*

—There was this whispering, like they were standing right next to me.

—*Who was whispering? Had you seen them yet?*

—No, but … it were like when I used to see that family. It were like Cornwall all over again … It … I knew. I *knew* it were them…

—*Who?*

—Those two kids – the ones I'd seen from the train. I could, like, see them in my head, stood outside the door.

—*Did you go to the back door and look?*

—I were so scared. I were almost in shock, stock still, rooted to the spot. I could hear one of them knocking and I knew it were the little one, the boy. It were like … it was like I could sense them *through* the door. I could see them already…

So I got down quick on my hands and knees, so they couldn't see me. I knew though – I knew as soon as I'd got down that it were pointless. I knew they knew I were there.

And that whispering. I could hear it like something shuffling in its nest, like something turning over in bed. It sounded like there were mice in the walls or something. I couldn't hear any words, just this whispering, as if the words were rustling together … I could feel it inside my head.

I crawled as quietly as I could over to the kitchen window. I were crouched behind the sink – I could smell the cleaning stuff that Mam kept under there. I didn't want to look – I swear I didn't – but it was like … it was like I had to. Then the knocking came again – *rat-a-tat-tat* – I poked my head up and looked.

—*And what did you see?*

—It was … they … I didn't see them at first, and I felt this sort of jolt in my heart, like when you wake up from a bad dream.

I could see the back doorstep through the rain – the edge of it anyway – and there were nothing there…

And then it appeared – *they* appeared, as if they were stepping back from the door, stepping back and waiting for me to ask them in.

I saw their legs first – pale and twiggy, white as bones in the darkness. The boy ... the ... the little boy was wearing shorts, and she – the older one, the girl – she had a dress on. It looked ... wrong, just all wrong, like they were from some history programme about the Victorians or something...

—*They were wearing old-fashioned clothes?*

—Yeah and you know, it were that ... it were *that* that really freaked me out, like it were a game or something ... kids from an old book...

—*A game?*

—Yeah, like knocky-nine-doors or something.

Just to clarify for international listeners, 'knocky-nine-doors' is an old term for the kids' prank of knocking on doors and running away. It's interesting that Arla uses such an archaic term, perhaps unconsciously mirroring the anachronistic appearance of the children's clothes.

—*Did you think you were experiencing something paranormal, Arla? At first, I mean?*

—No way. Not once ... they were too real, too ... solid. They were there ... right *there*. And then I were suddenly at the door and my hands, they were opening it, like I weren't in control or nowt. There was this cold feeling inside me, this icy pool at the bottom of my belly, dark and cold, a black, icy hole widening, and all my hope, all my *everything* was getting sucked down into that frozen darkness...

It were only when the door opened and the cold air came rushing in like it were escaping from something, right into my face, that I sort of woke up. I was standing there, the door a few inches open and I were looking out at them.

—*The children were still there?*

—Yeah. In the flesh, bold as brass. Stood there, the older girl and the little boy. They were pale and they were soaked, I mean drenched – those clothes of theirs were clinging to them like skin. But you know what was weird? Despite that, they didn't like look cold, if you know what I mean. They weren't hunched or shivering, they were just stood there.

—*Did they speak?*

—Yeah. They weren't, like, looking at me though; they were looking at the ground, as if ... I dunno, as if they were shy. And when he spoke, the little boy, I wasn't even sure he'd moved his lips – it were like a robot or something had spoken, like the words just sort of fell out.

—*What did he say?*

—It were something like, 'Please miss, let us in. We lost our mum and dad and we need somewhere to stay for the night. It's very cold out here. Please let us in.' But he wasn't *begging*, like; more ... I dunno ... as if he were *reciting* it, you know? As if he were in a play or something.

—*What did you do?*

—I sort of bent down to try and look at his face – you know how a teacher does. I could feel that horrible icy hole inside me getting wider with every second, but I ... I couldn't look away. I couldn't stop looking at him.

—*What about the other one – the older girl – did she speak?*

—No. She were a few feet back, looking at the floor, too. She had this long, black hair, dead straight, and the wind was whipping it all round her head, like ... like a blur, a scribble, a photo gone wrong or something.

He spoke again, the little boy: 'Please miss, it's so cold out here and we lost our mum and dad. Please will you let us in?' And you know something? That black fear inside me, it spoke, it spoke to every cell in my body. It told me that by no means should I let them in – no way. That if I did, something terrible would happen.

I dunno how I managed it, but I found my voice from somewhere and I were like, 'No, I'm sorry...' I felt bad. Like, how could I do that to a couple of kids?

Maybe it were the ... the *guilt* that overshadowed, that overpowered, everything. It felt so wrong to let them in; but it felt even worse to leave them out there.

Then the boy, he said it again, only this time, it were more like an … like an order. But still in that weird robot voice, like it were one of those phone lines which says *'Press hash now'*.

'It's COLD out here and we need to come in and use your PHONE.'

So … I … I couldn't even believe I were doing it: I opened the door, I pulled it wide open, I nodded and I stood to the side to let them in. Every part of me was screaming, was *howling* that this were a mistake, but I just … I couldn't do anything. I just watched them sort of … float … like they were walking a millimetre off the ground. They didn't look up, not yet anyway. They just walked past me and into the house.

I sort of snapped to my senses again, as if … as if I'd been hypnotised or something and I realised what I was doing. I had this feeling – this terrible, terrible feeling – that I'd done something awful; that this was the end … like one of those dreams where you've killed someone.

They were past me, gliding up the hall silently – too quiet, like their shoes weren't making any sound. I started to panic. I knew that if they went any further, that … that something really bad was going to happen. So I sort of called out in this … in this fucking stupid laughing way, like I were in a shop and had forgotten to give them their change or something. I were, like, 'Oh, I'm sorry, I'm afraid you can't come in after all…'

That's when that boy looked back at me. He turned his head and looked up…

There's a pause – a long, long pause. I don't know what to do, whether I should push Arla any further. Her voice has become increasingly agitated as she's describing the experience. I can hear her breathing. In and out, in and out. When she continues, it's in a whispery voice that sends a chill dancing down every vertebra of my spine.

—When he looked at me I saw his eyes. And they were black. All over. Just black.

There is a click and the line goes dead. I sit there staring into my phone for what seems like a very long time.

§§

Arla Macleod pleaded guilty to the manslaughter of her mother, step-father and sister. Her defence successfully argued that Arla's psychosis warranted that verdict. Two court-appointed psychologists, as well as a psychiatrist hired by Arla's defence team, agreed that she was unable to decipher reality from fantasy at the time of the killings.

Even if Arla herself tells us what happened, we'll never know for sure what exactly occurred that night in 2014. Below, I will lay out the Crown Prosecution Service's version of events based on the forensic evidence and analysis. This is your one and only warning: what I am going to describe to you is deeply unsettling.

Twenty-one-year-old Arla Macleod, at some time close to 2 am on the 21st of November, woke up and went downstairs to the kitchen. Her mother, stepfather and sister were asleep upstairs in their beds. Arla poured herself a glass of water before opening the kitchen door that led out into the garden. She then walked from the back door and across the lawn to the garden shed. She then unlocked the shed and took a hammer from a metal toolbox inside.

By the time Arla returned to the house, Stanley Macleod was awake and had descended the stairs to the hallway that led to the kitchen. This is where his stepdaughter attacked him with the hammer, dealing him a blow to the temple that broke his skull and knocked him unconscious. Arla continued to beat her stepfather with the hammer until her mother and sister, roused by the noise, also began to descend the stairs. Alice Macleod, Arla's sister, came first. Arla attacked her halfway up the stairs, and it is thought she fell, breaking her ankle and knocking herself unconscious. Her sister then repeatedly beat her in the face and head with the hammer until her skull was completely caved in and her face was nothing but pulp.

What happened to Lucy Macleod is less straightforward. It has been widely speculated upon – notoriously by the UK Television docu-mentary She Never Told Us *(Blamenholm Productions, 2015) – and unless Arla tells us, we'll never know for sure. Crime-scene investiga-tors and forensics have pieced together a sequence of events based on Lucy's injuries and the position of her body when she was found. It is suggested that Lucy saw what happened to her daughter and husband and stayed calm. It is thought she may have tried to reason with Arla, talking to her calmly, imploring her to put down the hammer, all the while walking down the stairs, trying not to react to the bludgeoned bodies of her loved ones.*

Lucy Macleod must have been stepping over, or have stepped over, her loved ones' corpses when Arla swung the hammer and hit her in the side of the head. There were no defensive wounds on Lucy; it was a single blow from the hammer that felled her as opposed to the frenzied attack on the other family members. This creates speculation as to why. There are three explanations, it seems: Arla was tired; her psychotic episode was drawing to an end; or her relationship with her mother was different from those she had with Alice and her stepfather.

I ask Dr White for her opinion.

—It's interesting isn't it? There's no definite answer to that question.

—*What do you think?*

—About what?

—*About why she did it that way. I mean, the rest of the family were bludgeoned, her sister's face beaten to a pulp. What do you think this says about Arla's relationship with her mother?*

—I think Lucy Macleod most probably stood and watched Arla kill her husband and her other daughter, or at least saw the after-math. For me, this suggests that Lucy probably knew more about Arla's psychosis than the family ever let on. And if she did, I imagine she'd have seen Arla have psychotic episodes and knew how to deal with her.

—*If that's the case, why do you think she never got any help for Arla?*

—I think the reasons are complicated. The Macleods were quite traditional in their views. Things are getting better but there is still, unfortunately, huge stigma around mental illness. My guess is that Arla never did anything too extreme – nothing to make her parents seek help. Lucy could manage her and no one else had to know.

Also, her stepfather was the dominant one, remember – his religious beliefs dictated everything that went on in the family. I wouldn't be at all surprised if Stanley Macleod refused to get therapy for Arla, but instead trusted in the power of God.

—*All this said, don't you think the fact that Lucy being left until last suggests Arla had a better relationship with her mum than with the others?*

—Actually I believe it was the opposite. But that's only what I think. I may, of course, be wrong.

—*But Arla only hit Lucy once.*

—In my opinion, that says a lot about Lucy and Arla's relationship, or the lack of one…

—*Really?*

—I can't give any definite answers, but the way you *could* think of it is that Arla didn't actually want to kill her mother.

—*I don't follow.*

—Arla killed her mother's husband and her mother's daughter. So Arla got to see Lucy Macleod's reaction to these deaths. Apparently, Arla allowed her mother to walk towards her – she didn't chase her. The single blow to the head was almost an afterthought. In my opinion, that shows a kind of disdain for her mother, as opposed to the passion she showed when she killed her stepfather and sister. Bear in mind, this was during a clear state of psychosis.

It's an opinion. Whether it's right, we'll never know. As far as I'm aware, Arla has not deviated from her version of events. Indeed, it could be said that her diagnosed paranoid schizophrenia-induced psychosis caused Arla to believe that her home had been invaded by these black-eyed children. It is important to note, however, that Arla has never blamed the black-eyed children directly for killing her family. At least not to my knowledge.

So let's focus on what we do *know. A young woman suffering from psychosis killed her family. It's tragic and it's sad and it's horribly straightforward.*

Or is it?

Before we end this episode, I want to briefly expand on Arla's sighting of these black-eyed children – or BEKs as they're known. Because this particular delusion isn't exclusive to Arla Macleod.

BEKs (black-eyed kids) are a fairly modern phenomenon, and sightings of them have increased significantly with the birth of the internet. The first sighting of archetypal black-eyed kids was reported by a US journalist named Brian Bethel back in 1996.

Bethel was sitting in his car in a Texas parking lot at around 9.30 pm when he was approached by two boys, around twelve or thirteen years old, who knocked at his window. Bethel describes one of the boys as being 'olive-skinned' and 'curly-haired', and the other being 'redheaded' and 'pale-skinned'. The curly-haired boy asked if Bethel would give them a lift to their mother's house as they had forgotten to pick up their money for the bus. The boy assured him it wouldn't take long.

A strange enough situation; but Bethel reports that, as he spoke with the boys, he became consumed by an irrational fear – something like a fight-or-flight response. Arla describes a similar sensation.

Bethel goes on to say that he was just about to open his car door when he noticed the eyes of the boy. In Bethel's words they were 'the sort of eyes you see on late-night television, on aliens or bargain-basement vampires. They were soulless orbs, like two scraps of starless night.' Bethel did not open the door; instead he drove away.

The story began to spread online and more and more sightings of black-eyed kids were reported on paranormal forums and the like. A 'typical' BEK encounter begins in a home or in a car, usually late at night. The person will hear a knocking on the door. If they have pets, these become agitated. And when they answer the knocking, they are met with children – usually an older one of around twelve or thirteen and a younger one. These children will ask to come in for a variety of reasons – to use the phone, for example, because they're lost and they need to call their parents. Everyone who has allegedly come into contact with BEKs reports the same feeling of irrational terror in their presence.

Online speculation about what these creatures are is rife, ranging from vampires to aliens to an elaborate internet hoax in the vein of Slenderman. What is certain is that BEKs are a very modern phenomenon. It is entirely possible that Arla was au fait with these stories; according to others we'll talk to, she did spend a lot of her time at home, online. Was it the story of the BEKs that stimulated Arla's delusions?

Whatever conclusions we draw about Arla Macleod and what happened that night in 2014, the outcome is, sadly, the same: three of the Macleods are dead, and one is locked away for life in a secure hospital.

It should be cut and dried – what else is there to speculate about? What else is there to discover in this tragedy?

The most obvious is the question 'why?' Why did Arla Macleod, who had no history of violence, suddenly kill her entire family that night? Was it a psychotic episode or something else?

Like most of the cases I cover, on the surface it's clear: a troubled young woman committed a terrible act and was duly punished. So why am I looking any further? Why am I asking questions? Why am I raking over old graves?

As has been widely documented – in the television documentary and the many newspaper stories about her – Arla Macleod was a troubled young woman, destined to enter the annals of true-crime history, where she would become a wonder, a figure of fascination. She has also come to be seen, particularly by those who glorify such crimes online, as a fist in the face of 'conformity'. Only recently, a young man from a high school in Swansea was suspended for threatening to 'do a Macleod' to his classmates and posting the infamous picture of Arla at fifteen on Facebook.

But I'm convinced there's more. You will have noticed in this episode that Arla says the first time she saw the 'kids' was on a holiday in Cornwall. Details of this holiday have never, as far as I know, been discussed before.

Maybe this holiday will prove to be insignificant, maybe not. But I hope to speak to someone who was on that holiday, alongside Arla, in a future episode.

This has been Six Stories.

This has been our opening story.

Until next time…

TorrentWraith – Audio (Music & Sounds)

Type	Name
Audio	**Arla Macleod Rec002 [320KBPS]** Uploaded **5 weeks** ago, Size 52.9 MiB. ULed by JBazzzzz666

Today were better.

Better?

Sorry, 'better' is not a word I should really be using, is it? 'What is better?' you once asked me. I remember that day; it was when I'd first come here. It was moody outside, the sky stuffed full of cloud like a fat teddy; the air tight and warm. Too warm. I remember cos the air-con were on. I hate that air-con unit, sat up on the ceiling – its shape: two screws like eyes on either side of the vent, making an upside-down face, like a ray. I remember feeling sulky, like I were a teenager again and being put somewhere I didn't want to be. Pouting.

We all used to do that – pout. Me and Paulette and Debs. We used to rob expensive lippy from the precinct, proper ruby red. The thing to do were make your lips up nice then blacken your teeth. Mam used to say it made me look like a Victorian street urchin. Alice said it was scary. Both of them said, 'Don't show Dad.' *As if.*

I spent a lot of time looking better on the outside, when I was broken on the inside. Paulette and Debs got it. They understood what it all meant.

Embrace your emptiness.

We were nothing. All three of us.

Until three became two.

And two became one.

One big fat nothing.

Like now.

I'm too cold when the air-con is on and too hot when it isn't.

That day – the day I asked when I would get better – seems a long time ago, and the question sounds childish now, something an idiot would ask. I remember your face when I asked it, how you went to laugh, stopped your-self, considered it and then did it anyway.

'What is "*better*"?' you said.

I remember feeling a little bit sad at first, like this were a test and I wasn't doing very well at it. I looked around the room, at that painting behind where you sit – with the pears falling out of a bowl. I always mean to ask where you got it; why you got it. Maybe you didn't get it at all. Maybe it's just, you know, there, like it came with the building or something.

I said that 'better' is when I don't see things that aren't there. And as if in reply, I could feel the hairs on the back of my neck begin to rise. It were like something … sorry … *someone* were watching me. It were like someone was glaring at me.

There's no window in your room. I always forget to ask why. So … Can I even ask you questions like this? Will you answer in the next session? If so, then why – why is there no window in your room; in room four?

Last session you were talking about the idea of 'better' again – about how I had to re-frame my idea of 'better', and that I can't always think that what I see is a failure, that it's me not being 'better'.

I was telling you about 'embrace your emptiness' and you got mad. You said that with kids today, the idea of being 'broken' is much more appealing than the idea of being 'better' – you were angry about it, you were angry with how 'broken' was an aspiration and 'better' was seen as weak.

You were saying all this but I was hardly listening. It's hard to concentrate, being on the meds; things come slow, like someone's turned down the speed. I know you see when I'm not listening – you say I'm zoned out. 'Arla!' you say. 'Arla! Are you still with me?'

I am usually; I'm usually with you, but it's hard. Especially after lunch, when I'm proper full and tired, and all those tastes are still rattling round my mouth.

The thing was, in today's session I was a bit clearer. It were less like I was in a room of clouds, of fuzz, and I were thinking, *Does this mean I'm getting better?* But I didn't want to ask in case I spoiled it.

You were talking, and I was trying, but…

I stopped you mid-sentence: 'Can I just…'

For a second I thought you looked hurt, like you were sad I'd stopped listening to you.

'It's just…'

'What can you see?' you said.

And I remember feeling a little bit bad – bad that I couldn't see anything, that there was nothing there. But it wasn't what I could see; it was what I could *hear*. There was this shuffling noise and it were coming from right outside the door of room four. I wanted you to hear it first – that's what I wanted. I should have said, and I'm sorry but inside me I were scared, I were praying that it wasn't *them* … I…

I remember my heart sinking as you made notes. For a long time I hoped I could get through a session without you writing one thing on that pad. Why? I have no idea, I have no idea why that was even a thing, but it was.

You often say to me that sometimes a thing is just a thing.

I've tried to hold that sentence, that prophetic statement, and turn it over, look at its underside, study its details, its parts, try and decipher its sentiment.

But, like you say, sometimes a thing is just a thing.

I'm sorry, I'm babbling again, aren't I? I know you said I could make these recordings as long or as short as I want, but I just can't help thinking of you, sat at some desk somewhere, watching, sighing. I imagine your study, a great red-velvet room lined with books and stuffed things in bell jars. It's not like that at all though, is it? I don't even think you take your work home; you do it all here. Your office here is minimal, I think – just a big table, white walls, maybe another painting: a pineapple in a salad-spinner or something; a framed photo of your family. Or one of those electronic frames that you can upload photos to, cycling through trips to the beach, smiles and sandcastles, all of you guys snuggled up on a rollercoaster. I don't know, I've never even seen your office.

You've told me you have a son, not outright, but you've sort of dropped it into our sessions. I wonder if you even notice you're doing it. You've said nothing else though – nothing about a wife or anything. Professional distance I guess. That's cool.

Your son will be older than me judging by the lines on your face and those nostril hairs that sometimes I can't stop staring at, and the way you, like, creak when you lean back in your chair. He's lucky to have a dad like you.

I just want you to know that I think I'm getting, not better, but I'm getting … I think that I'm better at handling things.

So I woke up last night and went to the toilet. It's never silent here – you can hear everyone's racket and nonsense. I've got my own toilet but I can still hear everyone else. It makes me feel safe, the solidness of my door. It doesn't feel like I'm being contained; it feels like I'm being kept safe.

I hate the light in the toilet. It flickers on, making the room seem, for a couple of seconds, like something out of a horror movie. Maybe it's cos I think that … that I saw something in that flicker last night. I know you said to record everything I see, no matter how small, no matter how frequent. But what if it's just imagination? What if I was dreaming?

OK. I'll say what I saw. I'll say it anyway.

That flickering light, like I say, it lasts for a few seconds, and a jolt of fear went through me as it sputtered into life.

They were all there, dancing, arms in the air, hands waving, hopping from one leg to another, shaking their hair over their eyes. All three of them.

I could hear music as well – that *thud-thud-thud* stuff they liked, that I pretended to like too.

Then the light came on properly and they were gone.

I'm putting it down to imagination, I promise, because it didn't have the same feeling as it does when it's a … thing.

A thing is sometimes just a thing.

So yeah, that was last night.

Which I think is 'better'. I know, I know, but remember when I pulled the emergency cord on one of my first nights here? Remember when I told you they were outside the window, all of them with their *tap-tap-tap* little fingers on the glass? Remember those little fingers? I bet you're rolling your eyes right now, thinking, *Yeah, the fingers – the little fingers that tapped on the glass but weren't there when anyone else came and looked. Yeah I remember them, Arla.*

I remember screaming and hiding in my bed, burrowing in like a hamster. And I remember what you told me after – the mantras that you taught me for when I hear them: to just wait them out, to let them do their thing.

A thing is just a thing.

Right?

I know you always ask me to tell you what they say, when they tell me how to make them go away.

But I can't.

Because it's my fault they're here. It's all my fault. I opened the door. I opened the way for them. And if I tell you they'll come back.

And if they come back … well, no one wants that.

Episode 2: Embrace Your Emptiness

—Mr Whitton, he had this … this sort of wasting disease, I think. It was pretty bad; he was all skin and bones, the poor soul. You would think that would make us a bit nicer to him wouldn't you?

Kids are little bastards though – evil. Especially girls. This poor fella, all skinny with these big glasses and a bowl haircut straight out of about 1963 in front of a bunch of fifteen-year-olds. Bad fifteen-year-olds too – year-eleven scumbags, that whole class. We were horrid. I feel bad for any teacher who had to teach our lot: eleven F. Those four syllables struck fear into the heart of any teacher at that school, I swear.

Except for Mr Whitton.

Mr Whitton, he thought that God could save us, which was fine I suppose, but he was, like, really *angry* about it. Like God would save us but only if we behaved in exactly the right way, which was exactly the way Mr Whitton wanted us to behave.

You know, I don't remember learning about any other religions in his lessons; it was always stuff about the bloody Bible! I tell you what, drawing a cartoon strip about Jesus feeding the five thousand wasn't my idea of fun; but it was his. It was him who used to organise the Gideons to come and do their assemblies. They were there every few weeks in their shabby suits and with their bad PowerPoint presentations, giving everyone a little Bible with a plastic cover. They were lethal those covers, if you ripped all the pages out and held the cover in your fist, one corner poking out between your two fingers … I saw a lot of lads get slashed up with those weapons of God.

The day Mr Whitton lost his shit. I mean, at the time, it was funny but now … hmm … a part of me wants to say it wasn't – that he was a vulnerable man, clinging on to his religion like a fanatical Rottweiler and dragging us all along for the ride. That he was a man desperate for redemption – for something outside his crappy life working in our crappy school with us bratty kids.

But if I'm honest, if I search my soul, I'm sad to say it was pretty funny. Yeah. It was pretty funny.

I remember his face that day – it was so red … his cheeks were *beetroot*. It was amazing – his glasses all steamed up and his skinny arms waving about. Sweat stains on his shirt.

I remember the moment we all started laughing as well.

She started it. She was the first one to start laughing. She was the puppet master – puppet mistress, whatever. It was her.

All of it.

When I heard what she did to her family, well, I have to say I wasn't shocked … No, that's not true: I *was* shocked, but I wasn't surprised, if you see what I mean. I didn't think she was *in*capable of it, put it that way.

§§

Welcome to Six Stories. *I'm Scott King.*

In these six weeks, we are looking back at the Macleod Massacre – the killings by twenty-one-year-old Arla Macleod of her stepfather, mother and younger sister. We're looking back from six different perspectives, seeing the events that unfolded through six pairs of eyes.

Then, of course, it's up to you to decide the reasons behind what happened.

For this episode, I managed to contact Tessa Spurrey (not her real name), whose voice you heard at the beginning. Without Tessa, episode two of this series may not have been possible and the entire series may have faltered.

Tessa attended Saint Theresa's Catholic School in Stanwel at the same time as Arla Macleod and was in many of Arla's classes. As far as I am aware Tessa has not previously spoken about Arla, or about what happened to the Macleods in 2014. Her reasons for speaking to me now will become apparent later.

First though, it is important we talk a bit about the newspaper and television coverage that emerged at the time of the Macleod Massacre. As soon as we start chatting, Tessa tells me about it straight off the bat. We talk on the phone.

—Oh ugh, yeah, it was almost immediate. Honestly, it was only hours after it happened, I got a message from some journalist. They were asking about Arla; about what she was like, about how friendly I was with her, everything. And you know the worst thing … the very worst thing? They didn't even seem to wonder whether this might have been a tad traumatic for me. They didn't care a jot!

Tessa is a lecturer at a university she's asked me not to disclose, and she's not disclosed what her subject is. I'll be honest here, Tessa was incredibly guarded and jumpy during our interview. As you will hear, she skips from subject to subject, never settling fully on anything, always careful of what she is saying, and not saying why. This perturbs me.

—Honestly, they wanted anything, anything at all. I'm sure you saw, didn't you? We all saw that documentary and the headlines – they were ludicrous, like something out of 1980s America. What was worse was the fact that it didn't even surprise me that there were people who didn't even know Arla, but who said they were her friends and were falling over themselves to tell the gutter press whatever they wanted to hear, all for a few pennies. It made me feel sick. Sick to my stomach. Now of course you've got everyone online treating her like some kind of anti-establishment hero. It's just as bad, it really is. None of these people even knew her!

—*But you'll talk to me?*

—Yes. Yes, because I've listened to your podcast so I know you'll give me a chance to speak – you'll let me tell my part of the story. And that's all I've ever wanted. You're not from one of those fucking shitrags, and you're not some fucking keyboard warrior either. Sorry. And you'll not tell anyone who I am.

—But surely there were opportunities before now to tell your story anonymously?

—Maybe. All I know is that when you speak to the papers, or to the television researchers, you tell them one thing and then off they go and turn it into whatever they want to, whatever fits the monster the baying crowds will flock to see.

Tessa is doubtless referring to the newspaper reports that were published in the days after Arla was taken into police custody and then to court, and the details of what actually happened to her family came out.

One particularly gruesome and sensationalist headline on the front of the Daily Express *read 'Satan's Sister in Stanwel Family Massacre', accompanied by the now infamous photograph of Arla looking suitably crazed, grinning sideways at the camera, her white teeth Ohaguro-style black, and her eyeliner streaming down her face. This picture was placed beside a stock photo of English shock-rock musician Skexxixx in a ghoulishly similar pose – right down to the running eyeliner and trademark teeth-blackener that had become a craze among his fan base in the early 2000s, including with a fifteen-year-old Arla Macleod.*

She Never Told Us, *the documentary I mentioned in episode one, made by Blamenholm, only just stopped short of citing Arla's brief flirtation with this image as the reason for what happened.*

Tessa's view is that the music and images that surrounded Arla are only the tip of the iceberg – something simple on which to pin the horror of what she did.

Extract from She Never Told Us
(Blamenholm Productions, 2015)

—Arla Macleod was a devoted fan of rock musician Skexxixx, often dressing in similar attire, adorning her face with crudely applied eyeliner and blackening her teeth. Some may see this simply as teenage rebellion gone a little too far. But was there, in fact,

something in Skexxixx's music that called to a vulnerable young girl? Certainly, there are themes in the
songs that speak to the vulnerability and low self-
esteem many teenagers in the UK share.

[*The chorus of 'Blighted Heart' by Skexxixx plays
over a scrolling display of lyrics from the song.*]

'Slice me open wide, pull back the bones,
Find sugar-plum fairies in the mulch of a dying mind.
For I'm your nothing, I'm your no one,
A walking flagrant,
A stalking irritant,
A failure not fit to fall by your wayside...'

[*This dissolves into a clip of Skexxixx standing
onstage at a concert, bathed in red light and dry ice,
screaming into a microphone.*]

'Embrace your emptiness! Embrace it! We are
   nothing! We are nothing!'

[*This shot then dissolves into a photograph of Arla
Macleod with her arms around two other girls with their
faces pixellated. All three are wearing torn clothing.
Arla has black eyeliner smeared around her eyes. She
is grinning; some of her teeth are blacked out. She's
wearing a T-shirt that reads 'I am nothing' with an
'S' insignia below it.*]

—The thing was, Arla's parents never even *tried* to understand
the music, how she used to dress, any of it. It was far too complicated. They threw everything they had into Alice – the pretty one,
the swimmer. They just had no idea what any of the music meant
to Arla. It was her *life*. At least my parents made an attempt; Dad
showed me his old Venom and Bathory cassettes from 'back in the
day', bless him. It was all an escape for Arla, it was the most important thing in her life and they didn't care. When she did what she
did, everyone seemed to miss the point entirely.

—*What was the point?*

—That it wasn't simple cause and effect. Why is that so hard to understand? You don't listen to music and then kill your family. If that was the case, all of us – all of Arla's friends – would have done the same. We all listened to that stuff, we all embraced it.

—*You and Arla were friends?*

—Not 'friends' exactly.

—*OK, so tell me about how you and Arla first got to know each other.*

—Alright … So what would you think if I told you that Arla … that it was clear to everyone that Arla needed help.

—*Let's rewind a little – I'm trying to get a sort of timeline here.*

—OK, so I was in the same school as Arla Macleod from year nine, when she joined. I didn't notice her – no one did, not until year eleven. So that would have been around 2008, 2009?

—*Go on.*

—So year ten, year eleven, it's the time when most kids sort of come into their own, when they start working out who they are, *why* they are, yes? I remember that there were a few kids at the school who were into Skexxixx – you know, they dyed their hair black, wrote the logo on their bags in Tipp-Ex, drew that symbol in their books, that sort of thing.

—*Were you one of them?*

—That isn't really relevant, to be fair. What matters is that Arla began year eleven … *different*…

—*She had taken on this image?*

—See, this is where it all goes skew-whiff, where what was actually going on with Arla is diminished into a 'phase' or 'rebellion'. The truth was that the whole Skexxixx thing could have been anything – it could have been any musical group, any obsession. But the actual subject matter wasn't important; what was, was Arla's attitude towards it.

The other thing was that, in this country it's different. In the US, after Columbine, the whole 'goth' image was demonised, when in actual fact those killers – Dylan Klebold and Eric Harris – had nothing to do with goth whatsoever. The Christian right blamed

Marilyn Manson, a singer who Klebold and Harris didn't even *like*. It was a convenient way for them not to look at the deeper issues. In this country, on the other hand, the whole Skexxixx image was ... Put it this way: the kids at Saint Theresa's who cultivated that image used to get the shit kicked out of them. It wasn't cool or dangerous to have that image, and, certainly, no one was scared of them.

—*OK, but Arla took on that image all the same?*

—For a while, yes. But she was ... she used it differently...

Tessa then tells me the story you heard at the beginning of this episode about the religious studies teacher – about how he lost his temper with Arla, who, up until year eleven, had been a quiet and conscientious student.

—*What had she done to make him that angry?*

—Not much – hardly anything at all. She'd only written things in the inside cover of her exercise book. We used to have these green exercise books and the inside covers were great for doodling in, if you had the right sort of pen – those black rollerballs or fineliners.

—*What had she written?*

—As you probably know, the whole Skexxixx aesthetic was 'embrace your emptiness' – a kind of call to disenfranchised youth. Arla had written all this stuff about God in her book: 'God is nothing', 'I am nothing' – all that stuff; and she'd drawn all these weird drawings, these – I'm not sure – they were like men, boys, with these black, inky eyes...

—*She got quite a reaction from Mr Whitton though, right?*

—Yeah, he went mad. He actually ripped the back off her book and threw it in the bin, started ranting. It was pretty scary actually. The rest of us were pretty freaked out. And that's when I knew there was something not right about Arla ... because she started laughing. It wasn't nervous, and it wasn't a reaction to Mr Whitton's shouting. It was ... it was like she just didn't care anymore. Like she didn't give a single, solitary shit. Just think how much those drawings would go for on Ebay now ... It's disgusting.

—*Tessa, you said earlier that you were shocked but not surprised about Arla doing what she did. That was about five or six years after the incident you're talking about, right?*

—That's right. But that thing with Mr Whitton was the first time I saw that Arla Macleod had changed – not just changed, she had undergone a complete metamorphosis. She had become someone ... something else.

—*That sounds rather extreme!*

—It was! There was this girl, this nondescript little nerd, this good girl, who suddenly became ... just ... someone else.

—*And this incident in the RS class was the first time you noticed it?*

—Yes, it was the first time *I* did, but there were more, I'm sure of it. What was disgusting, what just made no sense, was that everyone blamed it on the music; like, if Arla hadn't listened to Skexxixx, she would have been fine. That was what angered me the most. And ... I guess that's what drew me to her in the first place.

—*So talk me through the Arla you knew.*

—I'm not sure if I ever really *knew* her. Like I say, from the very start of year eleven, she was ... it was like *Invasion of the Body-Snatchers* or something. Looking back on it now, it was clear that Arla was suffering from some sort of mental illness.

Anyway, we had a lot of new staff that year. Maybe we were all starting again? A lot of the teachers were young; some of them good, some not.

Anyhow, we were year eleven, we were practically adults, right? We had our favourites and we weren't going to take any nonsense from these upstarts. So imagine having to try and teach us lot; it must have been hell. Those young teachers are probably older teachers now, some of them will be freezing classes with the raise of an eyebrow...

But with Arla ... she ... it was the male ones, the men, that's who she seemed to save her bad behaviour for. You could tell she relished it; that she couldn't stand ... well, the men. There was Mr Whitton for RS, who'd been there for years, and two new ones: Mr Larsson, who taught French, and Mr Mahlik, who was ... history;

yes, that's right. Mahlik was the first black teacher we'd had. He had a funny accent as well – Birmingham or somewhere. There was always a tension, a silence when he taught us about apartheid. I remember that. Not knowing where to put your eyes, a laugh building in your throat – if you met someone else's eyes you were done for.

—*And Arla?*

—Yeah, she was just … just awful … to all of them. Mr Larsson got it the worst though. He was young, enthusiastic, posh – sort of like a dog; a big blonde Labrador. You could practically see his tail wagging as he pranced around the classroom, pointing at people with a big stupid grin on his face and getting them to repeat '*je vais à la pêche*', '*je vais au théâtre*'.

—*Sounds like quite a fun way of teaching to me.*

—Remember though, this was Stanwel – a shit, little, angry mining town in the northwest. One of those mad, racist, indie councillors nearly got elected a while back didn't they? Mr Larsson's progressive teaching methods were looked on either with derision or indifference!

—*Where were you in all this?*

—Oh, I was a stuck-up little madam back then. Thought I knew better than everyone.

—*That doesn't sound like the sort of person who would associate with Arla Macleod, then.*

—No. And I didn't really. I did sit with her in French though. Thanks to Mr Larsson.

—*I have to say, you've been pretty careful about dissociating yourself from Arla – you don't want to be seen as one of her friends.*

—That's true. If you ask anyone else who was at school with Arla, you'll get the same view of her. It's the reason she sat with me – was *made* to sit with me – in French.

—*And what was that view?*

—Let me finish this story first, then you'll get your answer.

—*OK.*

—So, Arla had been sent out of French for the third time for

– I don't even remember: turning around in her seat, not listening, whatever. Anyhow, Mr Larsson was so desperate to be liked, we soon worked out that the worst he would do was send you out of the room, and you could either have a wander round the corridors, because he'd inevitably forget you were out there, or else you could pull faces through the window.

Arla usually did the window faces. But the thing that struck me was that none of Arla's gang were in our French class, so she had no audience. Which meant she was just doing it to be vindictive, for no good reason, you know. And she was only ever like this with the men. It made me wonder if something had ... happened ... to her to make her that way.

—*So after that third time she was sat next to you ... as a punishment?*

—Not really. It was more like ... I think Mr Larsson was hoping I might be good for her in some way.

—*You mentioned Arla had a 'gang'? Were these her friends – the ones we see in the photos in the documentary?*

—That's them: Deborah Masterson and Paulette English. I'll never forget those names.

—*Were you a ... victim of this 'gang'...?*

—Sort of. But they were hardly a gang, to be fair – just three little Skeks, ha! I'd forgotten that word till now – a collective term for a bunch of girls in ripped clothes and too much eyeliner who crept around the edges of the corridors and huddled in their little covens at break time, talking about how life was so deeply unfair and how no one understood them.

Anyway, having Arla sit next to me in that lesson was a godsend; it meant that there was a sort of begrudging truce between us. I also got a lot of insight into her as a person. I guess that's why I got in touch with you. I feel I can be objective about the whole thing, but still remain vaguely anonymous.

—*Why is it so important to you to remain anonymous?*

—I ... I guess that some fears don't leave you, not properly. Some fears leave, like, teeth marks that will never fade.

Imagine not feeling safe in your own home … imagine them…
Sorry. Excuse me. Can we take five, please?

*Both Tessa and the television documentary allude to the violence and
intimidation that Arla and her two friends dealt out at the school. This
behaviour seems utterly at odds with the current image of the UK's 'goth'
subculture, which is composed mostly of quiet introverts. When we start
again, I ask Tessa if the bullying seemed in any way strange or out of the
ordinary to her.*

—In retrospect, yes; but at the time, no. So, at the start of year
eleven, like I say, there were a few kids who shared the same sort of
aesthetic, the same look, as Arla. But they were your typical introverts, loners.

—*I'm a little confused; did Arla have a gang at school that people
were scared of or not?*

—The thing you have to understand about Arla back then was
that she wasn't like the others, she wasn't like anyone. Arla had suddenly become this violent, messed-up kid but no one wanted to
look at why. Saint Theresa's staff were quick to snap off any ugly-
looking heads that reared up from among the students; but as soon
as they turned their backs, two would grow back in their places. So
Arla would get in trouble and be punished for her behaviour, but
what did that achieve? An hour's detention after school for terroris-
ing teachers was all she got. Anyway, to answer your question, yes,
Arla did have friends – Deborah and Paulette. And no one messed
with her, so no one messed with them. Any power those two had was
granted to them by Arla. And I suppose they shared the more-or-less
immunity that the school seemed to allow her.

—*There was a lot of talk after the killings about some kind of external
influence playing a part in what Arla did. Do you think that was an
attempt to pin the blame on something – on someone – perhaps?*

—You're right. In that documentary, they were quick to blame
Skexxixx's lyrics and songs, weren't they? That all this stuff about

embracing emptiness, about being nothing, was preying on young people's insecurities. When actually what it was doing was simply making money. I mean, I hate to sound cynical, but it was. And no teenager can say they've ever felt wholly adjusted growing up, that they've never felt worthless. They didn't need Skexxixx to tell them that.

But there was something else going on with all that Skexxixx stuff – something that never even got picked up on.

—*What was that?*

—So, his second album – which was the one everyone was listening to at the time, by the way – was much less … controversial than the first one. It was much more melancholy and introverted, with less defiance than *Embrace Your Emptiness*, which was the one everyone knew him for, and that fitted nicely into Arla's story, didn't it? In my humble opinion, though, *Through the Mocking Glass* holds much more significance – and it was the album that I know for a fact Arla listened to the most. She was obsessed with that CD when the rest of Skexxixx's fans were just starting to grow up a bit.

Skexxixx's 2007 album, Through the Mocking Glass, *which Tessa mentions, saw much less commercial success than 2004's* Embrace Your Emptiness, *and received mediocre reviews in* Kerrang *and* Metal Hammer *magazines, which cite it as the beginning of the end for the artist.*

However, Tessa is right about the significance of some of the album's themes for Arla's case. Look at some of the lyrics to the title track, 'Through the Mocking Glass':

'…driven to the place where our world ends,
Never look back, never look back.
Where all that remains is a pale door,
Never look back, never look back.
And a mocking reflection that beckons us forth,
Never look back, never look back.
To a place where our failures are marked by ticker-tape scars,

And our mistakes, pedestals where we gaze at the stars...'
(Copyright Wormfood Records, 2007)

*The lyrics of many of the songs on this album are about disappearing
to a place where our mistakes and our failures are embraced and treated
as lessons. At least that's an interpretation shared by many on the numerous fan sites and forums surrounding Skexxixx, which often cite these
themes as the reason the musician made* Through the Mocking Glass
*his swan song. He seemed to vanish not long after its release, only making
a brief appearance on Twitter in 2015 before disappearing once again.*

—Arla used to listen to that *Through the Mocking Glass* album
constantly – she was obsessed with it. She used to write the lyrics
all over her books. Everything about failure, about mistakes, about
vanishing, disappearing. I don't know how much more of a cry for
help she could have made. Blaming the music for what Arla did is
just too easy, isn't it? People should look at what those lyrics really
said about her state of mind.

Extract from *She Never Told Us*
(Blamenholm Productions)

[*A montage of promotional photographs of Skexxixx
and footage of fans dressed in similar attire fades
in and then out. A shot of a priest shouting from the
stage in a school hall; below is the caption 'Concerned
Parents of America – Santa Barbara Division' meeting
2007.*]

'Parents! Teachers! I urge you to talk to your kids
about the music they're listening to! Go in their bed-
rooms! Read these lyrics that they're listening to,
listen to this music! Then you can come back to me and
tell me that I'm being hysterical!'

[*There are whoops and applause.*]

'Tell me I'm being hysterical when he's telling you

it's OK to embrace nothing! Tell me I'm being hysterical when he's telling your babies that they're nobody!'

[*Wild applause and shouts.*]

'Then, when you take these CDs and burn them, you
are showing your kids that you reject his nothing, that
you reject his emptiness!'

[*The audience give this a standing ovation.*]

*There's so much I want to ask Arla herself about all this, but Elmtree
Manor has very specifically told me not to. Which is unfortunate, because
this part of the story clearly goes so much deeper. And now I can see what
Tessa is getting at. Because I saw the photos of Arla from back then, and I
watched the documentary and read the newspapers, and I admit that, at
the time, I believed the simplified narrative they presented.*

Extract from She Never Told Us
(Blamenholm Productions)

[*On screen, a silhouetted teenage girl talks to the
camera. Her voice has been altered electronically.*]

'They would … they would just prowl the corridors,
wait till they caught you on your own and then surround
you. She – Arla – once told me that I'd been 'chosen'
as their 'sacrifice'. She was the ringleader, Arla was.
She had the others totally under her control … like,
totally under a spell or something…'

*—So let's go back to the tentative relationship between you and Arla.
You began speaking together in French lessons, correct?*

—Yes. Arla had this … I don't want to say aura, but this sort of
hum coming from her, this energy, like she was this restless soul
that couldn't be stilled. I admit I was scared of her – scared of her
unpredictability. The others – Paulette and Deborah – they were just
normal, I guess, but liked to pretend they were all messed up inside.
With Arla it felt genuine.

—Did she ever confide in you?

—No! Of course not! I don't think Arla ever confided in anyone. She was too … *feral*. Yes, that's a good word for her. I don't think she actually trusted anyone. But in those lessons we were in a delimited environment, where I could … study her. I'll make no bones about it – she fascinated me. She really did. It was like there was this terrible emptiness inside her that was screaming, constantly screaming.

—So what about this idea that she and her gang picked victims?

—Horseshit, if you don't mind the language. Like I say, it was a nice little narrative for the papers. And I suppose the people who were there at the time couldn't help exploiting it. Imagine getting a message from a *Sun* journalist on Friends Reunited promising you hundreds of pounds to talk about some girl you hated at school who killed her family. It doesn't matter what the truth is, then, does it? Her actions made her worthless, right? Imagine if you could get on prime-time television, tell a story with your face blacked out and your voice distorted, make even more money, look after your family, get your kids that present they're hankering for? Who cares if it's true – it's only Arla Macleod, that psycho who killed her family. Who's going to object?

—What about her friends, Deborah and Paulette – did they sell their stories?

—To be fair to them, they were as scared of Arla as the rest of us. As far as I know, they hid as far away as they could after Arla did what she did to her family. Cowards to the end, those two.

—So why didn't you make money from Arla's story? Why are you telling me all this now?

—Because I believe in what's right. Because I noticed something about Arla that maybe no one else picked up on – not the teachers, not the other students. I'm not an expert; I'm not bigging up myself here. I'm just saying that it was easier to dismiss Arla as trouble rather than try to work out why she behaved like she did. Maybe if I tell you all this, it'll exorcise some of my old ghosts? I don't know.

—So why do you *think she behaved like that?*

—Remember those two boys who killed James Bulger back in 1993? And what about those two brothers in Edlington in 2009 – ten and eleven years old – who tortured and almost killed an eleven-year-old and only stopped because their 'arms were tired'; those two were known as 'the Devil Brothers', for fuck's sake. Look, I'm not saying that any of them should be absolved of the horrific things they did – all four of those children deserve punishment – but no one wants to look at *why*, about how those kids had been failed, had been turned into monsters … by eleven years old. They were monsters, yes, but also victims – victims of abuse and neglect. Victims of parents who had also been abused and neglected; parents who didn't know how to parent. Monsters can only be made, monsters are not born.

—*So how do you think all that applies to Arla?*

—Look, I'm not here to accuse anyone of anything, I just think Arla Macleod killed her family for a reason. But I don't know what that reason was.

I will tell you about something I saw, though. I've never told anyone about it before because it's not exciting, and it doesn't fit the narrative. But to be fair it is a little bit strange.

—*OK…*

—Saint Theresa's was pretty good about calling parents in when kids were playing up. So it wasn't long after the start of year eleven that Arla's mum got called to a meeting. It was Mr Whitton's doing, as far as I know. How it worked was that the kid and their parent would have to meet with the head of year. I only knew Arla's mum was there because I was on my way to the toilet in the middle of maths. The girls' toilet was on the first-floor corridor. You had to walk along a kind of open balcony to get there, and from there you could look down and see the reception; they had this fancy new one – all glass and ceramics displays, trophies and signed football shirts, that sort of thing. Anyway, I was walking along to the toilet, and glanced down into reception and saw her sat there – Mrs Macleod, Arla's mum.

—*How did you know it was her?*

—Arla was stood next to her. Honestly, they were the double of

each other, those two. It was like a taller, fatter Arla had walked into
school!

Ms Caton, our head of year, was stood with them, her back to
me. I stopped and I was scared. I should have kept going, but I don't
think I could have moved even if I wanted to.

And I remember feeling there was something … wrong about it
all. Arla was stood next to her mum, all sweetness and light, none
of the tooth-blackener stuff or her Skexxixx hoodie; I'd never seen
her look so meek, not since the year before. I mean, I fully expected
her to be all attitude with her mum, but it was clear – no one was
messing with Mrs Mcleod.

—*What were you scared of? Was it what Arla would do if she saw you
and thought you were eavesdropping?*

—I … hmm … that's a good question. I don't think there was
any one thing that scared me. I mean, like I say, the girl fascinated
me and here was her mum too … I *was* scared, but I couldn't resist
listening. So I just sort of stood there, pretending to be fascinated by
the netball trials poster on the wall. I knew I only had a few minutes
to listen before either Arla, her mum or one of the reception staff saw
me and called up to see what I was doing.

So I stood, trying to keep just out of sight. I remember the sun
was beating down outside and the air was totally still. I could hear
Arla's mum talking; she had this strong Scottish accent and it was like
she was shouting and whispering at the same time. It came out like
a sort of squeak, like the air coming out of a balloon.

—*What was she saying?*

—At the time, they resonated, those words, but I had no idea
why; I was only young myself and had no clue.

'I hope you realise, Arla,' she was saying, her face really close to
Arla's, speaking almost through her teeth, 'I hope you realise how this
is making our family look.'

Arla was nodding; she was nodding but her face was absolutely
still, almost like a doll or a mannequin. She had tears pouring down
her cheeks, but she was utterly silent.

Mrs Macleod went on – I remember her teeth – they were bared, big, yellow and thick. It was like she hated Arla.

'Do you want them calling round?' she hissed. 'Do you want them talking to your dad? Is that what you want? You're making our family look awful. Is that what you want?'

Arla was crying and shaking her head fast, like little kids do. She looked utterly humiliated.

'What about your sister?' Mrs Macleod kept saying, and she was jabbing Arla at the top of her arm with a long finger. 'What about your sister? You want to destroy it all for her too? Everything we've built here. Is that what you want? You remember when we came here, do you? You remember me telling you about taking your chance, how you only get one? Well Alice is taking her chance, even if you're not!'

Something must have tickled my senses then because I ... I somehow knew that one of them was about to look up. I remember just turning tail and walking back the way I had come, head up, shoulders back. Even if Arla spotted me, it would just look like I was walking along the balcony towards the corridor.

But those words: 'how this is making our family look'. I remember walking back to maths with the weight of them dragging at me. It's like when you hear your parents swear. I thought about Arla's tears and there was something ... *something*, this flicker of understanding that everything wasn't right, that there was something wrong for her.

If you look at it and try to make sense of what she said ... well, I mean, her daughter was stood there, crying, clearly messed up and she was more interested in how it was making *her* look, all the trouble Arla was getting into, you see? 'I hope you realise how this is making our family look.' She was almost saying that they'd given up on Arla. Like, instead of asking *why* Arla was behaving the way she was, they'd given up and were now concentrating on her sister instead. I think it was then when I really started feeling sorry for Arla. I only wish I'd been mature enough to recognise that sort of narcissism back then.

But it makes sense now, I suppose. No wonder Arla wanted to escape to 'another place'.

—*So you got close to Arla after that day?*

—I was interested in her. We weren't proper friends. But even that's not quite right. Like I say, her whole … her whole *thing* fascinated me.

—*And you reached out to her?*

—In a small way at first. Like with a wild dog – you offer little bits of food to begin with, to show it you mean no harm. I'd sometimes point out answers, show her how to do little bits and bobs. We neither of us had much interest in French but, sat next to me, Arla didn't really have much of an audience and didn't disrupt as much. Soon enough, she began to treat me like I was … well, like she trusted me a little.

—*You and Arla talked, then?*

—Yes. Not intimately, not at first, but it was alarming how quick Arla was to share certain things with me. That's what it was like with her: she was either furious with you, trying to control the conversation, or she was curled into herself, tucked away inside a shell so you couldn't even get close.

—*Attachment issues?*

—Clearly. Again, I see that now, but why did no one see it then?

Tessa pauses for a moment. I can tell she's thinking carefully about what she's going to tell me next.

—Arla used to slash, she used to cut. Her forearms were crisscrossed with scabs and scars. She never tried to hide them, but she never showed them off either. They were just *there*. She told me she used to do it when she was so angry, or so sad, she didn't know what else to do. It would 'let some of the pain out' she used to say. I used to tell her I understood. It was a cry for help. To anyone who'd listen.

—*None of the teachers picked up on this?*

—I don't know. Maybe they did. In classes, though, I certainly never saw any sort of attempt to understand the way Arla was. But then again, they had thirty teenagers who all needed help, school inspectors breathing down their necks, and the government telling them they're crap and worthless. You can see why a troublemaker like Arla might have slipped through the net.

—*Did you ever bring up Arla's home life in your chats? Did you ever mention the incident with her mother?*

—I learned pretty quickly that if you asked Arla things she would clam up, shut down, retreat; you had to wait for her to volunteer information. And when she did it would be scattergun. So, she'd turn and ask me whether a word was masculine or feminine, then the next thing was, she'd tell me about how her mother hit her in the face the previous night…

—*She said that?*

—Yes. Just like, matter-of-fact. She wouldn't look at me; just said it. Just dropped it into conversation: 'My mum slapped me across the face last night.'

I never asked why, I never said that was awful or anything. I just nodded, listened. Maybe that was why she kept telling me stuff.

—*What else did Arla tell you about her home life?*

—Not a great deal. I know she spent a lot of time on her own. Her sister was forever being driven to sports training and Arla would just be left in the house. And she'd just drop these things in when she felt like it: her mum slapped her, her dad made them all pray for an hour when they got home, that sort of thing.

—*Being left alone, being hit and being made to pray – it doesn't sound like a happy home…*

—I suppose it doesn't. But – and this sounds awful – I was more *interested* than concerned. How cold is that? But I've had my comeuppance. I'll always live with the guilt that maybe if I'd said something, raised a concern, things may have been different.

—*So, do you think that some kind of intervention could have pre-vented Arla doing what she did to her family?*

—I think it's pointless to speculate. Arla was, what, twenty-one when she killed her family? Still not a proper adult really. Maybe it would, maybe it wouldn't. That's the thing about looking back and regretting; you'll never ever know for sure. It sounds so stupid now, but back then, if you'd have seen her, experienced her, this whirling dervish; all angles, all anger … I think a lot of people – school staff included – were more frightened of her than they wanted to admit.

—*Arla's younger sister, Alice – was the same thing happening to her?*

—Alice was in a very different world from Arla. She was a swimmer, wasn't she? Some sort of athlete. She was pretty as well – stunning if I remember right. She was one of the elite. She had the looks, the body, the winning smile. Alice Macleod certainly didn't associate with the likes of me. You know, Arla never mentioned her to me, not even once. What does that tell you?

—*You say Mrs Macleod said 'Alice is taking her chance, even if you're not!' What do you think that meant?*

—It's a funny one. At first it sounds like the Macleods had clear ideas of how they wanted their daughters to behave. Arla maybe was a prototype? Alice was the real deal? They'd failed with Arla so they stopped bothering with her. Like I say, we never once talked about Alice. I sometimes wish we had.

Tessa's account of the Arla she knew has now added a bit more to the picture we are building up here. We already know that Lucy Macleod fled an abusive home life in Saltcoats when Arla and Alice were very young, that she then grew up in a staunchly religious environment. Stanley Macleod seems to have used the fact he 'saved' the family from Arla's violent father as some kind of justification for the strictness he imposed. But Tessa's story is now suggesting that Lucy Macleod was not the nurturing type either.

Were these the beginnings – the touchpaper for Arla's psychosis? Possibly. But I still feel we're missing something significant.

—*Did Arla ever talk to you about things that sounded … odd. Seeing things that weren't there, for example?*

—See that's interesting. A lot of that was discussed when she was in court, wasn't it? That she'd lost her grip on reality; that her psychosis had taken over, that sort of thing.

Arla did used to talk a lot of rubbish about seeing things – demons, beings, ghosts, all that stuff.

—*Go on…*

—She used to tell me about the 'thin places' – places where you could go back and forth between here and other worlds.

—*To me, that sounds pretty significant.*

—Like I said earlier, Arla was obsessed with that second Skexxixx album. She spent her time on message boards, chat rooms, forums talking to other Skeks about it. All the theories behind it. To me, it seemed like just an escape to her … nothing more. What fifteen-year-old *doesn't* want to escape?

I'd like to take a moment to draw your attention to another track on the Through the Mocking Glass *album entitled 'Dead-Eyed March', which, after speaking to Arla herself, strikes a strange chord within me.*

Again, like much of Skexxixx's output, especially on Through the Mocking Glass, *the lyrics deal with isolation and alienation. 'Dead-Eyed March' is a rather experimental track, mainly instrumental; it reminds me of one of the more languid and indulgent tracks on* The Cure's Disintegration *album, but maybe that's me showing my age. On this track, in the midst of the whirling guitars and feedback, Skexxixx's voice wails a brief chorus:*

'A thousand black-eyed girls,
A thousand black-eyed boys,
Marching to a distant drum,
Looking for a place called home…'

It's conjecture, of course, but was there something in this track that Arla fixated on? Arla's story of the night she killed her family features a black-eyed girl and boy. Is this simply a coincidence?

According to the various reviews I've read, Through the Mocking

Glass *was an attempt to speak about conformity and how it can alien-ate those on society's fringes. But coming in 2007, it was seen by many as behind the times and even irrelevant.*

But this is what a great many other alternative musicians talk about in their music, and always have. Arla, by year eleven, when she was about fifteen, clearly felt this way, so perhaps it's no wonder she identified with the content of the album.

The link between this music and Arla Macleod cannot be ignored, therefore. Whether it is right essentially to blame music for heinous deeds committed by its listeners I don't think it's my place to say. But, I do agree with Tessa: things just aren't that simple.

Let's go back to Tessa.

—*You said earlier that you weren't surprised that Arla did what she did to her family. You also describe Arla as being troubled and intimidating.*

—I'll tell you a bit about what it was really like to be at school in proximity to Arla Macleod. Now, like I say, I was in this privileged position of not being 'in' with her, but being deemed 'alright' enough not to get the full force of her rage.

So I told you the story about Mr Whitton, the things she wrote in her book, the way she laughed and got everyone else laughing. That's what was frightening about Arla, she had no fear. She was not intimidated by anyone. She looked like this meek little thing; and I saw first-hand when she was with her mother that buried under all this anger there was a quiet girl. But there was one thing in particular that would bring the rage out. If anyone made a sexual remark to Arla, or said something about her body, she'd go … she'd go for them like an attack dog.

—*Can you give me any examples of this?*

—So the 'bully' at Saint Theresa's was a lad called Keith Jobson – or 'Jobba' as everyone knew him. Jobba was like a silverback gorilla, but an ugly, white one, more like a troll, with a big scar down the side of his face. I'd been to primary school with Jobba, so I knew that it was from having a birthmark removed, but he used to tell people in high school that it was from 'getting glassed'.

Jobba liked to pick on the quiet little introverts – the boys with long hair and 'Skexxixx' written on their bags in Tipp-ex.

—*I know the type. Every school has a 'Jobba'.*

—So right near the start of year eleven, Jobba and his mates were hanging around the corner shop near school, smoking. Jobba – inexplicably – had a girlfriend at the time; this pinched little thing in year nine whose face always looked like it had growths all over it because she covered her acne with such a thick layer of foundation.

I was walking away from the shop, up to get my bus, when I heard a commotion. I turned and saw there were loads of Saint Theresa's kids there and a few from Stanwel Grammar. And I saw Arla and Jobba's girlfriend standing face to face in front of a growing crowd. The two were clearly squaring up for a fight; and no one wants to miss a fight, especially when it's girls, right?

—*Isn't that rare – a girl fight?*

—Yeah. Especially when one was Arla Macleod. This was right at the beginning of year eleven, remember, before all her 'scary Arla' reputation was made.

—*So this was the first time you'd seen Arla be violent?*

—Yes. And the way it happened was … it just was so … I mean, it wasn't like anything serious, not really. What happened was Jobba's girlfriend, Tracey, was screaming, calling Arla all these names, and Jobba's stood behind her, chuckling like a drain. It looked for a bit like Arla was just going to back down, she was shaking her head, moving away. Then he said something.

—*Who? Jobba?*

—Yeah. I didn't catch it all but it was something … derogatory … something sexual. And Arla … you could see it in her eyes first, it was *scary* … she just lost it. She brushed Tracey aside and just started laying into Jobba. I remember she had hold of his ear with her left hand and with her right she was just swinging, hitting him over and over again … and he was screaming, 'Get her off me! Get her off!'

It should have been funny. It was at first. But then something …
something uncertain fell over the crowd. It was the childish panic
in Jobba's voice, I think, and the shrieks coming from Arla. Loads
of people just turned and began walking away. A few ran. No one
stepped in to help. It took the guy with the moustache from the shop
to come out and threaten to call the police before Arla stopped. And
she just ran – this lopsided, gangly run, like a half-squashed daddy-
long-legs – off round the corner while Jobba just stood there, blood
all over his face.

He came into school the next day with two black eyes. I was fully
expecting everyone to be laughing at him, but no one did. And you
would have expected Arla to become an almost-hero then. But that
never happened either. If anything, what had happened had been too
much, had gone full circle. It seemed that then everyone wanted to
challenge her, wind her up, to see what she'd do.

—*This sounds like quite unusual behaviour. And I hate to sound
sexist – but especially for a girl.*

—I think that's what first made Arla an … an oddity, something
everyone wanted to look at, to poke with a stick.

Including me.

—*So there were other, similar incidents?*

—Yeah. And it didn't matter if it was in a lesson, she would just
go…

But Arla wasn't respected. In a story, after that incident, she would
have been, right? I mean, she would have been seen as a sort of hero?
Maybe if she'd fought someone who commanded respect themselves,
then it might have been different. But, no – Arla ended up a freak
show and things only got worse for her…

—*Worse?*

—It was like, there seemed to be this sort of *sexuality* that ema-
nated from Arla after that. Like, her shirt was always unbuttoned and
she always wore a black bra and you could see the straps. I mean,
it's not like some other girls didn't, but – it's hard to explain – it was
much more *raw* with Arla.

—*But you said that any sexual remark directed at Arla resulted in extreme behaviour. This sounds like a huge contradiction.*

—Yes, it was. But isn't that another huge red flag, that kind of behaviour? I remember how wrong it all felt at the time. I was just too young to properly understand it.

—*You were a child too, of course.*

—If … if Arla was suffering from mental illness at the time, were people taking advantage of her? It feels … it's too much for me to say.

—*You're just reporting what you heard…*

—OK then. What I will say is that there were rumours of promiscuity; and not just that, it was also said that Arla was into certain *things*. I don't want to say what because there was just frankly ridiculous stuff flying about, it was horrible: that she was easy; that she would go with anyone; you just had to get her drunk. I don't know if any of it was true. It's just what I heard…

So … there you have it. That's me … that's all I know, really…

—*Are you saying that's the end?*

—I'm saying that's all I have.

We have to remember that all this occurred long ago. I'm also wondering just how significant Skexxixx's lyrics really are for Arla's case. I doubt Tessa's belief that Arla was completely unlike any other Skexxixx fan in the country, possibly in the world. What does stand out for me, however, is Arla's violence, her unpredictability; it feels like it's in this part of Tessa's account that we're really starting to get a feel for the origins of Arla's … what? … Madness? Psychosis? But overall I feel like I have come up against a blank wall, an account from a spectator rather than a participant.

I don't know what axe Tessa has to grind with Arla, if she has one at all, but I do get the impression that there's something she's not telling me. Exactly what seems buried under a mound of conjecture.

The longer I talk to Tessa, the more frustrated I have become. Her stories and memories are disorganised and fragmented. I feel she's holding

*back through fear of something, but I'm not sure what. As our interview
draws to a close, I can't help feeling a little disappointed.*

*I finish by asking her the question, the answer to which is perhaps
what I'm searching for with this series.*

   —*In your opinion, why did she do it? Why did she kill her family
that night?*
   —I couldn't say. I have no idea other than what was said in court.
Arla Macleod is mentally ill. She was at the time of the killing and
there were definitely signs of it in school. But I'm not qualified to
say anything. I can't make a diagnosis and I can't give you a definitive reason.
   —*Can I just say something, before we finish?*
   —By all means.
   —*I just feel like … I don't know … that I've only seen a little bit of
what you know; that you've only given me a glimpse into what it was like
to be close to Arla Macleod back in school.*
   —I've told you what I know, what I experienced. She wasn't long
out of school, was she, when she killed her family? Twenty-one – no
age really.
   But I have told you everything I know. I mean, I was never directly
involved with her really, so this is all I can give you. Arla was a troubled kid. It should have been obvious to everyone, but it was missed,
ignored, swept under the carpet. I'm not just blaming the school
either, it's all our faults – all of us who knew her, or knew of her.
   —*But the ordinary person can't be expected to—*
   —But they should. This is what I mean: there should be so much
more awareness of … of whatever was going on with Arla. All the
signs were there that something was wrong and as far as I know, they
were ignored.

*This is, unfortunately, the truth. There are no records of social services
ever having been alerted to Arla Macleod – not by the school, nor anyone
else in her life. It's hard to say whether these are failings of the system or*

failings in people, or, like most of the things in Arla Macleod's case, the two are entwined, tangled.

Tessa had no contact with Arla after she left school. Tessa stayed on for A-levels while Arla was cast adrift and left to her own devices. We will, in next week's episode, find out more about the years after school but it seems we have come to the end of the line with Tessa, which leaves me feeling strangely unfulfilled.

—I'm just … I'm intrigued by why you agreed to speak to me. I feel like there's something you want to say and you haven't … or you can't…

I immediately regret these words and prepare for Tessa to terminate our interview, even perhaps forbid me to use these last few hours of conversation. But after a long pause, she continues, in what at first sounds like an elaborate stage whisper. She drops her voice and its edge carries a very real fear.

—I'm going to tell you something. No, that's not right. I'm going to give you something: a warning.

—A warning?

—Yes. You're going to think I'm either insane or paranoid, but to be fair, that doesn't matter. You've promised me anonymity. I hope you'll respect that promise.

—Of course. You've been gracious enough to talk to me, I—

—Listen, I asked for that guarantee for a very good reason. And if you're going to speak out about Arla Macleod, you should follow my example.

—What do you mean? I should remain anonymous? Why? I can't really—

—Let's just say I'm surprised. I'm surprised you haven't had any … any *contact* yet.

—OK, I'm lost now. Surely you don't mean…

—You're not difficult to find – online I mean.

—Right … but I'm not online, not personally.

—You'll want to have a think about that. Like, you'll want to make sure. That's what I mean.

—*Are you talking about threats? Trolls? I've honestly never even considered that to be a problem. The internet's full of strange things…*

—All I'm saying is be careful. I don't know all the answers to the questions that'll be flying into your head right now. What I do know is that you need to be careful. That's why, after this is over, you won't be able to find me. No one will. That's all.

—*Can you elaborate?*

—No. I won't. I just … I can't have it happen again. No way. I won't.

—*Can't have what happen again?*

—I've already said too much. I'm sorry, we have to stop here. Just … just … It's like when you check your locks at night on all your windows and doors – do that online. Do it.

Our interview ends abruptly and Tessa vanishes back into the ether, behind the cloak she's spent a long time creating for herself. My immediate response is one of frustration. Our interview has been frustrating; Tessa herself has been frustrating, obscure and difficult to understand. Her warning is the clearest example of that.

If she didn't want me poking my nose around in the case of Arla Macleod, if I need to be careful, then why did she agree to talk to me?

What I'm really interested in are the reasons behind this warning, rather than the warning itself. I can only conclude that Tessa's final words are simply a deterrent – a way to put more distance between us, perhaps a final gesture to keep me at bay. I did notice that Tessa kept a similar distance from Arla in her recollections. Why?

It is while I am finishing the edits on this current episode and preparing for episode three, however, that things begin happening.

I often edit Six Stories *late into the night. Anyone who knows anything about the process of audio editing will tell you that it devours time, eats hours in great gulps, and before you know it, it's 4 am, your back is aching, a cup of cold coffee has formed a skin beside you and your brain feels like it's been between the jaws of a George Foreman grill for the last few hours.*

During these long periods of solitude, my reverie is generally uninterrupted, save for trips to the kettle or to the bathroom. Editing episode two, however, I am shocked from my hypnotic state by my phone. I must have been asleep, or close to it; the rendered audio on my screen is looping over and over again, and the buzz from my phone sends a galvanic jolt of something akin to horror right through me – as it always does.

I'll never get used to being notified of new followers or comments, which are few and so far have been, thankfully, pleasant. Of course, Six Stories is not immune to flame wars, but ninety-nine percent of the time these are between users in the comments section. Rarely is anything directed at me personally.

'Don't feed the trolls,' my friend told me. 'If someone's being horrid, ignore, ignore, ignore ... then block if need be.'

Thankfully I've not been trip-trapping too loudly over any bridges, yet when my phone buzzes, a long-buried, dusty verse from Poe fills my mind.

> *'Tis some visitor entreating entrance at my chamber door –*
> *Some late visitor entreating entrance at my chamber door; –*
> *This it is and nothing more.'*

The first thing I do, of course, is look at the time: 3.27 am. So I fully expect this to be a notification of a new follower – I wake up sometimes to a few new followers, sometimes in the US or Australia. Time difference – makes sense.

This, however, was a text.

Here I open wide the door.

```
From: [Unknown number]
Pack up. Pack in. Stop this now. There will be con-
sequences. This is your warning.
```

It's like something out of a bad thriller, yet the hour and the anonymity strike somewhere, niggle down between my ribs and find a sweet spot – the fear I've been talking about … its epicentre – and press with a sharpened point…

…as if someone knew exactly where to place the blade.

I shouldn't have looked. I should have trusted my instincts, waited until I'd slept, used the shock of the notification as an alarm that it was time to stop editing and go to bed.

But all of us know that it is impossible to ignore a text at 3.27 am from an unknown number. You *wouldn't have waited either; you, like me, would have felt the thing throbbing through your phone like an infection, the knowledge of it as intrusive and impossible to ignore as the tingle of a crowning wisdom tooth.*

So I looked.

This is your warning.

It has to be a mistake, it has to be. I've received mistaken texts before – we all have – and I've replied politely, even jovially, only to receive a tirade of abuse in return.

'Don't feed the trolls.'

I told myself not to open it, not now in this strange, dead time between night and morning, in this semi-consciousness where the slightest movement, the edge of a shadow can grow legs, become a monster and before you know it, you're being haunted.

Something, in that terrible morning half-light tells me that this is no mistake. A tiny, screaming, rational part of me is trying desperately to tell me this is a prank, but after Tessa's warning, that tiny, rational part of me is swamped in shadows. I feel myself beginning to shake.

Why such an extreme reaction? some of you may ask.

Maybe it's a generational thing; maybe it's a personality thing; maybe it's just me. It doesn't matter. What does matter is that there's a part of me – quite a significant part – that is unhappy with being visible, being available, online.

Why? You may ask. Everyone's online these days. You can tweet praise to your favourite celebrity on Twitter; argue politics with a stranger on

Facebook. And maybe it's exactly that – that little pocket in which I'm uncomfortable.

The thing is Six Stories *never was, never is and never will be about me. There are plenty of podcasters out there who have carved out a small niche of celebrity, and that's fine, well done to them. But it's a step I could never take. Sometimes I wonder what it must be like to be someone like J.K. Rowling, picking up her phone to have thousands of social-media notifications every moment of every day; dropping the veil of fiction and being a celebrity in her own right. The very idea of facing such a barrage of attention fills me with horror. Because that way lie the trolls, the rape threats, all that stuff.*

Imagine walking out of your house into a busy city centre to have every single person yell their opinion in your face; then those people arguing with each other. Imagine having people calling you names, saying personal things about you and your life and your family then vanishing behind a wall – the anonymity of the internet.

I admire J.K. Rowling more than ever for being able to withstand that. I never could.

I am ready to reply, my thumbs poised to type a wide-eyed protest: Why? What have I done?

Then I remember: Don't feed the trolls.

I go to be bed, but I don't sleep – I toss and turn and compose replies, playing out entirely fictitious conversations, each with a different outcome, all of which end in something terrible happening.

To me.

When I awake from a couple of hours of fitful slumber, I call my friend who helps me with social media and ask advice.

They tell me what I thought they would: ignore, keep on going, don't even acknowledge.

I wish it would help.

The truth is, a message on the Six Stories *Facebook page, or a tweet or an Instagram comment would frighten me less. But this was a text. My phone number is not and has never been publicly available.*

Now, I'm not so naive that I don't know there are plenty of nefarious ways to find someone's number, and, in those weary hours of the morning, I endlessly google myself, follow threads, read blogs, even trawl the comments on a YouTube channel where someone uploaded all previous Six Stories *episodes without my permission.*

Nothing.

I should feel at least some relief that there doesn't seem to be anyone publicly calling out their hatred of me online. I have never before dared to look, in case there is.

It isn't until lunchtime the following day, when the fear engendered by the text message has almost evaporated and I am tentatively continuing the edit, that my phone buzzes again. This time, that jolt in my stomach is not so harsh; a protracted text conversation with my friend during the previous few hours has readied me for incoming notifications. This same friend has advised me to be defiant, to update the Six Stories *media accounts, to tell my followers episode three will be dropping soon. I have followed this advice.*

However, when I read the text, my stomach clenches fist-like and tears prick my eyes.

From: [Unknown number]
Perhaps I need to make myself clear. Stop. Delete. Leave well alone. This is your final warning. There will be consequences.

This reignites the terrible fear from before and turns it into a whirling sickness. I'm not too proud to admit that my initial reaction is to lie down, curl up, hide, protect myself. You might think I'm overreacting, but those are my feelings.

So what to do? Well … the fact you're listening to episode two now speaks for itself. My social-media accounts remain open. I will not bow down to threats.

What I will say to whoever is sending me these messages, is that I am open for proper, adult discussion – on or off the record. Rather than hiding behind your anonymity, why not come forward and talk – explain to me in rational terms what I should be leaving alone and why. I am a reasonable person and am willing to listen. To debate, like an adult.

I will not, however, engage with threats or abuse. I will point out as well, that anyone who engages in offensive posts, comments or squabbles on the Six Stories *social-media accounts will simply be blocked or banned. I get that this is a recent and, perhaps, difficult subject for discussion, but really, what is at the heart of it all? Discussion is what.*

And that's where I want to keep it.

On that note, this has been Six Stories.

This has been our second.

Until next time…

TorrentWraith – Audio (Music & Sounds)

Type	Name
Audio	**Arla Macleod Rec003 [320KBPS]** Uploaded **4 weeks** ago, Size 52.9 MiB. ULed by JBazzzzz666

I'm going to be quick. I'm going to tell you straight away what I saw. I'm not going to mess about talking about other things.

I might start talking about other things.

You said it was OK to do that.

But I'm tired today.

You see, sometimes I just want to say it out loud, say it quick. I can feel the words in my mouth, filling me up, desperate to come out and then … then they just stay there, stuck around my teeth like toffee.

You said that that's normal too. You said when I saw them that I should treat them like they're real. The words will come easier then. Talking might change them, it won't stop them, but they might change a little bit. That's what you said. You said that I have to keep going.

You said if I did this, we might be able to maybe find a trigger. You said that this is new therapy, pioneering. You're proud of it. I was proud that you'd chosen me.

But it's hard.

The Quetiapine kept them away at first, kept them calm, like that film *Drop Dead Fred*. Have you seen it? Where the girl has an imaginary friend and every time she takes her medication it hurts him, weakens him, makes him fall over, become less strong.

It were like that at first. It were like, I had that feeling when I knew they were coming – that fear, boiling in my belly.

Then nothing.

Sometimes I remember those silly games I used to play. All those daft rules. I try and remember how to do them but I only get about halfway before I get tired and forget. Or I can smell dinner coming from the canteen and my mouth starts watering and that makes me forget.

You know, I mainly think about food these days. That comes first, before everything. Like, look … look at my mouth – it's watering just saying that! Maybe that's all the Quetiapine is, like, it's just a pill that makes you so hungry you can't think about anything else. Meatballs last night, oh my God those meatballs. Like, every time I ate one, every time it squished between my teeth and I could feel the juices on my tongue, I wanted to shout out, I wanted to cry about how … how beautiful it were…

We had trifle for afters last night. They put this stuff between the layers – I think it's sponge and it soaks up all the juice from the fruit, and if you get your spoon in just right and you get a layer of custard and jelly and fruit – all different textures and tastes at once – it's like the magic number, the secret combination, you know?

The size of me … the size of me now. No wonder, eh?

No wonder.

I'm so tired.

So I woke up at about three this morning and needed the toilet. I was half asleep, you know? Like, where the world is all a bit fuzzy on the edges and it's like you're here but not really here – you're an observer in your own reality. It never gets proper dark here, there's always that soft light that you can't turn off in your room. You can ask them to turn it off if you want but I quite like it. I were never allowed a night-light when I were a kid, so maybe that's why? Maybe I want to feel like a kid – grab hold of a bit of childhood I didn't have? I dunno.

I looked at my clock and it were midnight. One of those silly games from all them years ago was about midnight. You had to get up at midnight and make a phone call or something. I try and remember but there's something stopping me, like my brain clams up and won't let me peek in.

Anyway, and I'm sat down in the bog, like, you know, and…

When I came back out, it were sitting on top of the bed. I don't remember pulling the duvet back over but I must have done, you know, to keep it warm inside. It were sat … not *sat* but sort of kneeling; horrible it was, like proper *there*, you know, as if it had been waiting for the Quetiapine to wear off and … Well, we don't get given it till the morning.

Ugh … it were horrible.

I know, I shouldn't … you said I shouldn't personify them, but it's hard … it's hard. She … *it* were, like, kneeling on my bed. It were, like … I couldn't tell if it were wearing clothes or not cos it were … it were so horrible I couldn't keep my eyes on her … on *it* … for too long. It looked wet but it were definitely female – it had breasts and long black hair all plastered to its face, like that one off *The Ring*, you know? It were pale like her too, but not skinny. It were … all muscly and it had its arms up, like its elbows up and … and I could see all these, like, veins, all knotty, standing out on its arms. Her skin was pale … like she were dead, drowned.

There were something, I dunno, spidery about her … about it. It were like I knew she'd just sort of fallen off the ceiling and sat up on my bed. I knew that if I looked up at the ceiling I'd see a patch of wet, like she'd been in a cocoon or something … I dunno…

It were its face, though, that were the most scary thing. It was sort of old and young at the same time. It's hard to describe. You could only see a bit through the hair. Like, one moment its skin was wrinkly, like an old woman, and then it were smooth like a doll; and there was this one eye glaring out, all smooth and black like a shark's, you know? Like there were nothing behind it. And it were sort of … glowing. I know, right? How does black glow? But it was, like … like a sort of black-blue light, like something out of a rave. Like a strobe light or something. And I knew … oh, I knew that that were its only eye, that if you tucked back the hair you'd see just…

She was staring at me with that one eye, her arms up and her fingers spread, all her muscles tight. She were making no sound at all, like she were a TV programme turned down. I couldn't stop looking at her, she were so horrible. I just couldn't stop staring. Her lips were moving – she had these thick lips that were sort of black, like slugs, and I could see her teeth … they were … there were too many of them, all mashed together, all brown and yellow, like, not like fangs but all, like, squashed and sharp and crowded, you know?

She were saying something. She were talking. And every time she said it those teeth would catch her lips; they would catch those two black-slug lips, and it were, like, I could feel it too … I could feel the edges of those teeth on my lips. And she kept saying it over and over and over again, until those lips, until they burst and this … this stuff started dribbling down her chin. It were horrible.

I tried to make out the words.

'*Dar-oo-maa-san, dar-oo-ma-san*', or something like that.

It sent shivers through me and made my brain clench even harder.

When she … *it* went away, I got back into bed. I had to keep telling myself that I couldn't feel a warm patch on top – you know, like where it had been?

I were brave – I *felt* like I were brave not pressing the call button or owt, you know? Like, I knew she weren't real. But she was, she was there.

You know?

But, like I say, I'm tired today. Proper knackered.

It were like, when I tried to go to sleep, all those things that she were saying, all those silent words that she were mouthing, they all came back when I were trying to go to sleep – like an echo, you know? Like when you see something happen but you hear the sound a second later. Like that. As if her voice was coming from thousands and millions of light years away or something.

I'm the ghost that follows.

That's what she were saying. She were saying it over and over again. I knew it was her cos she had a sort of lisp cos of her teeth, cos she had too many. She kept saying it when I were trying to sleep. I recognised her voice.

I'm the ghost that follows.

And all I could think about were school – those times in school when Mrs Morris had a bull's heart up on her desk and we all had to watch her cut it open, and there were that horrible meaty smell like you get when you walk past the butcher's in the market. I remember a voice saying, 'Miss, I don't want to do it!' And Mrs Morris getting all exasperated and saying, 'For God's sake, Deborah, it's only a bit of meat – you eat burgers, don't you?'

That smell.

Deborah wasn't scared of meat anymore.

She was the queen of flesh, of muscle and organs and blood.

Dar-oo-ma-san.

She kept telling me, over and over and over.

She would never stop following me. She would never forgive me.

And that's why I'm tired.

Episode 3: The Ghost That Follows

—I remember once seeing this mam there one day with her little girl, must have only been three or summit. She was wearing one of them burkas and she's unwinding the swing; the lads used to wind the swings up, right to the top, spin them round till they were all looped up over the crossbar and it looked like barbed wire – God knows why. This mam, right, she spends about ten minutes, dead patient, unravelling the swing. The little lass is shouting 'Mammy, swing! Swing!' and the mam never shouts at her once; she never gets cross. That's maybe why I stopped and watched. Not proper staring, just kind of walking past slowly, but watching, pretending to look at my phone. This woman, right, she gets one of the swings down and she puts her little girl up on it and starts pushing. It's, like … it's weird cos it's someone with their kid using the park as a park, but still I get this sort of proper sad feeling in my belly.

Anyways, after a couple of minutes all these little lads go by on scooters and I can just hear them shouting 'Paki this' and 'Paki that', 'dirty Muslim', all that. One of them chucks a can of energy drink, half full, and it spins across the floor shooting it everywhere like a firework. That little girl, she looks all confused then she starts crying and the mam picks her up, dead calm and that, not even looking round, and the lads all scoot off, laughing. And, well, me mind did this sort of snapshot, this woman stood there in her burka, holding this crying kid, graffiti all over the swings, fag ends all over the floor. I was only fourteen and I thought what a shithole this place was. What a dump.

One thing's for sure – I'd never go back. Never. Not now.

I mean, I have to sometimes cos my parents live there, but I'm

never there for long. One night at most. If I can drive back the same
night I will.

It's a shit-hole. Just full of chavs and smackheads. Horrible.

The thing about growing up in a town like Stanwel is that you
get used to wanting to get away. There's a few ways you can get out:
you can work hard, do well in school, keep your head down and
make your own road out – you know, get to uni, get a good job
somewhere else. Or you can just let Stanwel take you, get you mad
and bitter, get on smack or booze and the dole. That's the way a lot
of kids go.

But there's another more common way and that's how most of
us did it.

You start fighting it. You start fighting back against it young. But
it don't really get you anywhere, not when you're young, but it starts
that fire, it ignites that flame and then you'll stay fighting. You'll stay
fighting all your life to get out.

The first drink I ever had was down Sage Park. We was young,
like twelve or thirteen or something. Sage Park was where I met
her.

There was this lad, everyone called him 'Goose', I dunno why.
He were big, older than us and he could get served in the corner
shop for voddy and cider and packets of fags. We all chipped in and
passed them round. Goose were probably only about sixteen at the
time, but to us back then he were like a proper man. We – us girls I
mean – we used to sit at the top of the slide. I feel proper bad now
cos when I take my little 'uns to the park round here and it's all fag
ends and broken glass, I'm proper raging. I'm, like, 'Why do these
kids have no respect?' Then I have to catch myself cos that were me
not long ago, back in Stanwel. I hope I never hurt a kid – threw one
of those bottles off the slide, left glass lying about. It would proper
break my heart, that. It would proper kill me.

Goose would get us a bottle, a quarter bottle of Russian Supreme;
it tasted like fuckin' paint thinner, I tell you. That and ten Mayfair
and we were away. My mam and dad didn't give a shit, they was too

busy fighting or drinking. Same with most of us who hung round down Sage Park. I hear they've done it up nice now, all new stuff and that for the kids. Back then it were grim – that cheap asphalt stuff and half the rides was broken. Our fault, mainly.

I would sit there with Chelsea and them, just shouting, winding up the lads who were always messing on, fighting and that, showing off. It were shite but it was summit to do; it was what we all did. It's what you did if you weren't a boring little saddo. If you grew up in Stanwel, you went down Sage Park and drank until you couldn't feel it no more.

Arla Macleod never came down till she were like, in year eleven. I never thought we'd be friends; I never thought I'd be mates with someone like her.

I never thought … any of it. Amazing what life chucks at you, eh?

This is the voice of Paulette English. If you haven't listened to episode two yet, I would advise you to do so. Paulette was one of Arla Macleod's 'gang' at school. She also knew Arla in the years after school, when they both attended Stanwel Community College.

Paulette no longer lives in Stanwel. She 'escaped' with her three young children and three excitable Labradors. Mr English is also a Stanwel ex-pat and works as a tiler for a large bathroom firm. He's out at work and Paulette's mother shepherds the children round the lawn outside while we chat over Skype.

—Arla and me, we only really became close *after* school, you know? Like, when we were older. Maybe we was just too immature back in school, so we only really started having serious conversations when we was in college, when it was just the two of us, when we were supposed to grow up, like.

I say close, but I suppose it wasn't really like that. We'd chat about lads and that, but, I dunno, you could never really get proper *tight* with Arla. She was so used to talking online, I think real people confused her.

She had her moments like we all do … but for most of the time she was just normal. Just an everyday lass.

That's how she was.

Mad isn't it?

Sorry.

§§

Welcome to Six Stories. *I'm Scott King.*

Over these six weeks we're looking back at the Macleod Massacre of 2014, the tragic killing of her mother, sister and stepfather by the then twenty-one-year-old Arla Macleod.

Arla Macleod has never denied her part in the killing of her family with a hammer on that fateful November night in 2014. Found guilty but for reasons of diminished responsibility, Arla remains ensconced in Elmtree Manor, a medium-security hospital for those who are deemed to be a danger to themselves or others. Court-appointed psychologists confirmed that Arla was suffering from psychosis at the time of the killings, that the acts were not premeditated and that Arla was not in control of her behaviour at the time.

Debate about whether this sentence was just abounds.

Six Stories *has never and will never push an agenda; what I do is present the facts and talk to those involved – people whose voices perhaps haven't been heard before. I am not here to crack a case or solve a crime. I'm simply here to help us all understand.*

In episode one, I talked to Arla herself on a monitored phone line from Elmtree Manor. In episode two I spoke to someone who was aware of and had interaction with, but was not close to Arla at school. So far, though, I feel there remains some significant distance between myself and this case.

An unexpected element to this series has arisen, however. I have been receiving text messages to my personal mobile asking me to desist from any more interviews or podcasts concerning Arla Macleod. I have been informed there will be 'consequences' to my actions. There have also been a flurry of tweets and posts to the Six Stories *Twitter and Facebook pages, which have been duly blocked and deleted. The content of these posts are not something I want to share; suffice to say that they were attacks against me personally. I notice, however, that there were no 'real' threats – nothing direct; nothing that could get the perpetrator into trouble. Someone knows what they are doing.*

I will not engage with abuse or online trolling. However, I am willing to have an adult discussion with anyone who wants to air their griev-ances, either in private or on the podcast itself. So if that's you, send a direct message to the Six Stories *Twitter handle or on the Facebook page, and I'll ask you a few questions to verify that it's the same person who's been texting me and we'll talk.*

That's where I stand.

That's all the airtime I'll dedicate to this issue, so let's proceed.

What we know so far about Arla Macleod is that there were some issues that could have, and perhaps should have, been identified in her teenage years. Some of these stem from allegations about the family dynamic itself. Unfortunately not a lot is known about the inner work-ings of the Macleod family; by all accounts we've heard so far, they kept themselves to themselves. Arla's parents had no close friends in Stanwel, Lancashire – the small mining town they moved to from Saltcoats, Ayr-shire when Arla was two years old. We do know that the Macleods were staunchly Catholic and that Arla's mother, Lucy, was very conscious of keeping up appearances. Sadly, Arla's younger sister, Alice, has barely even been mentioned in this series.

So it is Alice Macleod I am going to try to explore in this episode. And Paulette English is someone who may be able to shed some light on her.

I open our chat with a question about Alice. A tumble dryer clanks away in the background, and makes the room faintly steamy.

—I'm sorry about the racket, love. I hope it don't interfere with your whatssama-thingy there. It's on the blink, this.

—*Were you friends with both the Macleod girls?*

—Yeah. Well no, not really. It were Arla I was mates with; Alice was the more ... the more *sociable* one when she were younger, you know? Arla sort of floated round in her own little world, like she was always on the edge of everything, everyone.

—*Did you meet the Macleod sisters together, then?*

—That was a long time ago, but yeah, they was always together when they was little. You couldn't have one without the other.

—*Inseparable?*

—Yeah, but in a funny way, you know? Like, you know when you see chicks? Baby chickens, little fluffy ones all crowding round each other under those hot lamps – they sort of reminded me of that. Arla would pick up Alice from primary after she'd finished at Saint Theresa's. You'd see them both scuttling past, like, with their hoods up. All the other kids with their mams or dads or whatever and them two little girls on their own.

Mind you, my memory might be...

—*What was your personal opinion of the Macleod sisters back then? I mean yours rather than the general one?*

—This is going to sound well harsh, but it was hard to feel sorry for them. It sounds proper bad, doesn't it, but I'm only being honest. I'm like that, me – speak my mind these days, more than I did back then; loads more. Anyway, it wasn't just me who felt like that.

—*Are you saying that people thought badly of Arla and Alice? Did people pick on them?*

—Not so much picked on, but sort of not pitied either, like I say. It were more like people just ... people thought they were a bit strange, you know, but not in like, an interesting way, more in a sort of ... like they was, like, I dunno. There was summat odd about them, like, it were catching. I dunno, kids are funny aren't they?

—*Were there any rumours? Did anyone speculate about the Macleod sisters?*

—Oh yeah, there was loads of daft stuff floating about. People used to say all sorts. But it was only when I got to know Arla in year eleven that I found out that most of it was sort of true ... but ... but not in the way you'd expect.

—Can you expand on that at all?

—So there was this rumour going round – this was in year eight maybe – that Arla was only allowed to whisper at home. Honestly, I dunno where it came from; someone might have made it up. But everyone used to whisper to each other – ironically, I suppose – passing it on that Arla and Alice weren't allowed to talk properly at home. And ... it feels proper bad now telling you this ... but we used to, like, jump out on them – try and make them scream. It wasn't anything nasty – not *proper* nasty, not bullying, but just enough to give them a fright, you know? Just enough to get them to make a noise. And sometimes people would try and make Arla swear.

—Make her?

—We would just crowd round her and get her to shout 'fuck' or 'bitch' or something – it was just daft stuff.

—What were the other rumours about the Macleods?

—Oh, most of them were just stupid. It was cos her parents were proper Jesus freaks and that, weren't they? We heard things, like they had to get up at 5 am and pray, and that they didn't get presents at Christmas – that sort of thing, you know? Just stupid stuff.

—You said that when you got to know Arla a bit better, you were surprised that a lot of the school rumours turned out to be true.

—I tell you what, I only ever went inside Arla's house once. I always used to have to wait at the front door for her. No one told me to, I just got the feeling I had to, you know? And no one ever asked me to come in. Arla either poked her head around the door and was, like, 'I'll just get me coat' and would shut it again, not properly, just so there was like a millimetre open, and then she'd come out.

—What happened that time you went inside?

—Nothing *happened* as such, it was just uncomfortable. Inside the house it were dead, like ... still and cold, like a museum, and it smelled funny. You know how people's houses have a smell, like, if they eat lots of chips, there's that oily smell; or if they have a dog, that has a smell too? Arla's house was like ... it was like the smell of a museum or an antiques shop or something, like, cold, dusty stillness.

It looked old too, like it had dead thick carpets and all this tacky stuff – these oil pictures on the walls of like, the Last Supper and Jesus and that, and the sort of stuff you see in a charity shop, you know?

—How old were you?

—Oh, we were in college by then, and I was … me and Arla were in a sort of wilderness phase, you know? We were going out all the time and that. I remember Arla creeping around that house and keeping her voice dead low as if someone was asleep upstairs. I just remember thinking about all the things we used to say about them in school and if some of it was true, like, just a little bit. And … well … how sad was that? How horrible it must have been for them girls when they was kids.

I never properly met her parents. Me and Arla, we was pretty close as we got older, but it was like … not like they avoided meeting me or didn't want to; it was more like they just didn't care. My existence meant nothing to them. I was their daughter's best mate and that didn't matter in any way to them. That was sad. I sort of understood, then, where Arla was coming from.

—Are you talking about when she rebelled – in her teens? From what I know about Arla Macleod, she changed a lot when she got to around year eleven in school, is that right?

—Yeah. But the thing about that, you see, I watched that documentary and read all the papers and that, and that's what they all said – that something changed for her around that time, that she started listening to Skexxixx, dressing in black and became a maniac. But it was bollocks, all of it.

—How do you mean?

—Because what they *didn't* say, what they *didn't* point out was that that happens to pretty much everyone when they get to that age. They failed to mention that all over the world, loads of girls and lads start rebelling, start finding themselves. Every teenager does that at some point – every one of them. There was plenty of other things about Arla's life that they didn't want to look into. Things that would make the school, the authorities look bad.

—*What sort of things?*

—Well, the real reasons she changed. They never questioned how she went from this weird little nobody to … to what she became. They never looked properly at that. Instead it was all about the music stuff, the image: 'Oooh, blame nasty, evil Skexxixx and his lyrics for corrupting our kids'. Proper *Daily Mail* bollocks, that's what it was, but nearly everyone swallowed it. Everyone was *happy* to swallow it cos it were easier than looking at what they could have done to help her!

—*Not you though?*

—No. Like I say, I never properly knew Arla before year eleven, she was just this quiet little oddball, you know? We all knew *who* she was, her and Alice, because we'd most of us been through primary school with them. But once everyone were used to them, they passed us by.

—*So how did you two become friends?*

—It was a strange one, that. You see, it was Alice who kind of got us together. At a netball match.

—*How did that happen?*

—They were always together at first, them two, but by year nine, they'd started going in very different directions. There's no nice way of putting this, I'm afraid – Alice was the pretty one. Arla was gangly, skinny, wiry; her hair was always a mess and her skin was always, like, freckly and spotty. Alice though, she was, like, she was developing better and she never wore make-up and that; she just had this sort of natural beauty to her. I swear, even in year seven you could tell she was going to be a beauty. And Alice was on the netball team – she was good at sports, where Arla was just … she was different…

—*Do you think Arla resented that?*

—And that's why she killed her? Sorry, no. I mean maybe, but I dunno. I dunno what was going on in Arla's head.

—*Sorry, we will go back to how you became friends with Arla, but I must ask: do you think, in your heart of hearts, that there were signs back then – of Arla's problems, her mental illness?*

—I … You know when you're that age there are some kids who

you can tell have real problems? Then there's those that are just 'mad'? We all just thought, 'That Arla, she's proper mad isn't she?' Huh, probably not the best word to use, eh?

—*What was your personal experience of her? Who was the Arla that you knew?*

—OK love, look, I've talked about it so many times. I've said so much, and you know what? No one's listened. Those what made that documentary about her, all they was interested in was the violence, like, how she was with other girls and that.

—*But you didn't see that side of her?*

—They said Arla was this, like cult leader almost. They had her up as the female Charles Manson! Some of the claims were just daft. They said that she had, like, a harem of little Skeks who ran riot over the school. Bullshit, all of it; utter crap! I'll tell you the first and only time I ever saw Arla be violent was to that prick Jobba.

—*Keith Jobson, the school bully, right?*

—Yeah it was. It was early on, maybe the first week of year eleven. Not long before we became friends really. I can still hear what he said, his voice in my head, it were horrible. Sometimes, late at night it comes back. Arla had grown quite a bit over the summer – she'd got taller, skinnier. I'm not saying she wasn't pretty but ... but she was still just so gangly, like a stick insect – clumsy-looking. And she always wore that Skexxixx hoodie zipped up even when it was hot.

So, she's walking past the wall where Jobba and his mates are all sat and he shouts out: 'The fuckin' state of that! Walks round like it got shagged all over!'

I dunno what he was on about, what he meant, why he said something like that, but Arla just lost her shit and battered him. He had two black eyes for about a week afterwards. It served him right, the prick. Jobba used to call all the little Skexxixx kids 'vampire freaks' but he never said anything to Arla again after that. He made sure he never even went near her. Typical of him, the twat.

—*In the documentary, there was a notable scene where someone alluded to being 'intimidated' at school by Arla and her gang. Presumably that included you.*

—Ha! Yeah. And we all knew who was accusing us!

—*Who?*

—Jobba's little girlfriend. Tracey Allitt. A vindictive little cow. After it came out about what Arla did to her family, suddenly Tracey and her mates had all been 'bullied' by Arla and me and Debs. But everyone who went to Saint Theresa's knew it was *her* who was the bully – Tracey and her nasty little gang. She were just a female Jobba. Match made in heaven them two. But no one said anything. Because of what Arla did. Because then maybe … *maybe* it wouldn't altogether have been Arla's fault, right?

—*So was it ever true? About you and Arla and … I'm presuming you mean Deborah Masterson?*

—What do you think? It's pathetic isn't it? All those years, a family all killed and people like Allitt actually get money to go on telly and lie, just to wriggle out of any idea whatsoever that their bullying of Arla could have had any sort of influence on what happened. Pathetic. It goes to show that people like her, people like Jobba, they never really grow up; they never change.

—*Are they still together?*

—Oh yeah. They used to live near me when I were back in Stanwel. They moved to somewhere in the Midlands I heard. Filled another garden with rubbish and screaming kids. I mean, c'mon, they're both stupid, ugly, ignorant people. They deserve each other.

—*Was there not the opportunity for those of you who actually knew Arla to dispute what they said?*

—Well, like I told you, we tried, but the newspapers and that, they just weren't interested; it didn't make a good story did it? I was going to keep going, keep trying to fight for Arla, to try and stop this story that she was … that it was all sort of *inevitable* but…

—*But?*

—I dunno … I've got kids and that now, life gets in the way, doesn't it?

A part of me at this point wonders if Paulette has also been receiving strange communications telling her to leave things alone. I am about to ask, but something tells me it's not a good idea, not now. I don't want her to clam up, to ask to end the conversation.

So, for now, at least, I move back to safer ground.

—*Going back to when you first really got to know Arla: you said it was during one of Alice Macleod's netball games? Did Arla used to stay after school and watch her sister, then?*

—Yes. That's right.

—*What about the girls' parents? Were they ever there?*

—I never saw her mam or dad come to any of those netball games, not even once, save to pick her up afterwards if she had swimming training. That's proper bad that, isn't it? And before you say it was cos they worked, that's bullshit. Arla's dad did the bins and her mam was in a school but she wasn't even a teacher. And them netball games never started till four.

—*So Arla attended those games almost as a surrogate mother to her sister, you think?*

—Well, now I think about it, there was probably two reasons why she did it. She was either there to support Alice – to show her that someone cared; that someone gave a shit, you know? The other reason – and this was the more likely one, I thought – was that she preferred it to going home. Arla going to watch her perfect sister be brilliant at something was better than going home.

—*Maybe Arla really wanted to support her sister?*

—I doubt it. Anyway it was then, during one of those games, when me and Arla became mates.

—*How did that occur?*

—Well I think it started cos we was both wearing them Skexxixx hoodies, you know?

—*Those infamous hoodies.*

—Oh I know, it was just ignorant all that, just so ignorant. It made me proper mad. Did you notice on the reconstructions that the actresses that played me and Arla were wearing those leather jackets? Studs all over them. They cost more than we could have ever afforded. And it looked daft, I mean, like, they made it look like we proper stood out, like we were these proper freaks.

—*Not an accurate representation of your image then?*

—Ask anyone who was there and they'll tell you the same thing. None of us looked anything like that. Hang on … I got these ready to show you.

Paulette reaches across the table and pulls out a pile of printouts – old photographs.

—I did a bit of digging around and found a pen drive with these pics. There were a few from school of me and Arla. Look … We were hardly extreme, were we? I think the most expensive thing I owned, that any of us owned, was a pair of knock-off Doc Martens from Stanwel market! But they weren't even particularly rebellious! When you pulled your school trousers over them, they just looked like school shoes.

I'm not sure whether it's the way they've been printed, but Paulette's few photographs have a sepia tinge. It looks like they were taken in summer. She and Arla are half in and half out of their uniforms – school shirts on, no ties, black hoodies with the Skexxixx 'S' logo running down each sleeve. Both girls have cigarettes in their hands and both are sticking their tongues out at the camera.

These could be any schoolgirls in any summer, anywhere in the country.

—You see? That was about as daring as we got! Miss McKay used to tell us to 'tone down the eyeliner, girls' but that was about it. That was the most anyone ever said to us. In the documentary, me and Arla were sat at the back in those expensive leather jackets wearing spiked wristbands and that; it looked ridiculous.

—*You said that Arla adopted this, albeit not particularly extreme, look just after the summer holidays before year eleven, is that right?*

—Well, that was when I noticed her, yeah. That's how we started chatting.

—*Why were you at the netball game? Did you know someone who was playing?*

—That's the thing, you see: I was there for the same reason that I thought Arla was. Maybe it was intuition or something. Maybe I thought I saw it in her too…

—*That it was better than being at home, you mean?*

—Exactly. It's funny how people like us find each other, isn't it?

I don't press this point, and this seems to create a pause in the conversation. Throughout this part of the interview, my phone has been buzzing in my pocket, so I pull it out while we take what feels like a natural break. In front of our respective screens we both sip tea, and Paulette issues a few commands to her children, who have traipsed into the kitchen; they duly exit out into the garden to play with the dogs. Turning away from my webcam, I check my phone. There are a few text messages from a number I don't recognise:

```
From: [Unknown number]
I told you to stop.


From: [Unknown number]
I told you this was your warning.


From: [Unknown number]
You've had that warning now.
```

I can't help but feel a little sliver of fear pass under my skin. A part of me — some instinct — is desperate to reply to this unknown assailant, to insist I'm not scared. I do notice one thing that brings a degree of solace. These threats are entirely empty; they don't detail any specific consequence if I continue this case. This is not a direct threat.

It's a smart move I suppose. But it doesn't make me even consider stopping. I won't.

When Paulette has finished tending to her pets and offspring, we resume.

—*So the afternoon netball game ... when you got to know Arla...?*

—Yeah, I got to know her. Well, as much as anyone could get to know Arla Macleod.

—*What about Alice?*

—Ha! If Arla was distant, Alice ... she was something else entirely!

—*Go on.*

—It were like you was talking to a robot – it was like she had stock responses to everything. She had these wide, empty eyes and this great, big false smile. A proper little Stepford wife! There was no way in. And then there was Arla. Lived in a dream world. She was this gawky creature, stumbling through her life. And, like I said before, Alice was the prettier one: she had the looks and the body and everything, where Arla frankly just *didn't*. Alice could have had the pick of the lads, and I know for a fact that there were plenty of them after her. She looked considerably older than her sister: she had, like, proper boobs, a proper figure, where Arla was just skin and bones. When I used to knock about in Sage Park after school, I started noticing Alice there a few times. But I didn't know her. I never spoke to her.

—*So Alice was everything Arla wasn't.*

—Yeah, that's fair. You could see why Arla resented her. *I* did, for God's sake and I didn't even know her! Everyone else did too. Jealousy is a powerful thing, you know? Loads of girls used to say stuff about her behind her back. And it wasn't like she'd even done anything wrong. I mean, there was nothing *wrong* with her. She was just so *perfect*, you know? Inscrutable.

—*Did you try and get to know her?*

—Yeah. She was a closed book though, was Alice. She didn't let no one in. She spoke a lot through … like … it's hard to describe, but she spoke a lot with her eyes. It was the way she looked at you. Alice had these big, wide eyes with these fluttery eyelashes. She never pouted though, never made a big deal of herself; it was just, she was … one of a kind, you know? For all Arla didn't want to fit in, for all her rebellion, I reckon it was Alice who was the true rebel in that family, the silent rebel – that's what they should have called her. Where Arla would kick off, Alice would comply. That way she would get the attention, the praise. Alice was the one with the power in that family, I tell you!

—*So you started talking to them both?*

—I did, and you know what? For all the daft rumours and stories flying about, they was just like normal sisters – just like a normal pair of girls. They'd talk about girl stuff, argue and that.

—*Argue?*

—So, like, when we first got talking, me and Arla were just chatting on about Skexxixx and that, as you do. Arla knew *everything*, all the theories behind the lyrics. She used to spend a lot of time online you see, when her parents were out with her sister. Poor lass. And I noticed that the whole time we were chatting, Arla's phone kept buzzing, kept going off all the time, but she wasn't even looking at it. That struck me, you know: it was kind of polite, like, old-fashioned, sort of thing. If I'm honest, it made me feel good, like she was giving me her full attention, you know? I liked that.

But when Alice finished the netball game, she came over to where we was sitting and Arla just handed her the phone and was, like, 'There you go, you've got about a zillion messages', and rolled her eyes at me.

Now if you think about it, this was in the days before everyone had smartphones with Facebook and lock screens and that. Alice and Arla shared one of those old Nokias. Arla could have read all those messages if she'd wanted to. That's what I would have done – it was what pretty much every fifteen-year-old would have done. The fact that she didn't read her sister's messages told me that there was something more to Arla and Alice.

So I asked Arla who'd been messaging her sister and she was, like, 'Someone she met on holiday – her *boyfriend*.' And she drew the word out, proper long and slow, like she were wringing all the life out of it. That sort of reassured me, you know, like that was how sisters behaved, like Mickey-taking and that.

—*What was Alice's reaction?*

—Oh, she went proper beetroot red and put her head down, just stared at the phone. She didn't even say nowt.

—*Do you know who the boyfriend was?*

Paulette goes quiet at this and stares out of the window at her children. I can just see they have one of the dogs on the trampoline on the lawn. The animal looks like it's having the time of its life. She shakes her head. I move away from the subject for now.

—*So you became friendly with Arla. And Deborah Masterson did too. A lot has been made of you three at the school.*

—Ha! It's so ridiculous! All of that nonsense were cooked up in the mind of Tracey Allitt and her mates. Tracey said that me, Arla and Debs Masterson liked to 'intimidate people' or some bollocks. Do you want to know something?

—*Go on…*

—No one, not one, single, other person stood up after the papers and that documentary came out and said, 'No, it didn't happen like that at all.' Everyone knew that nothing like that happened, but it seemed like no one wanted to spoil the story about what Arla done to her family. Poor little pretty Alice and her good Christian mam and dad, eh? Their whole lives ruined by their bad daughter.

—*Why do you think that was?*

—I think … It's hard to put into words, but the story of Arla and me and Debs as this pack of psycho Skeks was like a shield or a cloak or something. It were easy to be quiet and get behind that story instead of looking a bit harder at the whole thing. It's sort of like a reverse mob-mentality – 'mob-silence', if you like.

—*Mob apathy?*

—Maybe.

—*But it's true you were also a fan of Skexxixx, yes?*

—Yeah. Not as obsessed as Arla, maybe, but yeah, I loved all that. I had his posters all over my bedroom. My mam hated it. Just like everyone else's mams did.

—*I've actually been looking into Skexxixx, specifically his* Through the Mocking Glass *album. I can see how a lot of the themes and concepts in the lyrics could have made sense to teenagers like you and Arla.*

—Yeah, you're right, they did. You see, that album, the whole thing was about escaping, about getting away from your life, the pain, you know? *Through the Mocking Glass*, Skexxixx himself, the whole thing… And it wasn't about suicide either; that's another misconception the papers and the TV gobbled up. It was deeper than that. There was more to it. But no one could be bothered to look into it. The whole concept of escapism, of not being accepted, of finding a place of your own, a world of your own, even – it was passed off as a silly teenage craze! Do you understand how insulting that was?

—*I think I get it.*

—You sound like you get it more than most other journalists and that who've looked into Arla. It sounds proper cringe, but that album literally saved my life back then, in school. They meant so much to me, those songs. I still put them on sometimes, if I'm having a bad day. And they still do the job. Sometimes, when I listen to them, I get sad cos I wish … I wish they could have saved Arla too. You see, whatever it was that were wrong with her started in school, you know? That were obvious to anyone. Then afterwards, when we became proper mates, I knew that … I knew that there was really something going on with her. Something really wrong…

—*Her mental health?*

—Yes and no. Like, both equally – yes and no. You know I blame myself sometimes. Like, I wish I could have helped her. But I just had no idea what to do. When she … done it … there were no warning or anything.

—I'd like you to have a think back to school. Do you remember anything significant, any incidents where you really worried about Arla?

At this point there is a distinct change in Paulette. She drops her gaze, twiddles her fingers, looks shifty.

—This isn't about blame, Paulette. You were only young too. Arla was—
—The games.
—The what?
—Just … I mean, we used to play all sorts of different games…
—Video games, you mean? I'm confused.
—It's silly really. We were just a bit immature. They were childish games … stupid. Daruma-san – the ghost that follows. Christ. I thought I'd managed to forget all that.

Paulette stops again. She looks out the window and her body slumps. I notice the tumble dryer has stopped, the dogs are quiet – all we can hear are the birds tweeting in the trees. In this moment, I can almost feel the past upon us, peering in through the windows. Things are starting, just starting to add up … twinges, hints.

§§

I want to use this natural break in proceedings to play you something that I recorded a while back. It's significance will become apparent when we hear from Paulette again. Interestingly, many of the staff at Saint Theresa's refused to be interviewed for the television documentary, and all my attempts to speak to them have come up against blank walls. I do, however, manage to make contact through Facebook with a man with the surname of Marsh. He agrees to answer a few questions about his days at Saint Theresa's.
Mr Marsh is around seventy years old and no longer lives in Stanwel.

I speak to him briefly on the phone. Please accept my apologies for the audio; the signal was very poor. And when I tried to call back, the number had been disconnected. So I'll play you all I managed to render from our brief chat.

—*You were the caretaker at Saint Theresa's for nearly twenty years. Were you familiar with the students?*

—You see a lot. You see more than folk think. You see ... [*Indistinguishable*] ... and the kids and that, like...

—*Were you aware of Arla Macleod and her 'gang'? Were they known throughout the school?*

—No, lad. No they ... [*Indistinguishable*] ... but I don't say nowt cos you get 'em .... [*Indistinguishable*] ... then they're knockin' on your doors. Knockin' on your windows all night. Bloody kids!

—*Excuse me? Knocking on doors? Did you ever get trouble like that from Arla Macleod and her friends?*

—No lad, no! You can't ... [*Indistinguishable*] ... and I didn't cos I don't want no trouble, me, you see.

—*Trouble?*

—Bad news, mate, bad news. You go kick a wasps' nest and ... [*Indistinguishable*]...

—*Arla Macleod specifically, though – her gang – do you remember them?*

—It's not about that though ... [*Indistinguishable*] ... be careful what you say. They'll come for you!

—*What? I can't hear. You're breaking up...*

—Just ... [*Indistinguishable*] ... It's more than ... [*Indistinguishable*] ... silly games and that ... [*Indistinguishable*] ... boiler room. That bloody boiler room ... [*Indistinguishable*] ... They're in your garden all night, every night. They don't stop. They don't shut up! They don't leave you alone!

After this the line goes dead and I couldn't get in touch again. Mr Marsh vanished. And I had nearly forgotten about the interview

*completely, until I talk to Paulette. When she mentions the 'games', I'm
reminded of something in the garbled audio from Mr Marsh.*

—*In relation to these games: did Arla ever talk about a boiler
room?*
—Who's told you that?
—*Someone who once worked at Saint Theresa's. It might be nothing.
But when you mentioned games…*
—Oh, yeah … Arla's games…
—*You say that with a degree of trepidation.*
—Look, I'm not sure it's a good idea to go into all that, really.
—*What makes you say that?*
—It's just … Oh it was silly really, all that stuff. It's not real, none
of it.
—*But it's an aspect of Arla that hasn't really been explored in any
detail. Can you give me an idea of what it was all about?*
—Well, I've always been careful not to mention any of it to
anyone, you know. You see, Arla was … For all she were unpredict-
able and angry, she were right childish at heart, you know?
—*How so?*
—Well the 'games' – she used to harp on about them. Maybe it
was something we *should* have taken more notice of. I don't know.
—*So, let's get specific: what sort of games are we talking about?*
—They were all, like, stuff she'd found online. All these daft urban
legends from Japan and Korea. Remember that film *Candyman*,
where you say 'Candyman' five times in the mirror and he turns up
with a hook for a hand and it … it doesn't end well for anyone who
does it? Arla's games, they were like that. Proper odd. Always about
ghosts and that. The way she went on about them was sort of embarrassing. She were like a big kid…
—*Did you ever play any of these games with her?*
—Look, it were all her – all that Daruma-san stuff, it was Arla!
—*OK, I believe you. Arla was … troubled. She had a lot going on.*
—She did. Look, all these ideas she had about escaping into

another world, it was like she was still a little kid. But when I look back now, as an adult, I see why she did it. It's all dead obvious. And that's why when I listen to that album, those old songs, and think about Arla, it makes me so sad. She took all that *Through the Mocking Glass* stuff literally, like, she didn't see it as a metaphor.

—*So that's the games. What about the boiler room – does that have some significance for you at all?*

—It does. It's … it's a horrible story that I've spent every day since trying to forget. I didn't know anyone else knew about it.

—*Do you think you can tell me about it? It may help ease the burden?*

—Can't make it worse, I suppose. You see, what happened down there in the boiler room, that was the beginning of the end. That was when Debs stopped hanging about with us.

—*Really?*

—I … I guess if you look back, that could have been thought of as 'bullying'. But it … it wasn't though, not really. We weren't like Jobba or Tracey Allitt or any of them. It *was* just a game…

—*Arla's game?*

—Yeah. Look, when we were at Saint Theresa's it wasn't like it is now. A lot of the buildings were still old – falling to bits. Me and Arla and Debs, we used to spend our lunch hour just sort of wandering around the corridors. When you were girls like us you would do anything to avoid Tracey Allitt and Jobba and all them. There was only so much we could take – getting called mingers, moshers, meffs, slags. It grinds you down, soaks you through like rain. Being a girl at that age, your ego's fragile enough without all that bullshit.

So, we found this one place on our wanders, and we claimed it as our own – just for one lunchtime. No one ever knew we'd even been there. Well, obviously someone did, but at the time we didn't know that. It was the boiler room.

—*Where was it?*

—There was this door just round the corner from the caretaker's office and it said 'boiler room'. We were wandering near it one lunchtime, and we heard someone coming. We panicked, thinking it was Tracey or whoever. And Arla tried the boiler room door and it opened, just like that.

We shut the door behind us and it were so weird, it were like stepping into an airlock or something. The air down there, it smelled different, it *felt* different down there. It were like, I guess you could call it another world. I was filled with that … you know, that excitement you get in your belly when you're doing something you shouldn't. It was so alien in there too; loads of exposed pipes and wires and stuff all over. There was this metal staircase going down and the ground just sort of *fell away* into darkness below. There was a few lights on somewhere down there, but it was still proper gloomy, proper spooky.

—*Was the caretaker there?*

—Mr Marsh? I doubt it. Marshy would have heard us straight away. He was like Filch in *Harry Potter*, but he'd have eaten the cat rather than had one as a pet! We were probably all squawking and making loads of racket, but we got all the way to the bottom of the stairs without anyone coming in. It were like that darkness just swallowed us up.

Arla didn't care, though. She just … the lass was fearless. She was in the lead and when she got to the bottom, she was, like, 'Come and look at this!'

We got down there, me in the middle and Debs at the back. Debs was proper shitting herself; she was all, like, 'We shouldn't be here … we should go.' But Arla wasn't listening.

Down at the bottom, it was huge – these great passages leading off into the darkness. There was loads of junk down there; all dusty props and old sets from the school plays and that. This was Marshy's little empire – all these piles of chairs and wood and metal, and tools all hung up on the walls. And in the middle of it all there was this old bath, like an old school bath with feet. It was just sat down there surrounded by all these piles of paint pots and junk. I remember we all just started giggling and laughing – it looked so out of place, this bath with these brass lion's feet, all stained with rust and paint.

The longer we spent down there, in that silence, with no one knowing we were there, the more we began to relax. Arla found this huge wall of light switches and started switching them on and off. Debs was screaming at her to stop, saying they might control the lights in the head's office or something. Arla told her to stop being such a baby. One of the switches set off this strip-light that lit up the bottom half of the boiler room properly. It was one of those fluorescent tubes but it didn't work properly, and when Arla hit the switch it kept flickering like it was a rave or something.

And that's when ... that's when it all went wrong...

—*What happened?*

—The tube must have packed in or something, because it stopped flickering and we were back in that half-light from before. But something had changed in Arla. She had this *look* in her eyes like it wasn't her anymore. And I was scared. Proper scared. Arla had something in her hand as well and ... God, this is going to sound just so ... You see, at some point Arla had picked up this ... this rusty hammer, like a claw hammer, from the rack on the wall and she was holding it in one hand and smacking the blunt end in her other. It was horrible. It wasn't Arla. That's the whole thing – it just wasn't her...

Paulette sighs and one of her dogs trots inside and nuzzles at her legs; she ruffles its fur and the dog seems to make a sympathetic sound in its throat.

—*Was this Arla playing a game?*

—See, it's going to sound wrong, but it was like being in another world down there, in the half-light with the bath and the junk and the dust. We were all sort of *high* somehow. We weren't on drugs or nowt. It was just ... I dunno. But when that bulb winked out and Arla was stood there with the hammer, there was something different about her.

She were holding that hammer and she were looking at me and Debs, back and forth. I were getting proper freaked out. But I didn't show it. I kept still, just dead still, it was like there was some instinct telling me that if I moved, if I spoke, she'd...

—She'd?

—I don't know.

But Debs … Debs says something – it were just something like 'C'mon let's go', something innocent like that – and Arla just lost it. It were horrible.

—What did Arla do?

—She still had that look – that manic look – in her eyes and she was, like, *slapping* that hammer in her palm. That's when Arla told Debs to come and stand in that old bath. I wanted to laugh but I couldn't. It was mad; it was crazy. It should have been funny. Debs was looking at me and I just … I kept my eyes down. It was like in a lesson when the teacher shouts and everyone goes silent.

Arla tells Debs to get in the bath and she's still slapping that hammer in her hand. I could see – I could *tell* – that Debs was scared too and she was trying not to show it. So Debs rolls her eyes and shrugs, putting on this show of not being bothered. She just gets in the bath, just as if she didn't give a shit, like she's in on the joke. I wanted to scream, to run, but I couldn't. I just stood there, saying nowt.

That's when Arla starts telling us about a game – this game she was obsessed with, something she'd read about on the internet. 'Daruma-san' it was called. Christ, I hate even saying it out loud!

So we're still dead quiet and Debs is stood in that bath. Arla starts telling us how she heard this story about a girl who came down into the boiler room in Saint Theresa's a few years before and killed herself. She said that it happened in the bathtub. We knew Arla was bullshitting, making it up as she went along. Arla said that this girl only had one eye cos she smashed her own face in with a hammer. Again, it should have been funny. I knew it was a story – Arla used to go on like that all the time. But down in that boiler room … there was something about being there. Neither me nor Debs wanted to speak up – neither of us said anything. The bottom of that bath had all these brown rust marks in it, and Arla was telling us they were dried blood. It sounds stupid now, doesn't it? But at the time, it was … it was like … like being in a dream or something. And Arla … with that look in her eyes…

—*Is this why Debs left?*

—No. It wasn't the story that made her go. It was ... it was what Arla did next.

—*Go on.*

—It was like we was in another world. Sometimes I wonder if any of it really happened. The bath, the boiler room. Debs was getting pissed off standing there in the bath. I could tell she were still scared but she was hiding it well. Arla told her to stand still, to stand absolutely still, and then she went back over to those light switches and hit one of them. Whatever lights were still on in the boiler room went out. It were pitch black.

I'm so ashamed, you know? I'm ashamed I did nowt – of being a passive observer. Let me tell you now, though, I never once thought Arla would use that hammer, not once. It was just ... she was just messing on, sort of thing. That's what I kept telling myself. She was just trying to scare us.

I could hear Debs blundering about in the bath and Arla's voice right by her. Arla was shouting, 'Close your eyes! Close your eyes and wash your hair.'

The bath wasn't connected to nowt but Arla kept saying it: 'Close your eyes! Wash your hair!' And in that darkness, it were proper creepy. Eventually Debs was, like, 'I am, I am!' It still felt like a game, but a really fucked-up one. It felt like none of us were in control – least of all Arla.

—*So Debs was doing as she was told?*

Arla was shouting at her again, making her say something, and Debs was chanting it over and over again. I'll never forget it, that voice in the darkness: 'Daruma-san fell down. Daruma-san fell down.' She was just shouting it over and over. And soon we were all saying it. It was like a chant and it just seemed to go on and on. 'Daruma-san fell down. Daruma-san fell down.'

—*What does it mean?*

—When she stopped, there was this horrible silence – like proper horrible. Worse than before. I'm not proud to have thought it, I swear to you, but I had this thought. I thought the lights would come on and Debs would just be *gone*. I used to dream of that happening, of searching for hours down in the darkness. Then Arla did turn on the lights. Debs was there and I felt this wave of relief. Debs was crouching in the bath with hair all over her face, her skin all red. I knew she'd been crying.

Arla was still holding the hammer. She was bending over Debs in the bath and said in this dead serious voice, 'Ask her ... ask her why she fell. Ask her why she died down here in this bath...'

And Debs does it, she says those words in this weedy little voice, this pathetic little voice. There was quiet for a second and then, suddenly, the spell was broken. All of a sudden we was just a few stupid teenage girls in a boiler room when we shouldn't have been.

—*What about Debs?*

—She just got up out of the bath, her hair all over, her skin all blotchy, and staggered away. She didn't look back at either of us. I wanted to shout, to say sorry, to tell her to come back, but I couldn't. I looked at Arla and Arla just sort of shrugged.

That was it. Debs never knocked about with us after that. And I get why. I get it. I nearly left too. It was too much. It were all just insane. But then who would Arla have had? She would have had no one.

—*Did Arla ever explain why she did that to Debs? Did she ever explain what Debs had done to deserve it?*

—No. She didn't say. All she did was, she nodded after Debs and said, 'She won't look back, her.' And I said, 'Why not?' Arla just shrugged and said, 'She'll see her tomorrow.'

—*What did that mean?*

—Arla said that the 'ghost' would now follow Debs. That whenever she looked behind her, she'd see her. That she'd spend the rest of her life running from her. I mean, *what?* Who *does* that?

—*What was your reaction at the time?*

—You know, I was more concerned we'd get into trouble for going into the boiler room! Like, if Debs went and told someone – a teacher – I was thinking whether I'd get in trouble too.

And I don't know to this day why Arla did that to her. I never asked. I wish I had. I just remember thinking that whoever was there with us in the boiler room with the hammer *wasn't* Arla.

—And did Debs tell anyone? Did she grass on Arla?

—I dunno. And that was another peculiar thing. As soon as it was over, as soon as we were back in form, by like, last period, I'd forgotten it more or less. Maybe it was too much for my little brain to take in…

—What about Debs? What became of her after that?

—What? Was she followed by a ghost? Sorry, no, I don't know. I saw her about and that. I don't think she ever told, though. I never spoke to her about it. Arla would have been excluded I reckon – me too. No teacher ever spoke to us about the boiler room.

—What about the caretaker? Did Mr Marsh ever find out about it?

—Marshy? Nah. He was just a little old oddball. He had this red face, all wrinkly and the lads used to say he was a convicted murderer on parole, that he'd killed his daughter. It was just another stupid story. No one who'd done that could work in a school, right? How would that even happen? Anyway, if Marshy had caught us, we'd have known about it.

⁂

Paulette's story about the boiler room, to my knowledge, has never been reported before. I ask Paulette why not, and she says that she was so disgusted by the coverage of the Macleod case that she felt if she spoke out about that day, it would be misconstrued, particularly as a hammer played a rather significant part. Paulette's reluctance doesn't sit particularly well with me though. Arla Macleod killed her entire family; what would have been the harm in sharing this story? Unless, of course, Paulette didn't want to be somehow implicated in the killings. There's also the shame that Paulette feels about her part in the game. Deborah Masterson was their friend and from Paulette's description of what went on, the game got out of hand – out of control.

There is also the possibility that someone was putting pressure on Paulette not to speak. I think again of the text messages on my phone.

After a cursory internet search I find the origins of Arla's bath game. It is known in Japanese as 'Darumasan ga Koronda' and is a sort of one-player version of Grandmother's Footsteps or Red Light/Green Light, in which you will be followed by a ghost of someone that supposedly died in a bathtub.

I don't for one minute believe that Arla indeed summoned a ghost, but I am interested in Paulette's description of her as 'not being Arla'. Could this incident be an early psychotic episode, perhaps – a psychotic 'break', as they are known? If this is the case, was there a trigger for it? Paulette mentions the flashing of the strip lights. That could certainly be a possibility. Paulette's assertion that Arla was 'normal' afterwards – almost apathetic – doesn't sit right though. It is common that people who suffer psychosis enter a state of depression after one of these episodes. Unless she experienced it in private, it looks like this did not happen to Arla.

Back to Paulette though. I ask her what she thinks was behind Arla's behaviour that day.

—It's like … there's a bit more education for girls now – about abuse and that, isn't there? I mean things aren't perfect, but there's posters and phone lines. I saw one just the other day when I was taking the little ones to the library: 'That's not love', something like that, and a phone number. That's more than we had back then.

—*Is that what you think was going on with Arla? Some kind of abuse?*

—Arla told me something, years later. I didn't know what to say, how to respond. But it might have something to do with it…

—*What did she tell you?*

—She told me something about being on holiday and that something happened with some lads. She got invited to a party and they got her drunk and … something bad happened with them. Something really bad. She never said, not explicitly. She couldn't. I think they took advantage of her.

—*So why didn't you say anything to someone about it after the killings?*

—Look, just imagine I'd said something … Imagine if I'd said something and Arla had got off scot-free somehow. It would have been like I'd *helped* that … I couldn't do it.

—*I understand. So can you elaborate on the story Arla told you?*

—It's a long time ago that she told me. And she only said it that one time and never mentioned it again. There was nothing more to tell than I've said really. She were proper rattled. Shut down right after she said it. You know what's so bad about that though? It's that … it's that for a lass, something like that is – I wouldn't say *normal,* but I'd say *common,* more common than you think.

—*Really?*

—I'm not being funny, right, but you're a bloke. I'm not saying you're ignorant or nowt like that, but it's different with lasses. We have to put up with all sorts and say nothing. You know there's a nightclub in the Midlands somewhere, right, where women are *expected* to be *grabbed.* Like, that's just *normal.* That's a *thing?* Like, the attitude is, if you don't want that don't go. But why? *Why* is that OK in this day and age? And then if we speak up about it, we're jumped on by the right, the trolls on the internet, who call us 'radical feminists' for not wanting to be treated like a hunk of meat. You can't win.

I think of the Gamergate controversy in 2013, in which a female games developer received a barrage of rape and death threats online – a campaign of misogynistic harassment. I think of a UK newspaper's headline comparing the legs of the, at the time, Prime Minister of England and the First Minister of Scotland (both female); the US President's comments about grabbing women – and as much as I try to understand the feelings, being male in a male world, I know I will never truly be able to feel what it's like to live in a world where these things are commonplace.

—*So that could have been something, you think? I've been told Arla's behaviour at school was often targeted at men and boys, wasn't it?*

—True, yeah. She really clashed with male teachers and she battered Jobba!

—*So why Debs? Why did Arla turn on her friend? I feel we still haven't got to the bottom of that.*

—That's another thing about Arla – you could never properly relax around her. She were properly skittish. Like, she was always testing you somehow, making sure you wouldn't sack her off. With Arla there was a friendship test round every corner. I don't know what Debs did. I honestly don't think she did anything. I think it were just … it was more about Arla.

—*In your opinion, though, as someone who was there: why did she do it? Why did Arla do that to Debs?*

—Looking back now, as an adult, I feel bad for her – Arla I mean. I don't think she could ever accept that we liked her. So she were giving us every reason not to. I guess that's what came of living in the shadow of her perfect sister. Maybe she had to show us she was a terrible person after all, and Debs just got caught in the firing line? That's the only reason I can think of.

—*You mentioned earlier about the netball match; about Alice having phone calls or texts from a 'boyfriend' she'd met on holiday. Are we talking about the holiday Arla and her family went on before year eleven?*

—Yeah, it would have been then. Devon or somewhere on the south coast?

—*Who was he, this boyfriend?*

—I don't even *know*. I've got no idea. But I remember the buzzing of that phone, like. The text alert was turned on and the way it was just buzzing over and over again, it was like there was a wasp trapped inside or something. I remember feeling that it was wrong, proper … *wrong*. Like no one should be texting someone that much.

—*Did you ever ask Arla about it?*

—Hmmm … no. It was, like … Arla never ever mentioned anything about anyone at home – not her family, nothing. And neither did I. We never said, because it was, like, when we were together, we could forget all that. We didn't have to think about it anymore, we could be free.

I didn't think about it at the time, but in editing this episode I see Paulette has managed to be excruciatingly vague about a couple of things. The first is why she didn't fight to try to explain Arla's actions, or even to clear her own name, which the media so blackened in its coverage of the Macleod Massacre. Then there's the question about Alice Macleod. So far in this series, Paulette's memories are the closest I've got to Alice, but that's not anywhere really. Still, something tells me not to be too explicit in what I ask.

My phone is still vibrating in my pocket as we chat – a grotesque synchronicity with our subject matter. These texts seem to permeate everything I try to do. And I want nothing more than to ask Paulette if she too has been receiving threats via text; whether she too harbours a strange feeling of being watched; whether she notices things slightly different outside her home – an open gate; rubbish in the front garden; dog shit in the drive? Does she too feel scrutinised? Does she wonder if this is just coincidence?

But saying it out loud, asking someone else would confirm my own fears; it would be admitting that I think something is going on. Also, if Paulette says nothing – if she looks at me as if I'm insane, as if I'm paranoid – what would that say about me and my ability to create these podcasts? So, instead, I carry on with the planned interview. I won't let … whatever it is win. I won't look at my phone.

Paulette asks me an interesting question next.

—You ever regretted doing something?
—*Many things. I think we all have.*
—Ever regretted *not* doing something?
—*I guess so, I think we could all do more.*
—Sometimes … sometimes it keeps me up at night, you see. Sometimes, I get proper terrors thinking about it. I just … I wish I'd been a bit more bothered about it. Not just Debs, but Arla. I should

have said something, tried to stop her. But I didn't. I had the chance – with Alice and the whole boyfriend thing – to intervene, to ask, to question what was going on. I could have asked her properly about what happened to her on holiday. Told someone. I wish I'd paid a bit more attention, you know?

–*Hindsight's a wonderful thing. We sometimes forget that we were young as well.*

—True, true. We didn't know anything back then; certainly I didn't. I liked to pretend I knew about boys, about love, all that, but I was just a daft young girl, same as Arla. Same as Alice, to be fair.

—*Was there a problem with this boyfriend? Did you get the vibe that he was controlling? Obsessive? Something like that?*

—Arla used to tell me that he was always messaging, constant, like, again and again. Alice would never tell no one what he said. I felt like Arla was perhaps was too far gone, but maybe I could have saved Alice? I dunno, it sounds daft.

—*'Saved' her? That doesn't sound good.*

—It doesn't does it? Neither of them could tell their mam cos they wasn't allowed boyfriends or nowt like that. I dunno if they was even allowed that phone. That phone they had it was shared, you know? They bought it with their pocket money.

—*So how did Arla know the messages were for Alice without looking?*

—Easy. It was cos Arla didn't get no messages. That makes me feel proper sad for her, that. Proper sad.

Suddenly I'm starting to put something together in my mind. Maybe it's my nature, or maybe it's because the crime this series is about is bereft of a solid motive, but it feels almost disappointing to conclude that Arla Macleod killed her family because she was suffering from psychosis – that she was simply mentally ill. The reason I created this series was to examine that particular bone of contention – the one that resulted in Arla's supposedly 'lenient' sentence in Elmtree Manor, and the subsequent uproar.

If Arla's mental health is not the whole story, is there something else – something about this boyfriend of Alice's that the Macleod sisters were hiding? They certainly hid him from their parents. Did this shadowy character somehow have something to do with what Arla did to her family all those years later? It's a sliver – barely anything – but I know that it hasn't been mentioned, to my knowledge, during any of the legal and investigative proceedings around the Macleod Massacre.

Then there's the question of what happened to Arla on the holiday to Cornwall. That holiday keeps coming up, and now we know Arla claims that she was taken advantage of then.

—I suppose I have to ask, finally, why you think Arla did it? To her family. The judge passed a verdict of diminished responsibility. Where do you stand on that?

—It's hard. I understand why folk were angry.

But, despite everything, Arla was simply just … just a bit weird. That's why I reckon all this Skexxixx stuff was blown up by the press. I trusted Arla, you know? And the hardest thing about all this is, sometimes I feel *responsible* in some way. I feel that I should have talked to her a bit more, been a better friend. But in another sense I soothe myself by thinking this could have just happened without any intervention from me, like I didn't have *any* impact on her life whatsoever, like I meant *nothing*.

—Why her family, though? Was it really that bad at home do you think?

—Like I said, it's odd, but I never knew. She never said and I was certainly never *welcome* there. This is all … this whole thing is making me feel like a bad person, a bad friend.

—I'm sorry about that.

—It's not your fault. If it's anyone's, it's mine. I wonder if anyone knew what was going on in her head? Anyone at all?

I begin to think about wrapping things up but I get the sense that Paulette's still holding back. I take my time and stay quiet and eventually she says something – it's quiet and she seems self-conscious.

—Can I tell you something? Something Arla said that … that just freaked me out a bit once?

—*Of course, please do.*

—It was … it was years later, in college. We were sat down at the table and I plucked up the courage to ask if there was anything wrong. She'd been quiet all day. Listless. That probably sounds daft doesn't it? We were mates, and everything, so it shouldn't have been difficult. But Arla never … You could never have those sorts of conversations with her; she'd clam up, start acting up, like a kid. But that day … that day it just felt right.

—*What did she say?*

—Not a lot … not a lot, just something about 'bad memories'. I sort of hinted about, you know, what happened to her in Cornwall, and she … I was tense, I was expecting her to kick off … but she just nodded. She just nodded and then didn't say anything else.

Then, after a minute she sort of half whispered something to me. She said, 'Don't tell no one … don't tell…' And I knew what she meant. I knew she were talking about what had happened to her with those lads in Cornwall. She didn't need to say it out loud. But her voice when she said it was all raspy and I could feel all the hairs on my arms sort of rise up.

I said I wouldn't, I promised. I said no way, and she was quiet for a bit. Then she said, 'If you tell … if you tell anyone, they'll come for you…'

I got a little flicker of fear then. I asked her what she was on about, *who* she was on about. Surely some lads from down south wouldn't come all the way up here? Arla was just dead quiet for ages and then she whispered something that proper shit me up.

—*What was it?*

—She said something about the 'black-eyed kids'. She said, 'Don't let them in, no matter what they say, no matter how much they beg. Whatever you do, don't let them in…'

That was it. That was all she said. And it's shameful to say it, but in that moment I was scared of her. Imagine – just because of that.

—*Did Arla ever speak of the black-eyed kids at any other time –
before or after that day?*

—Not that I remember. She stopped all that sort of stuff after
school – that Daruma-san game thing in the boiler room was the last
really odd thing she did. That comment, though … I knew in my
heart that it wasn't real. It was just some Skexxixx lyrics or something
like that. But it really scared me, it really did.

Maybe if I *had* asked her more, if I'd pressed her, then things
could have been different … I don't know…

§§

We leave the interview, unfortunately, on this sad and uncertain note.

*Paulette poses a good question here: Did anyone really know Arla
Macleod? The picture of her painted by the media seems still very different to the one I'm getting through these interviews. From Paulette's
account, Arla seemed more troubled and sad than dangerous and angry.
But what to make of the way she treated Deborah Masterson? I am convinced that this could have been an early sign of Arla's latent psychosis.*

*I find myself looking back at the link between Paulette's account of the
Daruma-san game and something Mr Marsh, the Saint Theresa's caretaker, said to me. My phone conversation with him was a few weeks ago
so I google Mr Marsh's full name. Just in case there's anything relevant.*

What I find shocks me.

*The first hit is a news story about the suicide of a certain Mr Marsh,
not in Stanwel but in a place with the same area code as the man I spoke
to. The article mentions, and links to, a video that appears to be an
online 'sting' by a group of paedophile hunters.*

*For those unfamiliar with the concept, online paedophile hunters are
a relatively new phenomenon, which has come to prominence in the last
few years. Their MO is to trawl online social-media platforms, posing as
children – a lure for the twisted individuals who then arrange to meet
them for sex. It's disturbing how little effort the hunters have to make.
Many hunter groups say that they do not have the time or resources to*

deal with the sheer volume of attention their decoy accounts receive.
These men (it is nearly always men) are lured to meet the decoy, usually
in a public place, such as a train station, and are then confronted on
camera by the 'hunter' group and their details given to the police. Many,
many people have been put away due to these groups and their work.
While still unregulated, it is a necessary service. It is as simple as that.

I watch the video. It begins with the camera pointing down to a
pavement and a voice telling the viewers that this is being broadcast
on Facebook live. As the camera position rises, we see it's not in a train
station, but at the front door of a house. A hand knocks on the door
which is opened by a red-faced pensioner.

The rest of the video is self-explanatory: the hunter group tell the man
what he has done and show him printed records of the chat log between
him and the decoy. The man, like most who are caught in this way, pleads
his innocence throughout, despite being shown the evidence which he
claims he's never seen. The video is disturbing to watch and effectively
questions your morals and your sense of justice. If Mr Marsh is guilty,
then he has waived his right to dignity and privacy – in my book anyway.
If he's not guilty, then … well … I don't know…

Of course, this sort of thing attracts controversy, with some saying these
groups are nothing more than vigilantes. It poses the question 'what if
they're wrong?' But it seems, with the evidence the hunter groups collate,
unlikely they are.

The news article below the video explains how, not long after the sting,
Mr Marsh apparently hanged himself, after being questioned but not
charged by the police.

Seeing this story is obviously shocking and poses many questions. It is
even more disturbing when I look at some of the messages on my phone.
One of them chills me to my very core. It makes me call into question
whether Mr Marsh is guilty at all.

```
From: [Unknown number]
U have seen what we can do :)
Now back off.
```

After this episode airs, the privacy settings on my social-media accounts will already have been upped, my earlier defiance having dissolved somewhat. However, I will not be bullied or intimidated and stop this series midway through. I feel the weight of the Macleod family on my shoulders. If some of the things that I've discovered had been out there before, then I think lots of people would have been asking some big questions about the case and Arla's conviction.

⁂

I want to break down a little bit of what we know so far.

Arla and Alice Macleod went on holiday to a hotel in Cornwall when they were teenagers.

At some point on this holiday, Arla alleges that some older boys got her drunk and took advantage of her. It is sometime before or after this incident that Arla also reports her first sighting of the 'black-eyed kids'.

Back in school after that summer, Arla's behaviour changes: there are episodes of violence and the incident in the boiler room.

This changes again after school and in college, when she warns Paulette about the 'black-eyed kids' coming to get her.

Then, at twenty-one, Arla bludgeons her entire family to death with a hammer. She claims that, before the incident, she allowed the black-eyed kids to enter the family home.

Arla is convicted of manslaughter with diminished responsibility and remanded in a secure unit for the rest of her life.

With my phone buzzing relentlessly, I realise that I'm close now, that I've reached a tipping point in this case. My instincts are telling me to keep on and the constant abusive texts and threats that are yammering from my phone only enhance this sense.

I feel that my most important port of call is Cornwall – the holiday that the Macleods took. It's going to be a long shot but I need to find out more about what happened there. The chances of finding anyone who was there at the same time as the Macleods are remote, but with every threat I receive, I feel I'm getting closer … closer to something.

I feel I have to keep on.

But at the same time I feel that I've inherited Arla's 'Daruma-san' – a ghost that is following me. The question is, why?

This has been our third…

Until next time…

TorrentWraith – Audio (Music & Sounds)

Type	Name
Audio	**Arla Macleod Rec004 [320KBPS]** Uploaded **3 weeks** ago, Size 57.3 MiB. ULed by JBazzzzz666

Today I've seen nothing so far – just shadows, dancing, moving shadows. Does that count?

And eyes. Glowing eyes.

They're under things, in spaces between things where there's black, where there's shadow. Sometimes I don't see them, I just know they're there, looking out at me from the dark places. Because there's dark places here, despite the white walls, the smell of polish and the *crick* of the plastic under the bed sheets. Under shelves, in the corners of cupboards and between the creases of sheets … you can't escape darkness.

It's my fault, I know. I should have listened to the warnings. You spend a long time opening a door and when you finally get it open, you stand before that opening, staring at the place you've always wanted to go. You don't realise, you don't even think, that maybe something's looking back at you, that something's been waiting on the other side and wants to get through that door too.

You can't escape darkness.

I dreamed last night, I dreamed vivid. Maybe it were a waking dream or, like, a lucid dream … whatever it was, it were clear as day.

I were a bird. I were … free. I were flying. I could feel me wings rattling, the wind under them, and I were above the sea … for ages. Maybe it's a sub-conscious wish for freedom, but it weren't like that … it were like I was *going* somewhere. There were cliffs, just sort of rearing up out of the sea. And that's it – that's where I were going.

A house. Not my house but, like, one you might see from a train – one sat in the middle of a field, or on top of the cliffs, and you look at it through the window and think, *Who lives there? What do they do all day?*

The house were in the middle of a field – it must have been a cornfield or something. There were long grass, anyway, and it were all green with like, those tractor marks running round the edges.

It were nighttime in the dream … or more like an evening in summer, where it's late but still light, but that little house in the field had all its curtains closed. And there were a terrible feeling, a feeling of horror, like a nightmare … cos the grass, the long grass – or crops or whatever – around the house, it were moving, like waggling like there was something in there. And I could see shapes … I could see these black shadows like a swarm, like a crowd of figures coming from every direction, approaching the house from all angles. And … and I knew … I knew what they were. I couldn't see them, not properly, but I caught a glimpse of a hand, a head.

I were sort of hovering now, you know? Right then I could feel how small I was, how fragile. You know when you touch a bird and you can feel its bones and you know that if you just closed your hand, you'd break it, kill it? I felt like that. I could feel that.

When you see this you'll say something about a lack of power – lack of control … I'm getting better at all this, aren't I?

I focused and I could suddenly make out what were moving through that long grass. It were children – raggedy children moving through the crops, making them wiggle. A swarm of them, a mob of them – they were coming from all angles through the field towards that little house. I felt tight – a tightness in my tummy – and I wanted to scream out, like, I wanted to warn whoever was in that house, tell them to get out. But my throat was all closed up, my throat was burned closed, and when I tried to speak all that came out was a whistling, croaking sound.

I think it's cos they've altered my medication, you know? I'm not seeing … *whole* things as much anymore, like I were before. Now they hide; they flicker in the corners. Shadows and eyes always peering out.

I know that later on we'll talk about my dream. You're going to say that you wonder why I had such a dream, and I'm going to have to come up with ideas.

It's going to be hard for me to put it into words, but what I'll say is that I can feel something's … coming; 'approaching' might be a better word for it.

Something's approaching – maybe that's what the dream was about. It were about things approaching weren't it? In the dream.

I got woke up by voices today. I think that's the medication too, cos I were proper down today, like it felt like I were dragging my feet through treacle. I've got a headache. It's cos I've not had a proper sleep.

It were the same voices as yesterday. But I didn't do a video yesterday cos you said I should make them when I *saw* stuff, you didn't say to do it when I *heard* stuff.

So, I were down the garden, in the polytunnel. I like the smell in there, especially after it's been raining – plastic and soil, and the air is warm. There's a stillness in there that you don't get anywhere else in here, even at night in my room. I love that stillness, especially when there's not many people around. It's like being somewhere else … like being in another…

Anyway, I was in the polytunnel and Sandy was there too – you know the big lad who wears the yellow T-shirt? He says he's getting out soon, going free. He's 'crossing the road' – that's what they call it here cos if you look out onto the main drive, you see the road just sort of disappearing into the trees, and there's a bit that goes over the motorway – a bridge – and once you go over there, you're free.

Sandy doesn't like gardening, he's too impatient and doesn't like getting soil on his hands. When I first came, he used to get angry about it, whining like a little kid. Sometimes he'd chuck a shrub against the floor or kick a flowerpot. He's not done that for ages now.

So, Sandy's stood over there in his yellow T-shirt that's too small for him now – his tummy pops right out of the bottom – and he's got his tongue out between his lips cos he's potting. I remember when Mam used to tell me off for that when I were little: 'Put your tongue in, Arla!' she'd snap. 'You look like you're simple!'

I were only five or six.

So, I'm replanting some of the strawberry plants, and the polytunnel's like a sauna, with that soily smell and the still air pressing in on you and making your face damp … but I like it. I'm being careful with the plants, pulling them gently out and pressing them into the beds, pouring a bit of water on them.

He hates you.

I look up. I look up and I know I've got my mouth open.

Close your mouth, Arla!

It snaps shut and I'm still looking about.

*He hates you and before he crosses the road, he's going to snap your bones –
your little bird bones.*

I nearly say something. It's such a surprise, I nearly forget. I nearly slip up
and shout out.

*All of them hate you, Arla. They hate you cos of what you did. Scum. You're
nowt but scum.*

Die, Arla, just die.

A memory came back then, a proper harsh one, like a flashback. I remember sitting in Paulette's bedroom when I was young. Her mam didn't mind
us having the music on and that, and we used to be able to smoke fags out
her bathroom window. I remember we were all sat on the floor – me and
Paulette and Debs – and Skexxixx were on and the air smelled of nail-polish
remover. We had a bottle of voddy that we kept passing round. All we were
getting ready to do was go out to wander about the streets!

Anyways, I remember that voice from back then. But back then it were
only a whisper.

*They want you dead, Arla, both of them. When you go to the bathroom, they're
planning how to get rid of you. They're going to stab you up and burn your body.*

I remember leaving Paulette's bedroom and crouching outside the door,
but I couldn't hear nowt. Then I burst back in.

I remember their faces, they were looking at me as if I was insane!

It were so hard to hold on, to not act out like that, down in the polytunnel. So hard, because I knew who it were who were saying those things, but
I didn't want to acknowledge them, you know? But they just kept going –
over and over and over – and I could hear *them*, the voices of those kids, their
questions, asking me, *Why, why, why?* Then the dancing boys' voices after
them – those were the loudest ones. They were telling me I was nowt but a
slag, calling me all these dirty names, all those dirty words. Their questions
and those names and their hands were rolling all over me – over and over
like waves. And I stood there in the polytunnel with sweat on my face and
my hands all covered in soil.

And I knew they'd all come through – I'd let all of them in, each one with each game I'd played. It were all my fault…

And I were screaming, screaming and screaming and screaming.

That were yesterday when I had to go to my room with a pill and just wait until they all stopped.

I lay on my bed and closed my eyes. And I knew they were outside the window – I could hear them crying. And I knew if I opened my eyes the dancing boys would be there…

They would all be there and they would all be telling me why everyone hates me, they would all be telling me to die, to just end it. It'd be better for everyone. Cos everyone knows what I've done…

I let them in.

But you'll be proud of me, cos I did open my eyes.

And there were nothing but shadows – shadows and eyes in the corners.

Which is better, I suppose.

Episode 4: Brown-Eyed Girl

—I saw her around, yeah, but I never had … I never had any reason to go and talk to her. Like, we were both girls, yeah, like, the same sort of age, so why didn't I just go talk to her? Man, it's hard to explain now I'm older – it just doesn't make sense anymore. Maybe I was just shy or something? Maybe I had no idea what to even say…

Back then I didn't know who I was yet, you get me? Like, I wasn't comfortable with myself. I used to run with *bad boys*. And I was horrible to girls, yeah? So I wasn't gonna go up to her and be all like 'hey', you know?

But I knew I liked them, you get me? Girls. Like, I liked them in *that* way. I'm cool with it now, yeah? But not then – not when I was fifteen, yeah? It's not easy when you're someone like me.

I tell you what, yeah: the thing is with girls like her, when you're young, like, when you're a teenager, you think everyone's like you. When you're young you think everyone just wants attention. Cos that's all *you* want when you're a teenage girl. Man, you want attention, but at the same time you want everyone to leave you alone, yeah?

The voice you're hearing is that of twenty-four-year-old Angel Mawson. At least that's the name she's given me. Angel has allowed me only to reveal a select few details about her. And these details are all I know as well. Angel lives in London. We meet in the back room of her friend's hair salon, and it's in this tight room, with the tang of chemicals in my throat, that we talk. Angel wears her hood up the whole time, shading her face. I'm surprised she didn't want to conduct this inter-view via phone or audio-only Skype, but Angel point blank refused those suggestions.

I had no idea of Angel's existence in the story of Arla Macleod until

she got in touch with the show and told me a few things – things that
have driven me to this place in the capital to conduct our interview.

It's evening time and the salon is closed. The lights are low in both the
back room and out front. Passers-by are visible through the slats in the
window shutters – ghosts dancing beyond the empty, hulking chairs and
treatment tables in the other room.

—So I'm out, man – I don't give a fuck, you know? I don't make
a thing about it, though. I just get on. But back then? Man, I didn't
even know what I was doing, yeah? I didn't have any idea what I was,
what I wanted.

But we're not talking about me, are we? You're not sat there
wanting to know about *my* life and shit, right? I don't matter. You
want to know about *her*, don't you? Arla Macleod.

It's been long since then, though, man, yeah? Long since then.

But yeah, I knew her. No one else knows that I knew her. Sort of.
At least I thought I did. For a bit. For that week.

§§

Welcome to Six Stories. *I'm Scott King.*

Over these six weeks, we are looking back at the Macleod Massacre
– a tragedy that occurred in the year 2014, when a twenty-one-year-old
woman killed her mother, stepfather and younger sister. We're looking
back from six different perspectives – seeing the events that unfolded
through six pairs of eyes.

Then, of course, it's up to you. As you know by now, I'm not here
to make any judgements or draw any definite conclusions. I'm just the
organ-grinder, the facilitator.

For newer listeners, as frustrating as it may be, I am not a policeman,
a forensic scientist or an FBI profiler; and this isn't an investigation. I
don't reveal new evidence. My podcast is more like a book group, a discus-
sion at an old crime scene. We discuss things with the help of others, those
who have agreed to look back on a tragedy.

Angel Mawson is dubious about me. We talk about any possible legal ramifications – whether she would have to answer for anything if the Macleod Massacre case is re-examined. I tell her it's possible, but I don't know. I can't say.

I'm not doing this to find a killer – that's been done already. I'm here to look at why Arla Macleod killed her family on the 21st of November 2014.

—So, like, what? You want me to go way back, yeah? So, like, way back about *me*? This thing ain't about me though, is it?

—*I guess it depends. But I'm not going to tell you to say anything you don't want to.*

There's a moment of tension after I say this. Angel pulls her hood down further and glances out through the salon, towards the street. I catch a glimpse of her face, momentarily. Her expression is serious, hard.

It's rush hour in London and the rain is lashing down. The lights of the passing cars drift by.

—Let me ask you something, man? So … like, have you ever recorded one of these things and it has been, like, I dunno, like it went nowhere? Like, you had a case and that, yeah, but you got nothing? It was too … easy? Like, someone killed someone and they just *did* it – like, there was nothing else?

It's a good question. A really good one. I'm honest when I tell Angel that my breakthrough series – the one about Daniel Murphy, the teenage spree-killer who shot several of his classmates in Devon – nearly floundered. I actually thought I'd bitten off more than I could chew then – there was just so much to consider in Murphy's case. I tell Angel I nearly gave up halfway through.

—*There's always something though – always a detail that gets overlooked: a person, an opinion that pulls these cases tight like shoelaces. At least that's how it feels for me.*

—Am I that person?

—*I don't know yet.*

—OK, man. So let me tell you a bit about me, yeah? I grew up in the care system. I was bad, I mean *bad* – a fighter. I had all this … this rage inside me that I just didn't know what to do with, yeah? I mean now I know what was fuckin' me up – I was angry at my mum, yeah? At my dad for giving up on me. Like, for them, having a kid was too much hard work. It was too much for them so they just got rid of me, yeah?

—*I understand.*

—Also, there was the gay thing. Like, they say you should come out to someone you trust, but I had no one back then, man, no one! Any adult who tried to get close – teachers, social workers, foster carers, all of them – I just pushed them away, like. I made myself unlikeable so they didn't even have a chance, you know. That way they couldn't be disappointed, yeah? It's fucked-up logic but it was what it was back then.

—*So were you still that angry girl when you met Arla? What were the circumstances in which you met her?*

—I'd been moved again for fighting – this time down south. I went to these carers, Emma and Gary Young. They were good to me, man, they were chill. It didn't work out in the end for me with them – I was too angry, too hard … too damaged. And Gary and Emma, they were too soft, too nice.

—*The Youngs were the ones who took you to Cornwall on holiday, right?*

—Yeah man, they did. They were good like that, you know – they meant well, taking this bratty little care kid to this, like, big posh place on the coast. I think they thought it would be good for me, you know? But I saw the looks we were getting, I saw the way the staff pulled their lips tight and whispered to each other whenever they turned their backs.

From what I can gather from a combination of Arla's and Angel's

scattered memories, the hotel was one of many all-inclusive family hotels
perched on the Cornish coast. I have an idea which one, but I don't
think it is right to reveal its name – it's not relevant to what happened.

It seems there weren't a great deal of activities for young people going
on during the day there – a games room, giant chess and an adventure
playground in the grounds. And there was entertainment at night as
well. The Macleods' holiday was in the peak of summer, so there must
have been a lot of young people and their families there.

—I stuck out like a sore thumb. That's how it felt anyway. All the
other kids were all so wholesome – privileged, rich. They stank of it.

Gary and Emma, man, they'd saved for this for a long time. They'd
arranged for me to do all this stuff – scrimped and saved and paid for
me to do all these activities. It was sport and archery and shit, you
know? I wanted to join in, but I just *couldn't*. However much Gary
and Emma tried, I was never that type of kid. But I felt so bad – this
was their holiday too. And I knew they wanted a break from me as
well. They'd go for little walks down the beach, have afternoon tea
and that. And I'd tell them I was having a great time and they would
look so pleased.

—*What were you actually doing?*

—Ah man, you see, people like me, people like I was back then,
we find each other.

—*And you and Arla found each other?*

—Not at first, nah. I found the bad boys, didn't I?

The 'bad boys' that Angel describes I cannot account for. Angel says she
can't remember if they were locals or hotel guests. At the time she didn't
care. She describes walking around outside the grounds of the hotel and
meeting the first 'bad boy' – a young man of around eighteen years old
who introduced himself as Kyle and gave Angel a cigarette. We'll hear
more about Kyle later, but right now, we'll concentrate on Angel's first
meeting with Arla.

—That first time I met Arla was well weird. There's loads I don't remember about that holiday, man, but I remember meeting Arla. It was like a dream or something. So it was, like, afternoon sometime, you know? It was hot, man, like it was abroad, and everyone was dozing and that. All the kids were out in the pool and the hotel was dead quiet. It was kind of like being in another world – all these long, empty corridors. The walls were like marble or something, and I was wearing those jelly sandals that everyone had back then, yeah? My feet were making this slapping noise that was echoing around. I could see this, like, vivid blue sky through all the windows, the staff quietly tidying up the breakfast stuff in the dining room. It was like I was in a dream. I just kept walking around.

I was just wandering round the hotel and I was waiting for the lift and, like, it opened, yeah, and there was ... man ... there was, like, this vision stood there. It was like something from a film, man. That was the moment! That was the fuckin' moment when I knew it, man – the moment I knew I liked girls. That's why ... ha! That's why I wasn't freaked out.

—I don't follow – what would you have been freaked out about?

—What that girl was doing in the lift, man! It was some witchcraft shit. She had a load of the buttons pressed, and she was just riding up and down to all these different floors, man, waiting for the doors to open and close and then going to the next one. It was mad!

—Why was she doing that?

—She didn't even say! At first, she wouldn't even speak to me! I was, like, 'What's up?' and she just put her head down and ignored me.

—Wasn't that a bit strange?

—Maybe, but I didn't even care. I was just, like, mesmerised by this girl. She had these big brown eyes, like a cow, but, like, not dopey. She ... like, she was from another world or something, you know? I just, like, stood there, arms folded and attitude out, yeah, just looking at her. It probably looked like I was giving her evils.

—So how did you two get to know each other if Arla wouldn't speak to you?

—I was just, like, I'm staying here, man. I knew stubborn – I'm just as stubborn now.

—I'm thinking, the way you were back then, you probably saw Arla as a challenge, right?

—Yeah! That's right – you got it in one! After a minute or something I was, like, girl, you're gonna talk to me no matter what?

—And did she?

—Of course.

—What happened?

—It was, like, we got to the tenth floor. I remember cos, like, it was either the very top floor or one from the top, you know? I was planning to go up there myself sometime, just to get away from people, yeah? We get there and she just looks at me with those big brown eyes, as if she expects me to say something, you know? I'm, like, 'What?' And you know the first thing she says to me?

—What?

—She's, like, 'Oh it's OK, you didn't get on at the fifth floor anyway.'

—What did she mean?

—I dunno, man – long time since then, yeah? It was like a game or something she'd made up. You had to go to all the different floors or something, yeah. Then, like, you'd go to another world. I wasn't even listening to that shit. I would have gone anywhere with that girl, you know?

What Angel has described here rings a bell – I think I have an idea about what Arla was doing in the lift: she could have been playing a game that appears to have originated on a Korean paranormal website. I discovered this particular game when researching the Daruma-san bath game I discuss in episode three.

This game is entitled Elevator to Another World and has very specific instructions. I'll summarise them briefly.

Elevator to Another World can only be played alone. You enter the lift from the first floor. If someone else enters with you, you must wait until they've gone and then start the game alone. (I believe Arla must have been some way through the game when she encountered Angel; the reason for that will become clear soon.) Next, press the button for the fourth floor. When the lift reaches the fourth floor, do not get out; instead, press the button for the second floor. Do the same again, stay in the lift and press the button for the second floor again. Do not get out when you reach the second floor. Press the button for the sixth floor. Do not get out when you reach the sixth floor; press the button for the second floor. Do not get out when you reach the second floor. Press the button for the tenth floor.

At this point in the game, people have allegedly heard a voice calling to them on the second floor. If that voice is heard, you must not acknowledge or reply to the voice in any way. I believe that Angel entered the lift with Arla at this exact point in the game. According to Angel, the hotel's restaurant and reception area were on this floor.

The lift should then reach the tenth floor. Again, do not get out; instead, press the button for the fifth floor.

Arla saying to Angel 'you didn't get on at the fifth floor' confirms, at least for me, that Arla could well have been playing this game. According to the numerous websites and blogs surrounding the game, at this point in the proceedings, a woman may enter the lift on the fifth floor. This woman may be a stranger or someone the player knows. I believe the reason why Arla ignored Angel at first is because, according to the rules of the game, you are not supposed to even look at this woman — you must stare at the floor or the buttons of the lift. If you engage with the woman she will 'keep you as her own'. What that means, I'm not entirely sure. I have been able to find no credible account of anyone who has 'come back' and reported what happens if you speak to the woman in the lift.

Now for the last element of the game: press the button to the first floor; the lift should go up instead of down, reach the tenth floor. That's when you have performed the ritual 'correctly'. However, it is important to know that, if the lift does indeed go down to the first floor, you should exit immediately.

If the ritual has been performed correctly, you will have a choice when you reach the tenth floor: you can exit or not. The woman may try and engage with you by screaming or asking you questions. If she does, you must still avoid her. Apparently you'll know if you've reached another world when stepping out of the lift as you'll be 'the only one there'. My guess is that, if the lift woman 'keeps you as her own', this world is where you'll see out your days – at least according to the supernatural rules of the game.

There are many similarities between the accounts of those that have supposedly completed the game and visited this other world. According to their accounts, the building looks the same as the one they began in, but all the lights are off. The other common feature is that all that can be seen outside is a red cross in the distance. There are no other living things in that world except the player.

There is a plethora of these 'dangerous' games floating around online, but Elevator to Another World rose to mainstream notoriety after the death of Elisa Lam in 2013.

To summarise what is a complex and troubling case, Elisa Lam was a Canadian student reported missing when she failed to check out of the hotel in which she was staying – the Hotel Cecil, Los Angeles – on the 31st of January 2013. Lam's body was found in the water tank on the roof of the hotel on the 19th of February after other guests complained about a lack of water pressure, and discoloured and foul-smelling water coming from the taps in their rooms.

There has been no definitive explanation for Elisa Lam's death, but what is widely concluded is that she suffered a psychotic episode from the medication she was taking for her bipolar disorder.

This podcast is in no position to comment on the death of Elisa Lam. Many other crime podcasts have covered the case, and I don't know enough about it to go into any great detail. But before Lam was found the LAPD released a video from a surveillance tape filmed within the hotel. The video shows Lam acting strangely inside one of the lifts: she presses a number of the floor buttons before moving back and forth to the open lift door and looking out.

As one would expect, the security tape has come under much scrutiny, and is easily accessible on YouTube. It is claimed that as much of

*a minute of the original footage from the video has been removed – for
reasons unknown. There are many theories about the case of Elisa Lam,
ranging from demon possession to a hit by the Illuminati. However, the
link with Elevator to Another World can be dismissed in the first ten
seconds, as it is clear that Elisa Lam presses the buttons to the floors in a
linear order rather than the sequence from the game's rules. The video is a
disturbing watch, granted, but any link to this 'game' is, in my opinion,
clutching at straws. I only mention it to demonstrate the power of online
speculation and the prominence of the game that I believe Arla Macleod
was playing in Cornwall.*

Back to Arla Macleod or more specifically, Angel.

—*Did Arla tell you what she was doing in the lift?*

—Yeah man, she was giving it all this about some 'gateway to
another world' or some shit, and I was like, 'whatever'. But I knew
what she was *really* saying, man. I knew what it was really about.

—*And what was that?*

—It had nothing to do with other worlds or witches or any of
that shit, yeah? The thing with Arla – she was like me, man. She was
like me...

*Angel pauses here for a long time and I follow her gaze out across the
salon and into the street, where people still pass by, oblivious to us sat
here in the back room. When she continues, it's as if the years leave her:
a softer voice comes out from behind that hard exterior. It's almost child-
like, and I think I can detect tears. I feel a pang of sorrow for Angel; she's
dropped her guard, albeit momentarily, and I wonder if there's something more to all this. And I wonder again why she's so adamant about
keeping herself anonymous.*

*Angel's phone buzzes in her pocket. The sound pushes a gasp out of
my chest. She looks at the screen for a second and then places it on the
worktop beside her. I see her face for a moment in the light of her screen,
see her guard snapping back – vigilant once again.*

—The thing is, yeah, when no one wants you – when this world tells you that you're not important, that you don't matter, that you're an inconvenience – some people start to believe it; they make themselves unlikeable.

Let me tell you a story, right. It's not about Arla, but … well, it is in the end, you'll see. I remember this boy, man, he'd just come into the home where I was when I was about fourteen, yeah? Somewhere near Ipswich. Like, this boy was younger, like eight or nine. He was way too young for the home. But that's what it was like, yeah? You don't get much of a choice.

The first night, this boy, he was wearing like, super-hero pyjamas – like any kid. But by his second night, man, he was in his boxer shorts shouting like the rest of us. I remember hearing one of his care team who came into the home talking to one of the staff. She was saying that Robbie – that was his name – she was saying that Robbie was used to having a story at night. But she'd asked him, and he'd told her he hadn't had a story since he got to the home. And that … man, that just broke my heart, you know? It just got inside me. So I went to his room that night – me, this angry girl, I went to his room and told him that I'd read him a story. Maybe I was, like, trying to recreate a childhood I'd never had or something. I remember feeling it so strong – that if I could just read this kid a story, man, that it would like … fix something in me…

—*What happened?*

—He's in bed, just lying there, and there's screaming coming from Tyrone in the next room and Jordan in the floor above stamping about. And this Robbie kid, he just looks over to me, and his eyes, man, they're just … empty; just …dead. And he says, 'Fuck off out of my room, you cunt.'

It was too late for him, man. The damage had been done. He'd lost out on the last thing that made him feel safe, so he created armour. People used to say that was me too. And I guess it was until I met Arla.

—*And do you think that was Arla too – was she putting on armour?*

—You ever see *Return to Oz?* Man, that shit is brutal.

—*You mean the wheelers and the queen with all the heads? It certainly is!*

—Yeah man, that shit's scary. But it's not the worst of it. The worst of it is little Dorothy, man. They all think she's lost her mind so they want to give her shock therapy. Her only escape from that shitty little farm in Kansas was Oz. Dorothy went there to escape a world where she didn't matter, where they would get rid of her only friend – that dog – and where they would fry her brains without a second thought. Dorothy Gayle was like Arla – or Arla was like Dorothy Gayle. All she wanted to do was get the fuck out of here and into Oz.

—*Why do you think that was, Angel? What was it about her world that Arla was trying to escape from – to protect herself from?*

—Man, we all got stuff we're running from. We've all got wheelers after us – evil queens.

Angel won't elaborate further and I take the hint; she's right when she claims to be stubborn. 'It's not my story to tell,' she repeats and lowers her head. Angel seems deeply reluctant to talk about anything more than this particular time in her life. I get an urge to share with her what's been happening to me, wondering if that will encourage her to open up. But I stop myself, although it takes a lot not to ask who Angel's 'wheelers' are.

—So me and Arla … we just, like, roamed about, you know? Aimless, just wandering round.

—*Where did the two of you end up?*

—It's mad down there on the coast – it's like tropical heat and shit; palm trees and that, you know? That summer was hot; it was like being abroad. Gary kept saying it was like being abroad but everyone spoke English.

The hotel was right above the beach, hanging off the cliff. To get down, you had to take this path. It was like a long zigzag down the cliff and there was, like, loads of older people and that with sticks. Arla and me, we just wandered down those paths. You could see the sea behind you, this big green wall, all the waves like paint flecks and that big blue sky above you. There was all sorts of mad flowers and weeds and that growing alongside those paths and you could smell the salt of the sea as you walked. It was like something out of a book or a film or some shit.

—*So the two of you walked to the beach?*

—Well, yeah and no. You could get down to the beach that way, but there was more than one path, you know? It was a huge cliff and there were all sorts of paths snaking down like veins or something. We just wandered those paths and as soon as we saw other people, we'd take another path. It was like a game.

—*Why did you do that?*

—I dunno, man. We never said we'd do it, we just did. For me, I think that if I'd seen Gary and Emma, like, I'd have felt bad. They'd paid for me to do all this shit, you know, like activities and stuff.

—*Did they ever find out? That you weren't there I mean?*

—Nah. Trust me, they were good people; they weren't like … They cared man. But they were tired; it was their holiday too. They trusted me.

Angel turns away and goes a little quiet again, overwhelmed by emotion. I get it; Angel has told me a few times that Gary and Emma were the only carers that she ever really felt a connection with. I haven't the heart to ask her what happened with her and them in the end.

—*So when you and Arla were exploring, I imagine you did a lot of talking.*

—Yeah, just chatting about our lives and that. It was well weird cos we didn't even know each other and we started talking deep shit, like, really early on. We talked about our lives and our dreams. She had a lot.

—*Did Arla tell you much about what things were like at home?*

—A bit. I can't speak for her, you know, but I will tell you that she had it hard … She was under it at home.

—*Under it?*

—Yeah, man. Her parents, man ... her mum, yeah? They really had that Catholic guilt thing going hard.

—*Go on.*

—Just, like, Arla's mum didn't trust her an inch!

—*Why do you think that was?*

—I dunno, man. Arla was a good girl, you know? The opposite of me completely. She was one of those girls that got As, man, that, like, did their homework. It sounded like her mum and dad was a bit ... tapped, you know? It sounded like neither of them were right in the head.

—*What made you think that?*

—Maybe it was just that we were from such different worlds, me and her? Arla wasn't allowed to go out with her friends or anything. When everyone was down the park and that, she would have to stay in. A boyfriend? That was out of the question, you know? She just seemed to spend all her time in the house on the internet and stuff. That was her place, the internet – that was her one place where her mum and dad couldn't watch her. They didn't even know about it. They spent their time driving her sister about and Arla just hung about online. That was her world. That's probably why she was into all that mad stuff.

—*What mad stuff?*

—Like, those games – like the lift game. And all that Skexxixx stuff – that music. I'd never even heard of it till Arla played me some.

I remember it was this beautiful day. We were walking down those paths and, like, she was telling me all this deep shit about these songs and about how only certain people could properly understand them. I wasn't even really listening, man. I guess I was falling in love with her, you know? It was like something out of a film, with the flowers and shit. I could smell her skin ... the sun cream ... and, man, all I could think was that this doesn't happen to girls like me, you know? I told her a lot, man; I told her stuff I don't normally tell.

—*Why was that? Why would you open up to Arla? It seems a little out of character, don't you think?*

—I've sometimes thought about that, man. At first I thought it was cos I was attracted to her, yeah? Maybe I wanted her to see this part of me I didn't really show anyone else, like it would impress her or something. But now I'm older, I think it was something to do with Arla herself. She was like a dream; like, she was not quite real. I knew I'd never see her again after this holiday, that we'd never hear from each other again, so we were in different worlds and that sort of made it OK, you know? That made it easier to just talk.

—*Did Arla talk back to you in the same way?*

—Sort of, I guess. She was an odd one though, like she wasn't quite of this world.

I've heard people describe both Alice and Arla in this way – as if there were something ethereal about the sisters that seemed to draw people in and push them away in equal measure.

I should also say that I realise that so far Angel hasn't even mentioned what happened in 2014. This is deliberate; she told me before we started the interview that what happened shocked her deeply. When she heard about it on the news she remembered Arla's name instantly. But she does not want to speculate about what Arla did to her family that night and anyway, she says she hadn't been in touch with Arla since they met on holiday.

It is also worth noting that Arla and Angel did not spend entire days unsupervised. Angel's memories are hazy but she insists they must have gone back to the hotel every few hours to make sure they were seen by their parents and guardians – and to eat meals with them. But otherwise they were granted free range of the resort.

—Me and Arla went down to the beach at the bottom of the cliffs a bit, but neither of us liked the feel of the sand on our feet very much. And there were too many people there, kids and parents playing out in the sun. Happy families.

—*So where did you go instead?*

—That's when things went wrong; that's why I wish I could just keep those first couple of days sacred. That what came next didn't happen, you see?

—*What did come next?*

—Man, there's so much of it – it's a lot to explain, you know?

—*Where's a good place to start?*

—Hmm … probably the games room.

—*The games room?*

—There was this tiny little room on the basement floor, next to the fire exit. It had pinball, one of those arcade games and fruit machines.

This is interesting. You will, of course, recall Arla's account from episode one of seeing the black-eyed kids in the very same room.

—*Did the two of you go there often?*

—Nah, man, we just found it one day after playing the lift game. We just went down to the basement and just sort of hung there for a bit. It wasn't our thing; it was just somewhere else to go that wasn't full of other people.

—*So what happened down there?*

—It's hard to remember exactly. There was some sports thing going on outside – you could hear it whenever you went out, some football match or something. So we must have been in hiding from that. That day there were a lot of new people in the hotel – families with suitcases coming in and out. Changeover day or something.

I guess we were just trying to keep away from all that. Just lying low, you know?

From what I can gather, Arla and Angel were kindred spirits of sorts and much of their behaviour centred around avoiding others, especially people their own age. This strikes me as a little strange when it comes to Angel. She hasn't long told me she almost found solace in the 'bad boys' again, but meeting Arla put a stop to that. Perhaps in Arla she found what she was looking for?

Angel sighs as she recounts the next part and there's more than a little bitterness in her voice.

—Then, like, this *boy* appears.

—*A boy?*

—Yeah, he was our age I think, or maybe younger. I dunno, man. I didn't give a fuck. One minute it was just me and Arla and next he was just suddenly there, ruining the vibe, you know?

—*Really? His presence was that intrusive?*

—From the very first second.

—*Tell me more about this boy.*

—OK. First, his name was Anthony. It didn't suit him! You know how some people just, like, don't suit their name, like, it just hangs off them like a bad coat? That was this guy, man. Anthony, it sounded just all wrong for him, you know?

—*What did he look like?*

—Ah, this guy was *big* and I'm not talking personality.

—*He was overweight?*

—He was wearing these big jeans, and you know his mum's got them for him from the fat-kid shop – Big & Beautiful or whatever. He was so fat his arms sort of stuck out, like a penguin or something, you know? He was breathing really loud as well – wheezing. It was disgusting. He had these red cheeks, sweat on his forehead. It was like even just existing was difficult for him, you know? He couldn't look at you, always had his head down. Weird man, just a big fat weirdo.

—*So was Anthony just another guest?*

—Oh we found out all about him immediately. You know, this is making me sound bad, like, shallow or something, yeah? But I'm not, because, like, I have no problem with fat … sorry, *overweight* people. I mean, I'm no model. But it wasn't about that with him – it wasn't his weight that was the problem.

—*Was there something else other than your attachment to Arla that this guy had interrupted?*

—So as soon as he walked into that room and we turned round I mean, I was taken aback by the sight of him at first cos the way he looked at us, it was creepy, man, like, up and down, slowly, both of us, one at a time. It was, like, for me anyway, you could feel his eyes all over your body. It made you feel greasy or something – *violated,* you know?

—*He was predatory?*

—See, I thought so at the time, but now I just think he was a bit sad, a bit lonely and awkward. But when he looked at Arla – man, I could see it written all over his face, and my heart just sort of sank.

—*Why?*

—You know what? I think I saw exactly what I had felt on his face. It was the feeling I had when I saw her the first time.

—*Why did your heart sink at that?*

—Because in that second I knew that we'd never be rid of him. At that moment I thought that whatever delicate chemistry was trying to happen between Arla and me was just about to get snuffed out. It sounds bad, doesn't it? Can you edit and shit afterwards to make me not sound so bad?

It is difficult, nigh on impossible, for me to locate the other guests who stayed at this hotel at the same time as Angel and Arla. Believe me, I've tried, but my sleuthing has only turned up maybes and dead ends. So unless the people themselves come forward, as Angel has, I am at a loss. All I have to go on are the words of Angel and Arla and I am aware that their recollections of the events are liable to bias and distortion.

Back in the salon, it's getting late, the rain is still falling outside, the darkness now swallowing the day. I am wondering to myself, as you are by now, what any of this has to do with what happened in 2014. I was hoping Angel could shed some light on the Arla Macleod that she knew. I was hoping that seeing Arla in her formative years might give us some insight into why she killed her family.

There have been hints. Angel has suggested that Arla's parents were strict, which is something we already knew, but there seems to be nothing extreme – that Angel knew about at least. To be honest I feel like I've learned more about Angel than Arla from this conversation. This is fine, but it wasn't what I set out to do here. As for this Anthony character, it feels like we're moving even further away from what I first intended to discover.

I decide to push Angel a little harder about Arla instead. There's a chance she might clam up, pull down her own shutters, but I have to do it.

—*I know you know what happened back in 2014 to Arla and her family.*

—Everyone knows that shit, man. It's the past now. God rest them.

—*What are your thoughts? People were angry when she was sentenced. People thought Arla got away with leniency, that her mental illness was perhaps an act.*

—People can think what they want. I've said nothing like that.

—*Was there anything else that happened? Anything at all you can remember that might help us understand Arla a bit more? I get that you had feelings for her back then. It makes sense. And you couldn't have predicted what she was going to do, no one could. But looking back, were there any signs?*

—Man, I've carried this round for years, yeah – so many years I've carried this, like a monkey on my back, you know? And I just never knew how or where I could tell it. Would the police even care? Would they even listen?

Then you came along.

—*And you reached out to me.*

—OK, look, I said that you had to edit this so I wouldn't look bad. What I'm about to tell you, it's bad, yeah. I mean it's not just bad, it's horrible, man. I've tried to stop it consuming me for all these years. I've held it off making me feel like shit every single day of my life. But the fact is I was young. I was stupid. I like to think I was streetwise and that, but no, man. I had been through a lot by then, but I wasn't anything. I was just a stupid little girl.

Fuck, man. Like I say, I've not talked about this shit before. Maybe if I do … it'll … maybe it'll do me some good?

—*OK, Angel, take your time.*

—This boy, this Anthony, he's just following us around – *Chat-chat-chat. What's your name? Have you got brothers and sisters? Where did you get that wristband from? Are you into this and that band?* All that. And I'm all, like, *OK, let's lose the douche bag, yeah?* I'm trying to say it to Arla with my eyes.

So, we're just walking through the hotel and I can just hear his breathing, this wheezing behind us wherever we go, you know? It's just relentless, man.

—*And how was Arla dealing with all this attention?*

—Well, that was the thing. Anthony was, like, barely even asking me anything; it was all about Arla: where she was from, what she was into, all that. I mean, I think she kind of liked the attention. She was all over it. I was like, *What about me, man?* I've just been giving everything these last two days and now this boy comes along and I'm nothing again.

But that was then. Now when I look at it I think, if that was me, suddenly being the centre of two different people's worlds … man, I'd have loved it, you know?

So I don't blame her now. But back then, man I was mad!

—*It makes sense, Angel. It really does.*

—The thing was, I could tell that Arla had never really had this sort of attention from boys before, you know? Cos she was just letting him ask all these questions, letting him get all interested. And you can't do that with boys, not if you know what you're doing. And she was talking about bands and all those 'games' off the internet with him. Cos, like I said, Arla was into all that too.

—*Did that make any difference to what was happening?*

—You know, I don't think she even knew what she was doing, yeah, but she had him in the palm of her hand, twisted round her little finger.

—*Wow.*

—Yeah. And that's where I should have stepped in; that's where I should have had a word with her – should have talked about it or something instead of doing what I did.

—*Which was?*

—I just thought *fuck this*, you know? I was so angry with that fucking wheezing fat kid. Why wasn't he interested in me? Why wasn't *she* interested in me anymore? That's why I did it. Just to show her. Just to show Arla that she'd miss me.

—*What did you do?*

—I just sacked her off for a bit man, like a big baby, like a princess – just took off on my own for a bit, you know? Just to see if she needed me.

Angel tells me she avoided Arla altogether for a couple of days. She spent a morning in her hotel room feigning a headache, apparently over-egging the pudding so much that her carers became a little concerned. It was this that drove Angel away from the grounds of the hotel and a little further afield.

—So I just started walking and didn't stop. I was pissed off. I was trying to forget both of them, and got further and further away until I was in the local village or something. Streets I didn't recognise. I didn't care. I could just get lost and no one would give a shit.

Then guess who pops up out of nowhere? One of the bad boys from before. Kyle. He was just sat there, just like before, man, just like, sat on a wall or something. And he looks up and he's like, 'You again.'

The look on his face man, everything about him, everything was just trouble. Because, trust me, I know trouble when I see it. I know bad boys when I see them, and he was one. Trouble.

Angel tells me she accepted a cigarette from Kyle. She then made a point of hanging around with him and his friends for the rest of that day and the whole of the next. She tells me they mainly spent it wandering around the streets smoking cigarettes. Bored teenagers.

—*How many of Kyle's friends were there with you?*

—I dunno, one or two. All the same, just like him: trouble.

—*Were there any other girls?*

—No.

—*Did that not strike you as a bit strange?*

—Nah, I'm used to that. I'm used to being one of the boys. Kyle told me about this party, and I got back a little bit of that feeling.

—*What do you mean?*

—Like someone finally cared enough to actually invite me to something, you know? I remember shrugging and doing my best to act cool. Then I remember the moment when I realised, when it all just came crashing down, when it was all destroyed.

—*How do you mean?*

—They had only told me about the party so I would tell *her*.

—*Arla?*

—I thought so at first but no. It was her sister. They asked me to go and hang with Arla again, to tell Alice, to tell Arla's sister about that party. I remember my stomach just folding in on itself, thinking *fuck you*, just walking away from them, just walking away from everyone after that. No one wanted me – not them, not Arla. I was good for no one.

—*Why Alice do you think? Did they know her?*

—She was beautiful. She was way younger than them, but still she was way out of their league, and none of them had the guts to speak to her. That's why they asked me.

After her day and a half with Kyle and his friends, Angel found herself back at the hotel. Alone.

—And then me and Arla, we just sort of bumped into each other again. Man, it was just ... I was pissed because it was like she didn't even care, man. Like, she wasn't even concerned that I'd been away. I know it was only a day or whatever, but still.

—*What about Anthony, was he still there?*

—Ugh, of course he was, wheezing away in the background, following her about like a shadow.

—*What had they been doing while you'd been with the boys?*

—It was like Arla had found her soul mate or some shit, you know? That Anthony, he was a little bit older but full of the same sort of mad shit as her.

—*Mad shit?*

—The lift game, those internet games. He loved all that stuff, too, man – all that other-world bullshit.

During those couple of days Anthony and Arla had presumably been comparing their knowledge of 'games' they had found on the internet. It is interesting to note the similarities between Anthony and Arla were stronger than between Arla and Angel. It is particularly interesting that both were into these games. Arla and Anthony seem to have been looking for an escape of some kind and these games heavily feature the concept of other worlds, of gateways between this dimension and others. A good example is Arla's Korean Elevator to Another World game. Angel believes Arla and Anthony played this on the days she was with Kyle and his friends. Angel's own escape was much more literal.

—*I bet that didn't go down well with you – that they got on so well.*

—You have to understand that for me, back then, all this was a lot. It was rejection, yeah? Another fuckin' rejection.

That's why it went down like it did. That's why it went down like that. Because of me.

—*Did you tell Arla or Alice Macleod about the party, like Kyle and his friends asked?*

—Fuck no, I didn't even know Alice! Alice was just like those boys, plastic and perfect. She was welcome to them! You know, my first instinct was to do it, to tell her and then go trotting back to those boys like a good little … But I didn't. If there's one thing I'm proud of, it's that I didn't do that. Not that it made much difference.

—*What do you mean?*

—One of the bad boys must have grown some balls because I started seeing Alice about with them, you know? They got to her somehow in the end. Guys like Kyle, they always get what they want.

—*Guys like Kyle?*

—Rich, entitled, spoiled. His dad was some sort of doctor and he knew for a fact he could do whatever he wanted. Money talks with guys like that.

So, anyway, I had no one and just found myself back with Arla. I couldn't resist her. And pretty much as soon as I start hanging around with her again, Arla starts telling me about this new game Anthony knows – this 'Hooded Man' thing.

The Hooded Man Ritual is similar in essence to the Elevator to Another World. We'll hear the details of it in due course. What is striking is that it too has a theme of escape, of passing from this world into another. I get the impression that Anthony was just as skilled as Arla and Angel were at finding ways to disappear. Angel's animosity towards him therefore seems odd. But that's teenagers, I guess.

—So I knew those two were going to sneak out of their rooms to meet and do that Hooded Man bullshit at midnight. They were just all hyped up about it. I was ready to walk away then and there, when Arla turns to me and says, 'Do you think you'll be able to sneak out?' as if we've all been in on this together all along. As if I was there too.

So I just nodded and she turns back to Anthony, yeah, just chatting on. I just left, man. I was, like, 'See you guys later, yeah?' And I just got up and left.

Arla didn't even turn around man. She didn't give one shit.

That's when I decided to actually do something. Not to Arla, yeah, but to him, to that Anthony.

—*What did you do?*

—See, I couldn't do nothing personally. If people like me do bad things, we get caught and we get punished. I knew that already back then. So I went and found Kyle and the bad boys. Alice was with them. This sounds just so stupid but I just started telling them about Arla and Anthony and the stupid baby games they were playing. They were all laughing and it felt good, man. Like, it was suddenly funny; like, it felt OK again. I regret telling them now. Course I do.

According to Angel, what she told Kyle and his friends was what she now tells me: that Arla and Anthony had agreed to meet in the hotel drawing room at midnight, a leisure area adjacent to the main reception, to begin the Hooded Man Ritual.

The Hooded Man is supposed to be a particularly 'dangerous' game and Angel says Arla and Anthony could talk about little else that day.

—The way they went on about that game! Like they were witches or some shit. I thought there was no way they were going to get out at midnight and go to the drawing room with no one finding them. Arla and Anthony, though – they were more concerned with the fuckin' game! They were more worried about being taken off by a ghost or some bullshit than getting in trouble. Different lives, different worlds we were from, me and them. I was, like, why can't you do that shit in your rooms? But they just looked at me, sat there with all these plans and bits of string and lighters and shit. They looked at me like I was a million miles away, man. So, after I felt good. I felt *good* that I told Kyle and the rest of them about their stupid fucking games!

There would be plenty of CCTV cameras in the hotel, not to mention hotel staff and other guests that could potentially challenge the youngsters. But the reason they chose the drawing room as the location to begin the game will become clear.

The Hooded Man Ritual's origins are sketchy at best, but my internet searches suggest it is Japanese in origin. For the ritual, you need an old telephone – one with a rotary dial. There was such a phone on a table in the corner of the drawing room, according to Angel – explaining why

Arla and Anthony planned to begin the ritual there. You also need some black cord – rope or string – matches and a watch.

The ritual begins on the stroke of midnight. Participants should count to thirteen before dialling a certain number with the phone still on the hook. I'm not going to divulge this number – people keen to partake in the ritual can find it out for themselves. I'll simply say that, apparently, this is one of the most dangerous of these types of games.

After calling the number, you must tie one of the black cords to the handset, lift the handset with the cord and dial another number. Count to thirteen and speak into the phone receiver: 'Hello, I need a cab.'

The black cord must be untied from the phone receiver and burned as soon as possible.

It's at this point that a black cab should turn up outside. According to the game's rules, you must exit the building, get into the back seat, close the door and go to sleep.

Like the elevator game, there are certain rules the participant must adhere to while inside the cab to make the game a success. For example, if you wake and see the time is anything other than 3.30 am, you must exit the cab and return home, and wait for another night to begin the ritual again. If you awake at exactly 3.30 am, however, you should see a hooded man driving the cab. It seems you must simply ride in the cab until he stops. That's when you must whisper in the hooded man's ear, 'I have reached my destination.' You will then fall asleep, waking back where you began.

It is ambiguous where the hooded man is taking you on your ride. Like the Elevator to Another World, it seems you enter another dimension. And the websites discussing the game state that the longer you ride, the harder it is to return to this one.

—*Did you try and connect with Arla and Anthony again that night?*

—So, those two were planning to go downstairs at midnight. Anthony's family were staying, like, on one of the lower floors and Arla was up on the fifth. I was on the ninth floor. We were nowhere near each other. They agreed to meet in the lift at 11.50 exactly. Arla would take the lift down to the first floor and wait for him.

I don't know if I even slept that night but I remember turning over, looking at the radio clock thing on my bedside table. Quarter to midnight: 11.45 – I'll always remember that, you know? Those red digits seared into my brain. I could have made it different. I could have got up. My carers were fast asleep in the room next door, so they wouldn't have noticed. But I didn't, I just lay there. All I could hear was my heart beating. It was hot that night – hot and muggy – and my duvet was caught up in my feet and I kept telling my body to get up, to swing my legs out of the bed, but they just refused.

—*So you never went with them?*

—I never even got out of bed. I just lay there, breathing, my heart beating. And then, just past midnight, I heard a noise. As soon as I heard that noise I jumped. I felt prickles all over me and this horrible feeling of dread – this horrible tingling, dragging feeling at the bottom of my belly. The only other time I've felt that was when I heard Arla's name on the news. I got that same feeling, and I thought, what if I'd got everything wrong after all?

What if they were right?

What if they were right about those other worlds?

There is a huge pause as Angel stares into the night, lost in her own thoughts. I almost don't want to ask about what she heard on that still night in Cornwall all those years ago, and I'm still at a loss to see what any of this has to do with what happened years later.

My phone buzzes, horribly loud from my pocket. We both jump. We then both laugh nervously, when a few moments later Angel's phone, which has lain silently on one of the work surfaces erupts in an even louder buzz. The ice seems broken – the shadows of the salon less dark – as we both turn our phones to silent and put them away.

—*What did you hear, Angel? In the middle of the night?*

—It was a car engine, man. It was an engine. I swear, as soon as I heard it, I put my head under the covers and started praying. I swear to you I have never prayed so hard in my life.

—*So what do you think happened that night? Are you saying you think it worked – the ritual?*

—I know – that car engine, it could have been anything, right? It could have been a night porter or something. One of the guests coming back late. That's logic – that's a logical explanation. That hotel was huge, man.

—*That's right. It could have been anything. Arla and Anthony were still there the next day weren't they? They hadn't gone?*

—Yeah they were, but neither of them even spoke to me. It was like something had changed.

—*Did you not ask about what happened?*

—I *wanted* to ask them, of course. But I have to admit I was scared. I was too fucking scared.

You know for years after that, for years, whenever I heard a car late at night I used to wake up terrified. To this day I close all the windows at night.

And that's why I never got in touch, why I never tried to find her again after that. I was just … scared.

And when I heard what she did to her family, you know what I thought? This is going to sound insane, but you know what I thought? I thought that something must have come back with her.

It sounds crazy but I thought they must have gone there … wherever 'there' was … and *something* came back with them. But maybe that was a defence mechanism, maybe that's what I wished had happened…

Frustratingly, this is as clear as Angel gets. She has no idea what the engine she heard outside was. And she doesn't even know for sure whether Arla or Anthony or both performed the ritual.

What Angel does explain to me, however, is that she's sure something bad happened to both Arla and Anthony that night and she is in some way culpable. And this clear sense of guilt makes me think that there is some finer detail she is neglecting to reveal – something she cannot bring herself to tell me.

I know by now, though, that Angel will only tell me what she wants to. She's told me a lot but she's also left a great deal of spaces between the lines.

There are, therefore, several questions that have emerged from my discussion with Angel – questions I was not expecting to ask.

What happened to Arla and Anthony that night?

Did they perform the Hooded Man Ritual, and if so, did it work?

Was there something else that Angel is, perhaps, not telling me about? Something to do with her snitching to Kyle? Some reason she felt so bad about that car pulling up; something that made her so scared?

What does any of this have to do with what Arla did to her family all those years later?

§§

Angel asks me politely if we can finish and when I look at my phone, I see, as well as several new text-message notifications, that we have been talking for hours. I'd be lying if I were to say I'm not a little unnerved, especially as a ghoulishly timed black cab races past, spraying up rainwater onto the salon's front window. However, I cannot leave without asking Angel a further question.

—*Angel, in your opinion, why did Arla do what she did to her family in 2014?*

—Man, that's asking, isn't it? That's the big-money question. Believe me, it's something that I've asked myself a few times. Did I have any effect on her? Was there something I could have done or not done back then? But then I think about it, man, and I'm, like, if Arla was gonna do it, she was gonna do it, regardless, right? Like, this is no butterfly-effect shit.

—*Do you have a theory?*

—Man, it's hard, you know? Because I didn't even know her well, you know? Me and her were so fleeting ... so brief...

What I do know is a couple of things: that her parents were strict.

Like, as far as she told me, they weren't crazy – like, they didn't beat her or nothing like that. I mean, she said her mum slapped her, but what's that? What's a slap? Plenty of kids get worse than that and don't kill their family, right?

And they were into religion, like Catholic or something. But each to their own beliefs, yeah?

But, I dunno man. Like, it's easy to look back and say there were signs, you know? There's always things that get missed. But with Arla there wasn't. I don't know if she was even – what would you say these days? – like, mentally unstable? She was just looking for a way to escape this world. She was just looking for a way out.

Or maybe something did come back with her from those other places she tried so desperately to go to? Maybe she did go there and something came back? Or maybe the real Arla never came back at all? Maybe she lost herself there. I don't know, man. I just wish I could have done something different.

I want to comfort Angel, some instinct in me wants to reach out to her, to tell her she's safe, that it'll be OK.

Angel looks up at me. There's a brief flicker of fear before she disappears beneath her hood and backs away into the shadows for the last time.

—That's enough now. That's enough for me, yeah? You promise you'll protect my identity, yeah? You swear?

—*Of course I will Angel, what…?*

—OK, bye now. Bye. I'll let you out. Don't call me…

We will, I assure you, find out more about the night when Arla and Anthony were planning to play the Hooded Man Ritual. We'll also uncover a few more nuances surrounding the Macleod Massacre. Then, of course, you'll be able to start connecting these frail endings – weave these frayed edges together to create a semblance of what was going on inside Arla Macleod.

This has been Six Stories.
This has been our fourth.
Until next time…

TorrentWraith – Audio (Music & Sounds)

Type	Name
Audio	**Arla Macleod Rec005 [320KBPS]** Uploaded **2 weeks** ago, Size 53.6 MiB. ULed by JBazzzzz666

The new meds are … I don't know…

I don't know if they're doing what they're supposed to be doing. Like, yeah, I'm not seeing things as much when I'm awake – shadows in the corners, eyes in the dark. But when I sleep…

Do you remember when your son was little? Did he have nightmares – monsters that only you could get rid of? I'm a grown-up and I still get monsters at night. Even with the new meds. Does that mean they'll never go away? What hope is there left for me, then?

I can hear them crying. And when I sleep, oh when I sleep, they all come trickling out of the cracks, out of the folds in my brain. In fact, I'd be dreading going to sleep if I wasn't so tired all the time. Sleep's like a marsh, a muddy bog that sucks at my feet. My life's like walking through this endless swamp.

I sleep where I fall, let the mud and the water close over me. I don't want to but I love it, it's like a hug.

Then I dream.

Last night it were that house again – me and Anthony looking over at that little house on the cliff top, in the middle of the field. We're side by side, passing a fag back and forth.

I'm a crow again. I'm a big, scraggly old carrion crow. Anthony's gone. I can feel my beak poking out of my face, can feel the tick-tick of my eyes as I stare round this human world. I can smell meat – old wiry meat on old bones. I can feel the fence post beneath my claws, my three toes, scaly like the feet of some dragon, some monster. Imagine that, though, if you've never seen birds before and you look at their feet. Scary as.

I'm sat on that post and it's suddenly dusk. Night's fallen and the long grass – the green, unripe corn or whatever it is – it's not moving. Anthony's gone and I can smell … I can smell the wind. It's sweet, carrying the traces of the wild flowers and the hedgerows. I can hear the evensong of nature – the rustlings and fussing of creatures in their beds; the hum of hungry mouths from concealed nests.

Anthony's gone.

All of this passes me by cos there's something else. My crow eyes flick and catch something.

Three of them. All holding hands and stood outside the front door of the little house. It's like something from a story book – some image from a long-forgotten story – and I ruffle my crow feathers. The windows of the little house are dark – curtains pulled, no lights, no music thumping. I wonder if Anthony's in there.

They're waiting, still and silent as the hunting animals; the silence before the spring of a cat; the stillness before the rush of an owl. All ending with claws and beaks and blood and teeth.

I want to cry out, to caw, to croak my rusted song across these skies – the ruffled purple clouds like furrows on a frown. I want to rise up, clatter my wings in warning. That poor little house, those closed curtains. I want to say no, I want to say, *Beware, beware!* My beak, though, it's all gummed up, all dry and sticky and it hangs heavy. My wings feel a sudden weight, heavy and hanging from me in a sodden coat.

I know they're waiting for their moment, those three black-eyed ones – their eyes like mine: birds' eyes, carrion eyes.

There'll be a signal, there'll be a call. And I know who it'll be from. It'll be from one of *them*, from somewhere deep inside them. Pale, flawless skin on the outside, but inside, horrible keening mouths, like little birds reaching from a nest. That's what it's like inside them; that's what it's like inside – all mouth, all desperate hunger.

When the time's right, they'll open their mouths and they'll cry, they'll wail and all the sorrow of the world will come spilling out of them like blood.

If Anthony's in that house he's fucked … he's dead.

Even if he's hiding, the black-eyed ones know it and that's why they do it. That's why they make that noise, that cry.

There's no escape for him in that little house.

I know because I'm the crow – feathers and feet and scales and beak. The smell of blood, blood, blood. It's all me.

Yeah. That was the dream. Does that count?

※※

I remember when we last had a meeting, in your office, you said that the more I recorded this, the more we'd be able to find out the *triggers*. And I wonder … I wonder if you're any closer? I'm just wondering – and I know it's brand-new techniques and that, and you'll say it's too early to tell and all that – but … but I just … I'm scared. I'm scared of next time I go to sleep that I'll see the next bit. I'll see what happens next.

That door will open and they'll let them in. It'll be all lit up inside like there's a fire and they'll be let in.

Maybe that's what happened back then. Maybe that's what the dream's trying to tell me?

I'm scared I've started something I can't stop. A runaway train. That's what Mam used to call me sometimes – a runaway train. 'Arla!' she used to say. 'You come in here like a runaway train.'

I remember that because it was the time I'd won best effort in swimming. I had a sticker and certificate – a proper one with that gold stuff on it – and I came in to show her, and that's what she said.

A runaway train.

※※

I'd rather dream about the dancing boys than *them*. The dancing boys in their thud and pulse of light. I remember that so deep, so hard. If I close my eyes I can see it, feel it again and again. The taste of cigarettes and … and what was it they used to mix with the vodka? Coke or Pepsi, one of those. I once drank a can of that when I was twenty. I just picked one up when I was in the shop. I felt the little warning flash through me but I ignored it. She wasn't there, but I could hear Mam sighing and muttering, '*You don't think do you, Arla, you just do.*'

I remember that tight feeling in my chest, when I used to choose sweets on the way home from school on a Friday. Her sigh when I took too long and how much it mattered, how much it really fucking mattered if I got a white mouse or a bon-bon, and how she used to harp on at me afterwards. How it had made her look daft in the shop cos there was a queue behind us. How it never mattered in the end whether it was a white mouse or a bon-bon cos they both tasted like chalk. I could feel her eyes on me when I was eating it later.

'*Alice doesn't even* like *sweets.*'

A paper bag in the bin, sad face of a white mouse poking out.

The taste of chalk and guilt.

So I bought that can of Coke and I was sick, all down myself. I washed my clothes myself so Mam wouldn't see.

When the dancing boys were there they watched me too. When I was on the other meds and the dancing boys came, they watched and there was no scowl, just the smoke from their cigarettes and their teeth flashing in the pulsing light. They watched me when I danced and they nodded and they nudged and they never told me to hurry up or told me that I made them look daft. They said keep going, that I was beautiful.

The taste of tongues, of cigarettes, of Coke and vodka.

§§

I'm frightened if I go to sleep again that that's what I'll see – the black-eyed kids being let in, disappearing into that house, where there's music and cigarettes and tongues and hurting. I'm frightened that that's their world and that I'll be taken back there too.

Episode 5: Empty

—We were on the beach.

Stupid really. Me, that is. So stupid. How on *earth* had I not worked it out till then?

It was evening, late afternoon. All the cliffs were way above us and we were walking back towards the hotel. It wasn't that hot anymore, just nice, calm. You could smell the sea. There was loads of families still playing on the sand. Dads and little lads building up the defences for their sandcastles. The smell of salt and sun cream, the tide encroaching further and further up the beach.

We were by the caves though, far away from all of that.

I could hear the others sniggering, and I sniggered too, as you do. Like you do when you're joining in. It didn't matter what we were sniggering about, did it? We were just happy under that dappled sky with the harshness of the sun all but gone.

I was thinking about *her*, that girl. I don't even know how we'd done it, but we had. Talked to them I mean. The girls. Those local girls. There was probably nothing else for the people who lived round here to do anyway save to talk to the likes of us at a bus stop.

There was only three of them. Those girls. All older than us. We thought we were playing them against each other but they had their pick. They knew it too.

Why did I even...?

Why did I even *think* I had a chance?

Oh fuck. Sometimes, I wake myself up at night cringing at this, you know? That cringe has got harder as I've got older, if anything.

She was called Anna, that girl. I remember that. I remember her name. She wasn't ugly or anything, I just didn't have any attraction to her. I guess she wasn't my type. But back then, I didn't even have a type. Anna was the only one the others weren't sniffing around and that made her mine. It didn't matter anyway cos she was actually talking to me. *Me*. I think I was talking back as well, like a real proper person, like a fully functional human being. Nothing interesting, just chat, you know. The sort of chat when you're sixteen and you're hanging about a bus stop in fuck-knows-where-ville on the south coast. I remember there being palm trees everywhere, and it didn't matter what she looked like because this was a holiday – this might even be a holiday romance. Suddenly all the songs, all the records that my dad played me, all of it started to make sense.

And Anna *was* pretty. I mean, it might be rose-tinted glasses and stuff, but she was. I thought things had finally changed for me.

Like I say, I was stupid.

So we were on the beach, beside the caves, sniggering, and I remember holding my tongue before I said something stupid about how happy I was. I nearly blurted out that I'd never had friends like this before and how we could all meet up again here one day, like, when we were older. Like in that song.

I'm so fucking glad I never said any of that. Imagine. That sort of cringe would never ever go away.

I remember all three of them, but the one who sticks in my mind the most was Jack. An apt name. I often wonder what he's doing now. For me, he'll be perpetually fifteen – tanned, hairy legs, tight blonde curls and a round face, straight out of the *Hardy Boys*.

I remember how he looked at me, out of the corners of his eyes, turning from the others.

'Which one did you like?' he said.

I remember his voice was reasonable, sincere, and his face betrayed nothing. He said it again: 'Which one did you like then?' And I could read nothing in those eyes of his.

The others – Kyle and Greg – were scuffing sand at each other.

'Anna,' I said.

This was it, this was talking about girls with other lads. This was finally what's supposed to happen.

'Anna, eh?' Jack said and his smile widened. I remember thinking, what did he have that I didn't? He still looked like a little boy, apart from his hairy legs, that is. Did girls like hairy legs?

Jack turned back to the others and we were starting to move now, sloping off towards the cliff path that led up back to the hotel. Kyle and Greg were gobbing up in the air, letting them fall like bird droppings, trying to shove each other underneath. The sea was whispering in the background and I could feel this sudden uncertainty come over me. I remember suddenly being aware of my clothes, how my jeans clung to my arse cheeks, how my belly pushed at the bottom of my T-shirt. How my belt buckle pressed against it. I became aware of a layer of sweat under my black beanie hat. Why the fuck was I wearing a beanie hat when it was hot? Why was I wearing a hoodie as well? It all hit me right then.

I looked around and Greg was doing something with his trousers. He was wearing jeans too – these skinny ones – and he had them pulled up over his stomach.

'Who's this?' Greg was saying.

Greg, the quiet one with the sandy hair and that smell of aftershave or cologne, the T-shirt that clung to his arms, showing off his muscles. Greg who'd been the only one to kiss one of the girls, who had sat with his arm around Kirsten, like they'd been together forever. Greg was waddling around with his jeans pulled up. Jack and Kyle were laughing now, really laughing.

I felt everything begin to slide.

I tried to laugh and nothing came out. Just air, like a cough. My mouth was really, really dry and I was suddenly aware of my whole body. I could feel my flesh hanging off my bones. I remember praying – *praying* – that Greg wasn't doing an impression of me.

But it all started to dawn on me. I looked around and all of them were wearing those board shorts or skinny jeans, where the crotch sort of hangs down. Mine were from the supermarket cos they did the bigger sizes and they were cheaper. It didn't matter what jeans I had on, did it? But it did. Of course it did. And I realised that I was wearing my

Skexxixx T-shirt – not the 'S' one that most fans had, but the limited-edition one that just said 'EMPTY' in these big white letters.

'It's *Empty*,' Jack said, pointing at Greg's waddle walk. And they all burst out into louder laughter. The high of hanging out with Anna and Kirsten and the other girls at the bus stop with the palm trees was now replaced with this horrible sense of dread.

'I told Anna, you know,' Jack was saying. His eyes kept flicking to me, like a lizard's. 'I told Anna that Empty liked her, and you know what she did?'

The question was to me – he was looking at me and the others were holding their breaths.

I was in paroxysms of shock, of horror. This was school – this was school all over again. Everything I had built up in a year – all the belief that Mum and Dad had helped instil in me that I wasn't worthless, that I was someone, despite my weight – was gone. Thundering back came the days when Mum and Dad had to drive me to school to escape the names and stones hurled at me by Darren Hayfield and the rest of his goons. This holiday, *this fucking holiday* was supposed to be about celebrating how far I'd come. And it was all unravelling faster than a lie…

'She *ran*!' Jack finished, bent double.

The others exploded into laughter and I felt the tears coming. I had to get away and I just began to walk, fast as I could, not looking, not saying anything, a great big lump swollen in my throat, tears clenched like fists behind my eyes, ready to spill out. I could hear them cawing like crows, caterwauling with laughter as I started along that path up the cliff, cursing myself, hating myself. *What did you think, you stupid, fat idiot? What did you think would happen? They've been laughing at you this whole time, calling you 'Empty'. How long's that been going on – that running joke? I bet it seemed like a hilarious piece of irony, considering the size of you. You go on holiday, far away from everything, celebrate how well you're getting on at college and look – look what happens. This is your fucking destiny and you deserve it.*

Then I heard someone running behind me, breathing heavy.

'Anth … Anth mate…'

I knew who it was and I couldn't look.

'Anth mate, I'm sorry. I'm sorry…'

'S'fine,' I said and I could barely even speak cos a lump of agony filled my throat.

I wanted to say, *Fuck you. Fuck off away from me, you. You of all people. You were the one who was my friend before Jack and Greg came along. You and me wandered out here and smoked fags and talked shit and it was like I had a friend. How could I have been so stupid?*

I saw him out the corner of my eye. I saw him turn back to the others, to Jack and Greg, shrugging, raising his hands in a *what-can-I-do?* gesture.

As if I was just an irritant – a problem that he couldn't fix.

'I'm sorry Anth…' he said. Then turned around and ran back down the track to the others. Free of me at last.

I *was* crying then, all the way back up to the hotel. I just let it all out, all the last year in tatters and all of it my fault.

Kyle had been my friend. For a time at least. For a couple of days I had had a friend. Now I had to tell Mum and Dad that, yet again, I was on my own. They wouldn't shame me – they weren't like that – but I could always see the sadness in their eyes when yet again I fucked something like this up by just being me.

That's when I met *her*.

That's another person whose life I fucked up, just by being part of it.

❋

Welcome to Six Stories. *I'm Scott King.*

Over these six weeks we are looking back at the Macleod Massacre – the infamous killing of the Macleod family by the eldest daughter, twenty-one-year-old Arla. We're looking back from six different perspectives, seeing the events that unfolded through six pairs of eyes.

Then, of course, it's up to you. As you know by now, I'm not here to make judgement, or draw definite conclusions. I simply present what information I discover.

For newer listeners, you should know I am not a policeman, a forensic scientist or an FBI profiler; this isn't an investigation and no new evidence is revealed. My podcast is more like a book group, a discussion at an old crime scene. We look back on tragedy.

The person whose voice you heard at the beginning is Anthony Walsh. If you listened to the last episode I'm guessing you have inferred that already. He is another person who was present during the Macleod family's holiday to Cornwall. A holiday, I am convinced, holds the key to why Arla Macleod did what she did. Anthony has come forward himself to tell his part of the story. I'll leave him to tell you his reasons for doing so.

Before we continue with this episode, I want to mention something. As those of you who have been following this series know, my investigation of the Macleod case has provoked a lot of vitriol online. I am aware that, for some reason, there are those out there telling me I should be leaving this case well alone. I called for reasoned debate and discussion in the previous episodes, and I'm still waiting.

Let me tell you, there has been more communication, but none of it has, as yet, been of a measured nature. I will not read out what I have received, and I will also not respond to threats. I will only reiterate that I am still waiting for an opportunity to have a reasonable discussion.

I also apologise for having to temporarily close down the comments section on the Facebook group; those who participate in that particular community know the reasons why. I will not stand for intimidation, insults and discussions that are inflammatory in their nature. I realise that there is lots of intense and potentially distressing subject matter within the realms of Six Stories. *True crime, is, by its very nature, horrific. But that's why we need to be able to debate like sensible people.*

If you don't like it. No one is forcing you to listen.

That's all I'm going to say on the matter.

Back to Anthony Walsh.

Anthony speaks to me from his home town, which he has asked me not to disclose. Twenty-six years old, Anthony still lives with his parents in the same house and lower-middle-class suburb he grew up in. He works mostly from home as a freelance graphic designer and makes enough money to pay for his board and lodging. His mother and father have always been supportive and Anthony emphasises the value he places on his relationship with them in our Skype chat.

—Yeah, Mum and Dad are good. They always have been. We've always got along. I think I've never wanted to be too far away from them. Maybe that's because of how they've always been so supportive. They've always looked after me.

Anthony's been through the mill. An unusually shy child, he found it hard to mix with others from a young age. This timidity resulted in Anthony becoming a target of bullying as far back as primary school.

—It was my weight as well – we can't skirt around that. Literally and figuratively! I'm nearly seventeen stone now and only five foot seven. That's overweight. That's obese. But it's how I've always been – heavy. And you know what? Mum and Dad never got on my back about it; never tried to get me to lose weight. They never planted the message that I'd get friends if only I was slim. That happens to so many kids and it's awful. So many parents project their own experiences onto their children. As I've got older I understand why. I don't have children and never would. I would never want anyone to grow up and be remotely like me.

The bullying of Anthony Walsh at school is something that we could spend much longer on. A lot of the previous series of Six Stories *have dealt with perpetrators who were bullied and perpetrators who were bullies. That's not to say it's a cause of crime but it's definitely involved somehow.*

You will notice from the clip at the start of the episode that Anthony appears to have been, like Arla Macleod, a fan of Skexxixx. It's an aspect of his life that I will discuss with him later. I am in no doubt that there

were many others like Arla and Anthony – young people who felt like
outcasts and who could identify with the lyrics of Skexxixx.
  Anthony is a quiet and well-spoken individual. And there is a softness
to him – a vulnerability – that induces real empathy. Anthony does not
wear the scars of his life like medals. He does not draw attention to them
or make himself out to be a pariah or a martyr. Anthony talks about
what has clearly been a battle with a sense of reason. The trauma of what
he has been through is unmistakable on his face. When he recalls events,
such as the story of what took place at the beach, it strikes me just how
much damage living your life as an involuntary victim can do.

  —I got through it. I got through school. I never wanted to take
time off, to get my parents involved – that would have only made it
worse. Every bullied kid knows that. We just have to keep our heads
down and take it until we can get out and get better jobs than those
who bully us.
  —*Was anything ever done about it? At school?*
  —Let's say it wasn't a priority. And it was never *that* bad – it was
never, like, people beating me up or anything. I was too pathetic
even for that. It was just a consistent, low-level unpleasantness that
didn't go away.
  —*What could have been done? Something, surely?*
  —Perhaps. I mean, sometimes teachers would … I hate to say
it, but some would join in, especially some of the younger ones. It
was the men especially – male teachers trying to be liked, to be 'one
of the lads'. Again though, it was always like, under the radar, snide
remarks. You had to feel sorry for them. Imagine being a grown adult
and trying to endear yourself to teenage boys by picking on the fat
guy?
  —*You're remarkably together about it all.*
  —I've been through a lot of therapy. No, really, that's not a joke.
I have. Everyone should. People need to talk.
  But you see, I can't just blame all my problems on other people.
I'm just naturally quite an anxious person, always have been. I think

I showed signs of depression in childhood: shyness, difficulty making friends, that sort of thing. I never slept properly as a baby. I don't know how Mum and Dad coped with me – up and down all night; bad dreams; night terrors. Back when I was a kid you just didn't equate these things with illness. That's the other thing. Something like depression – people always seem to want a root cause, as if your illness has to be quantified, like it can't be enough that your brain chemistry is skew-whiff, I don't know. It's not really relevant I guess.

It's a shame – the more I talk with Anthony, the more I glimpse how endearing he is as a person. But as soon as he takes one step onto his soapbox, he climbs down, cuts himself off. I almost want to tell him it's OK, that what he has to say is important, that I want to hear him. It saddens me somewhat that this learned behaviour – not getting above his station – is now just his way of life.

—*So let's go back to the holiday you and your folks took to Cornwall.*
—Yeah. I was sixteen. I'd completed my first term at college and I'd done it without any problems. I was getting the bus there on my own without having a panic attack; I was weaning off my meds – everything was going in the right direction.
—*That must have felt like an achievement in itself.*
—Yeah, totally. I remember the first day, Dad drove me into the car park and when he said goodbye I just wanted to cuddle into him and ask him to walk in with me, to hold my hand. I just saw all these other people – all these kids who all looked so much older than me – and I just thought, wow, these folk are just a world away from someone like me. But I did it: I walked in there; I knew what building I had to be at and I just stood there. I was waiting ... waiting for the first comment, the first insult, the first bit of bitten-off rubber thrown at my head. But then someone just came up and started a conversation – with *me*! Imagine that! Some girl just walked up and said 'Hi,' like it was the most normal thing in the world. A *girl*!

From what Anthony tells me, he was enjoying college. He had a small group of friends and a sense of confidence beginning to emerge. Green shoots. Anthony was undergoing cognitive behavioural therapy for his anxiety and was beginning to see results.

—I'd got myself out of these cyclical patterns of negative thinking. I had strategies. Of course there were setbacks – there were bad days – but I really felt like I was making progress. My main problems were isolating myself, spending too much time online, falling into internet worm-holes ... do you know what I mean?

—*Was the internet a place of refuge for you?*

—It was, but I knew it was negative. I used to read all sorts of strange things on there. I was making an effort to try and forge real friendships offline too. That was one of my targets – self-imposed, I may add! It's so easy to just stay at home, in your little bubble, your safe place, a place where you can hide out, you can *rage-quit* a social interaction online but you can't in real life. My parents, they'd helped me realise that there *was* a way out, there was a place I could be after school – a place for me in the world. Does that sound stupid?

—*Not at all. Everyone deserves their place in the world. No matter who they are.*

—Yeah. I believed it too. What happened in Cornwall set me back a long way. Then a few years later, when it all came out in the news – all the stuff about the Macleod Ma— sorry, about what happened to that family, I turned it all inward. I turned it all back on myself. I guess I blamed myself for all of it.

—*Really? You blamed yourself for what Arla Macleod did to her family?*

—Sounds stupid, doesn't it? But that's just how my brain works. It makes these ridiculous neural connections. I'm so used to feeling like I'm the problem.

I was so scared when the ... when what Arla Macleod did became big in the news, when it was all over the internet. I was terrified.

I mean, I was being disproportionate, hysterical, but … did you see what happened to that guy? The caretaker from her old school?

—*I saw the end result, yes.*

—It's like … complicated … hard to explain. I … I don't want to say too much…

—*What's holding you back?*

—I'd rather not say. It's not my business. That man topping himself was the end of it, the only bit that we got to see. I wonder if anything else happened.

—*Like what?*

—I wonder if there was anything before all that? There has to have been, right? I just wonder what he might have seen, that's all.

—*I find myself having little sympathy for a man who groomed children online…*

—If he even did it at all?

—*Do you have doubts about that?*

—I do. I'm sorry but there was a lot more going on than just that. It's … I'm not sure it's my place to mention all that.

—*All that?*

—Yeah … kids, but not … I'm sorry, can I … can I have a minute?

A change comes over Anthony as we speak. His face goes pale, his eyes glaze over and he begins to tremble. A text message I have received swims into my mind, silent and deadly, like the tentacles of some terrible jellyfish:

```
U have seen what we can do :)
Now back off.
```

Anthony's alluded to the notion that the paedophile hunter sting on Mr Marsh may not have been all it seemed. Is Anthony implying that the old caretaker of Saint Theresa's may have been set up? I consider this and realise just what an involved and complicated process that would have to have been. If Marsh was set up, then whoever did it would have had either to hack some form of social media or else create a fake profile. Seeing as Marsh was older, I imagine his online presence was minimal. Whoever did it would have to have known where the man lived, tracked him down – found his address when he moved from Stanwel. That speaks of a vendetta to me.

But the question is why?

The only reason I can think of is that Mr Marsh was guilty of some sort of misdemeanour, or a perceived one at least. Someone had a good reason to do this to an old man.

I try and get back in touch with 'Tessa' from episode two, but to no avail. I want to know whether she had any encounters with Mr Marsh or even if she has heard rumours from her time at school or afterwards. Unfortunately, all the online profiles I used to contact 'Tessa' before as well as the phone number she gave me all seem to be dead.

I do, however, contact Paulette English again and refer her to this comment she made in episode three:

'[Marshy] was just a little old oddball. He had this red face, all wrinkly and the lads used to say he was a convicted murderer on parole, that he'd killed his daughter. It was just another stupid story. No one who'd done that could work in a school, right? How would that even happen? Anyway, if Marshy had caught us, we'd have known about it.'

Paulette clarifies.

—I just meant … I never had anything to do with him really. You never even saw him. Occasionally, between lessons maybe, just pottering about and that.

—*What did you mean by saying that if Marshy caught you you'd 'know about it'?*

—In that context I see what you're getting at. But no, it wasn't like that. Marshy was just a little, angry bloke – hated the students. He had that grouchy-old-man thing going on, you know? Like, if the lads kicked their ball up on the roof and that, Marshy wouldn't get it down. The year sevens said he had a cabinet full of old footballs he'd burst on purpose. I don't know if any of that was true, but no one liked him. He was old school. If he caught you messing about, he'd give you both barrels, screaming in your face and that. It never happened to me.

—*Do you think Arla ever had an encounter with Mr Marsh?*

—She could have done I suppose, but she never said anything. I would have remembered that. And it would have been all over the school if she had. It's a bit of a cliché really, isn't it? The janitor did it in the end. Just like something out of *Scooby Doo*.

Another blunt nib, another frayed end. More frustration. It feels like every lead I follow ends up with faded footprints in falling snow – just enough intrigue to keep me grasping before being obscured. The feeling that I am close to the resolution of this mystery comes and goes; it swims around my feet, a silent, hulking shape in dark waters, occasionally brushing my skin, sometimes diving deeper. Chasing this leviathan, I never know when or if it will end.

Then there's the threats. I take my privacy seriously. I am in the public eye to some extent and my attitude towards Six Stories *is that the podcast is about the crimes, the victims, the people involved. Not me. My role is the facilitator. I have nothing that can be taken from me personally. And I owe no one anything – not in terms of* Six Stories, *anyway.*

Yet these sustained and relentless text messages are still bothering me. How do they have my number? What have I done to provoke this? It makes me think of Mr Marsh.

It is true that Arla Macleod agreed to speak to me rather than the press, which has clearly not gone down well. Arla's sentence for what she did to her family is as divisive as the woman herself, so perhaps by agreeing to speak to me, she has made some people think I'm guilty by association. What I think personally matters very little on Six Stories. *I always try to present each case I cover in a balanced and fair manner. So for me to suddenly become the target of this unparalleled aggression online is unjustified, and very unpleasant.*

There are parts of me that want this to be over, to give in and say this was an open-and-shut case: a woman with mental-health issues killed her family in a state of psychosis. But then I think of the ripples that Arla Macleod has made; how who she is and what she's done affects those who are still here. Long after Arla's hammer blows subsided, the echoes still reverberate.

I realise that I too have become part of these ripples, and that maybe I am perpetuating this resonance, intensifying this echo. But for that do I deserve the abuse, the threats?

Perhaps there are those who think that somehow I am giving Arla a platform. That because of what she did she doesn't deserve this. To that I would say that I am only interested in how Arla Macleod became the way she did – in what triggered the psychosis that led to the events of the 21st of November 2014.

In the spirit of which, let's return to Anthony Walsh and his story.

—Can you remember the first time you met Arla Macleod?
—Actually, no, not really. That's kind of blurry.
—*Oh. Really?*
—Yeah, sorry. I can, however tell you about the first time I saw Alice, though. Her sister.

It is in this moment that I realise something – a spark of light when all seemed to have been dull. My phone is now mostly on silent and I have blocked several numbers as well as notifications from anonymous social-media accounts that pop up quicker than I can stop them. The cons of doing this were starting to outweigh the pros – that was until now, the moment when something makes sense to me, right here in this interview. Anthony's face changes, colour rises in his cheeks and his voice becomes wistful.

—It wasn't long after the business on the beach with Kyle and Jack and Greg – in fact it was the next morning. After they'd humiliated me the night before, I woke up with this feeling I'd never had in my life. I remember it so well. It was this black feeling, this heaviness that sort of hung from my soul. I know it sounds rather overdramatic, but it's true. I remember spending the day with my parents, just me and them, and it was so weird because I felt like a shadow. I felt like everything I was had just been emptied out of me, I was nothing but a puddle evaporated by the sun.

I was so scared of seeing them – Kyle and the others. I was so worried I'd bump into them in the hotel and they'd laugh at me. I was scared that I'd just break down, just weep. I remember packing that stupid 'Empty' T-shirt right down into the bottom of my bag, along with the beanie hat, and begging my mum to take me shopping for some other clothes. Everything I had just looked terrible, just stupid. I couldn't believe I'd dressed like I did – 'Empty' on the front of a fat kid's T-shirt – I mean, come on…

They had destroyed me. They'd skinned me alive and shone a bright light into me, forced me to see everything I was and realise how terrible it was. And they didn't care.

'I told Anna that Empty liked her, and you know what she did? … She *ran*!'

Of course she fucking ran.

—*You met Alice Macleod that day?*

—I did. The sun was beating down. It was almost subtropical outside, and I was in my jeans and one of my stupid band T-shirts, my stupid clothes. I felt so fat and disgusting, I thought the whole place would start laughing at me if I went outside. Mum and Dad were starting to get worried, I could tell. I was saying I had a headache but I had to come out sooner or later. I couldn't ruin this holiday that they'd worked hard and paid for. I couldn't mess this up as well.

They were both suggesting some swimming thing in the hotel pool. Inflatables or some such. I knew for a fact Kyle and the others would be there. They were always in the pool – 'scouting out the talent' was what they called it. I joined them a couple of times and it made me feel sick. Sick and embarrassed with the things they said about the girls in the hotel.

Of course I couldn't tell my parents what had happened, so I just said I was feeling a bit sick and that I would go back to my room. I remember just wandering about instead, walking up and down the stairs, as if that would somehow make me lose weight. In a day.

I eventually ended up on the basement floor. I didn't even know there was anything down there except the car park until I found this little room, this alcove where there were a couple of gambling machines and this girl just stood there all by herself.

I remember this sort of rush running through me like electricity – so powerful that all the humiliation from before was momentarily relegated to the back of my brain. I was simply blown away.

—*This girl was Alice Macleod, right?*

—It was, but I didn't know that yet. The other thing was, I thought she was way older than me. She was only fourteen I think but she looked at least twenty! She was so … *developed*. Ugh, this is all sounding so *bad* isn't it?

—*Maybe if you were an adult, but you weren't. Not back then. It's important to remember that.*

—You're right, of course. Yeah. She was perfect. She wasn't glamorous like the girls we were chasing all those other nights – make-up and revealing clothes and stuff. Alice's beauty was all natural. She was the only person to make me feel that rush. I've never felt it since. I don't want to say it was love. I just remember my own voice in my head, like a whisper … *Who on earth is that?*

—*Did you speak to her?*

—Somehow! Despite everything that had happened to me on that holiday so far, somehow my lips formed words and I said something. I have no idea what it was. I had nothing to lose you see. I felt so repulsive, so terrible, I'd lost all rhyme or reason. I just figured that nothing else could hurt me now. I was numb.

I don't remember my opening line at all. I was probably red and sweaty, after all those stairs. I remember she talked back – she spoke to me without laughing, without poking fun. I remember she seemed just so innocent, so fragile. I'd found this little lost creature, this beautiful thing, this rare flower that no one else had discovered … and … and I just wanted her for my own.

That sounds terrible as well, doesn't it? It sounds so wrong. But it wasn't like that – it wasn't sexual at all. I think back then I thought it was love. I think I fell in love with her on the spot.

I have to say a pang of empathy echoes from somewhere inside me when Anthony says this. He looks beyond the screen, lost in his memories. I feel sorry for the young, naive Anthony, still reeling from what happened to him at the mercy of Kyle and Jack and Greg.

—There's a saying isn't there? 'Fool me twice, shame on me.' I should have learned; I should have been more guarded, but I just wasn't like that and Alice completely had me in her thrall from the first moment I laid eyes on her.

—*So the two of you struck up a friendship? I imagine that couldn't have been easy.*

—We were both shy, so it was such a task, a chore, to get a chat going with her. But her shyness was another thing that enthralled me. I couldn't understand it; someone like her, shy? Every time we met, we would almost circle each other, like cats, but once we got talking it was great. I felt like I was spilling open, releasing all this tension. I told her all about my anxiety and all the problems I'd had before the holiday. She was an amazing listener. I always felt so at ease with her.

—*Did the two of you ever go anywhere together, like you had with Kyle and the boys?*

—We stayed down there in that room – always down there! Alice would go above ground to do activities and swim and stuff, with her family. I would just hang about down there and wait for her to come back. How pathetic is that?

—*Did Alice ever confide in you about herself?*

—A bit. I think I probably just blathered on, but from what I gathered about Alice, things weren't easy at home. Her parents were strict, religious; her sister was always in and out of some sort of crisis, all the attention focused on her, that sort of thing. Alice felt like

Arla was ruining her life, her future career, everything. Whenever they tried to get Arla involved in any of Alice's interests, Arla would spoil it.

It's interesting that Alice Macleod appeared to tow the line with her parents yet here she is, hanging about in the games room, just like her sister. I wonder if Alice in some way wished she could rebel like Arla did.

—*Did you ever see the Macleod sisters with their family?*

—Yeah, once. It was one of those entertainment nights in the hotel – you know when they put on a show? A load of staff in gold waistcoats sing songs from the shows and the adults get drunk. It seemed like everyone who was staying in the hotel was down there that night. I didn't even look out for Kyle and the rest of them. I didn't dare. I do remember seeing the Macleods. They were sitting on the other side of the stage, and I remember Alice turning and looking right at me, and I remember looking right back at her. I smiled, fully expecting her to walk over. I had this fantasy of her sitting down next to me, putting her head on my shoulder, our lips touching as the gold-coats sang a ballad. Ridiculous, but I was sixteen, I was in love.

And that was it.

—*What do you mean? What happened?*

—She just turned away. As if I wasn't there. She never looked at me once. I know because I spent the whole show staring at her. That's when I finally gave up. She was way out of my league. I had no chance. The boys had made me absolutely sure of that. That's all it took. For me to give up. I was back on my own.

—*And then you met Arla?*

—And that's when everything went wrong.

All of this fits the vague timeline that I've established for the events at the hotel in Cornwall. Arla at this point would have been spending most

of her time with Angel. Spurned by the other boys and now by Alice,
Anthony switched his attention to Arla.

—*Tell me, how did you and Arla meet?*
—It was pretty much an accident. Like I said, I was doing my
utmost to keep away from Kyle and the others. I knew it wasn't long
before they'd discover Alice, or she'd discover them.
—*Did you just stop hanging about with Alice then – did you just*
cut all ties?
—Yeah. I thought she'd be glad not to have me hanging around
her like an odour. It was obvious as well. I stayed in my room –
didn't even go down to the fruit machines again. I just read a book
– my dad's copy of *The Rats* by James Herbert. I just lay on my bed
and read that. When I did go out of the room, I stayed close to my
parents. I barely even looked up from the floor.
One day, though, I saw her and my heart leapt before withering
into a little ball. Alice with the boys. It was inevitable really. I used
to see them everywhere after that. She'd changed as well. Down there
with me she was withdrawn and shy. Up there with them she was
someone else entirely, always seemed to be laughing at something
they'd said, draping herself all over them, you know? The thing was
that she would always glance at me while she was doing it, as if to
let me know that she was with better people, that I was nothing and
I should know that. I realise now what a good little actress Alice
Macleod was.
—*That must have been painful.*
—The worst of it was the way they were around her. I just couldn't
bear it.
—*What do you mean?*
—When her back was turned they'd be trying to look up her skirt
or they'd be making gestures to each other – sex stuff. And she was
totally oblivious to it. I was too scared to say anything. I'll never
forgive myself for that. I thought she was older, I thought she could
handle herself. But still I felt protective of her. Especially as I knew

what Kyle and the others were like. I heard the way they talked about girls, about women. The things they said. It was revolting.

—*Did you ever try and intervene?*

—I knew I should have. I knew that was the right thing to do, but … but every time I went anywhere near them, I just kept hearing them saying 'Empty'. Whether they were actually saying it or it was all in my head, I don't know. But that humiliation just crushed me. These boys, they were all from rich families; their fathers were highly paid and powerful – doctors and executives and stuff. They had money and they had privilege. What was I going to do? No one was going to listen to 'Empty', were they?

I am yet again filled with sadness at this. To me, it seems that Anthony may have got this all wrong. Perhaps Alice Macleod was acting this way as a reaction to Anthony spurning her friendship. All she did was look away. And then he didn't speak to her again. Perhaps she felt rejected by Anthony and was punishing him for it? That's my instinctive thought, anyway. Let's not forget that Anthony's self-esteem had been shot into a million fragments and turning inward and punishing himself was his way of dealing with such situations.

Of course, I may be wrong. Alice Macleod could have been, deep down, a manipulative and unpleasant person, deciding to goad Anthony on purpose for reasons known only to herself.

—*So where did you and Arla meet?*

—Oddly enough, in the same place I met Alice. It was in that little games room down in the basement of the hotel. It's amazing, so many people in that hotel and I never saw anyone else down there.

—*Was Arla with anyone else when you met her?*

—Yeah. It was her and this other girl who was staying at the hotel. It was late-ish I suppose, like, maybe eight or nine. Mum and Dad still thought I was friends with Kyle and the others. I kept up that pretence by just going out of the room with my swimming stuff and wandering around. Or else just walking up and down the stairs.

So I was doing that when I wandered out into the basement floor, and there she was.

—*What were Arla and her friend doing?*

—They weren't bothered about the fruit machines or the pinball; they were messing about with the lift. When I first saw Arla she was standing there, looking at it, hands on her hips. I didn't even know she was Alice's sister. She looked nothing like her. Arla was tall, skinny. I very nearly just walked away but then I noticed something. I noticed she had a Skexxixx wristband, one of those black tennis-style ones, embroidered with that 'S', and I thought that, finally, I'd found someone like me.

—*That's a big assumption based on a wristband, no?*

—See, it's hard to explain unless you're a Skexxixx fan. Back then, if you saw someone else who liked Skexxixx, more often than not you knew that you shared something. It was like most Skexxixx people are on the fringes, the outcasts. You would never catch Jack or Kyle listening to stuff like that. By then though, Skexxixx wasn't as big as he had been, so it was rare seeing someone wearing Skexxixx stuff then.

—*After his second album had been such a flop?*

—Oh my gosh, are you a…

—*No. But I've researched him.*

—Oh. I hope you're not going with that whole 'music makes you evil' narrative. It's so nineties. So ignorant.

—*On the contrary. What I've surmised is that, while* Through the Mocking Glass *had a limited appeal, many Skexxixx fans found it really spoke to them, perhaps more than his earlier work. Would you agree with that?*

—Yes … wow … OK. It's nice to have someone understand like that. That's what it was like when I started talking to Arla. As much as I liked Alice, we didn't actually have that much in common. It was infatuation – puppy love. With Arla it was different, it was like we were kindred spirits or something. We became friends easily. We bonded with our love of Skexxixx…

—*Was it like that from the start?*

—Right off the bat. Just that one thing – that wristband. It was like a calling card and I remember hoping, *praying* that she got it, you know? So many people didn't.

—*What was it in particular that Arla understood?*

—She understood why that album made so much sense. The songs on that album were long, they were sad. You could get lost in them.

—*The overriding theme in* Through the Mocking Glass *is escape, isn't it? Other worlds.*

—Yes. That's why it appealed to me, that's why it just made sense to me – and loads of others like me! That's why me and Arla connected so much. We were both … we were both in a bad place. We were both looking for an escape. She'd spent a lot of time online too, reading about the theories behind the lyrics, the albums. I often wondered if we'd actually spoken before – online I mean!

Serendipity, sliding doors, aligned arts, all the clichés – but this certainly is a situation bound by coincidence. Anthony, while he had support at home, was crippled by anxiety and his self-esteem was non-existent. He was entombed within the hotel, with Alice and the boys flaunting their friendship in front of him, showing him how much they neatly fitted into the moulds that society builds for the young. They were the beautiful people, part of a world that Anthony did not belong to. Arla though, clearly did not fit in with the rest of the young people at the hotel and, unlike her younger sister, was defiant about that. Whatever it was, both Anthony and Arla met each other at a time when both were at a low and vulnerable ebb.

—So we started off talking about the BEKs.

—*BEKs?*

—Sorry, the black-eyed kids.

—*Sorry, I know what they are but, why? I'm not sure I follow…*

—Oh, I just thought you knowing about Skexxixx, that's all.

—Are you talking about the lyrics in that song where he mentions them?

—Well that and … Oh, it's a stupid story, just an internet thing. It doesn't matter in the grand scheme of things. Let's move on.

—Hang on. What if it does? This is what these podcasts are about – exploring all the apparently irrelevant stuff.

—Well, if we must. So you must know about the rumour? The one about Skexxixx and the BEKs?

—No.

—There's this theory that someone posted online, on Reddit, I think, or Tumblr – probably both. It's this theory that Skexxixx let them in. That he went to their world and that he came back and it sort of … It made him what he was.

—What was he? What was he to you back then?

—The thing is, I know he's now just a rich musician with good PR. I sort of knew it back then too. But that sort of thing doesn't come from nowhere. There was a lot of cross-referencing of his lyrics with the symbols on the inlay cards and that hidden track on the Japanese import version of *Through the Mocking Glass* that all adds up. Looking back it was probably just a really smart way to get everyone to buy the album twice.

—But…

—I don't know, you only have to look at him. I've heard interviews and stuff. He's a weird guy I suppose. And, I don't know, I guess it doesn't matter, but me and Arla, we were always on about it.

Despite his protests, I'm suddenly on my guard that Anthony might be playing me here. I haven't yet asked him if he knows about Arla's account of the night of the 21st of November 2014. Of course, there's every possibility he's listened to episode one, in which she describes the black-eyed children at the back door of her house on the night of the killings. So has he dropped this element into our discussion in response to that? Or is he in fact being entirely open and honest. After all, it is true that Skexxixx

mentions the BEKs in an oblique way in his music. I think back to the
lyrics of the track 'Dead-Eyed March':
  'A thousand black-eyed girls,
  A thousand black-eyed boys,
  Marching to a distant drum,
  Looking for a place called home…'

—So you said Arla was with another girl when you met her – someone
else from the hotel?
—Yeah, she sometimes knocked around with this other girl. But
she just seemed … well … not like us – nothing like me and Arla.
This girl was streetwise, she was hard. I had no idea why she was there
with Arla. She was more like Kyle and the boys.

How interesting. For all Anthony is amiable, humble and forthcom-
ing, it is a shame that he's guilty of being as close-minded as those who
picked on and bullied him. Notice he only talks about Arla and doesn't
even mention Angel by name. If only he'd spoken to Angel properly rather
than focusing on Arla, he'd have found, like Arla did, that they had
much in common. But it seems like the story of Arla Macleod is one that
is filled with what-ifs and could-haves.

—So back to what Arla and her friend were doing with the lift. Did
you recognise anything there?
—Yes. I'd spent a lot of time reading about that sort of thing online.
Arla was doing the elevator game. Again, it was something that just
clicked between us, it was something that we had in common. Like it
was destiny or something. I found a new sort of lease of life, as you might
call it, just talking about Skexxixx and stuff with Arla. She was always
asking about the games. She wanted to try the more dangerous ones.
—*Dangerous?*
—Well, yes. I mean, these games mostly originate from Japan and
Korea and there's warnings and disclaimers all over the internet not
to play them.

—Had you ever played them?

—No. I'll admit that. I was too scared. I always wanted to try the Hooded Man Ritual or something like that, but I just couldn't bring myself to do it. Until I met Arla.

I leave a pause to allow Anthony to expand on this. He doesn't, so I decide to change tack – for the moment.

—What did Arla tell you about her life?

—You know, that's another thing I beat myself up about. Like with Alice, I was so obsessed with telling Arla about my own problems, I guess I didn't listen too much. But, like Alice said, her parents were odd, religious. Arla thought Alice was the favourite, the 'normal' one, the 'pretty' one. Arla said that her mum used to tell them she had the brains and Alice had the looks. When they took Alice to her swimming training, they'd leave Arla behind at home. She was an embarrassment to them. All of them. I think that's what they used to say. What sort of thing is that to say to a kid? A young girl especially? The Macleod sisters were never allowed boyfriends – hardly allowed friends. Their entire worth was based on how pious they were, how well they did at school, how much they conformed. Their parents' love was conditional. I remember that so well. How horrible.

—Did Arla ever strike you as being ill – mentally, I mean?

—There's no way I could say. She was odd, I remember that. Like no one I'd ever met before. But I liked that, I thought she was great. When I found out what she did to her family I wished I had been more sensible. But there I was, failing at life again.

—Earlier, you said that everything went wrong when you met Arla. It doesn't sound that way so far; it sounds like the two of you were close. Surely that was a good thing?

—That's what I thought, yes. That's what immature, naive me thought, but in reality, it was no good for either of us.

—How so? You didn't find solace in each other?

—We did, but that was the problem. Instead of the holiday making us better, making us more *normal*, better at being *social*, it didn't. It drove us further underground. It made us.

It saddens me again that Anthony thinks that it was a bad thing to meet someone more like him than the other boys who treated him so poorly were. From what I have learned about Anthony, he is a bit of a paradox: in some ways he was desperate to fit in; yet he also kept his identity as a Skexxixx fan in full knowledge that he wouldn't be taken seriously by most people. It seems that, unlike Arla, who flaunted her identity as an outcast, there was always a small part of Anthony that wanted to be universally liked.

—*So how did it feel to find someone like Arla? Did it help how you were feeling about yourself?*
—It was liberating. That's the word. Finding someone who liked all the same stuff as me. Who didn't judge me for liking it.
—*Did Arla's parents know she was into Skexxixx, the games and all that?*
—It wasn't hard for them to see it, it was right in front of them. Arla just felt like they didn't ever try to understand the things she was passionate about. They weren't tangible, like church or school or swimming. It didn't make sense to them, so they just ignored it. I mean she never said anything about wanting to kill them! She said nothing about what she eventually did. It was, I guess, normal teenage stuff, you know? Rebellion. It was sad, though, the way she was always looking to escape, to get away from the world.
—*And you joined in with that?*
—Yeah. There was always a part of me somewhere inside that knew it wasn't real – that we were sort of playing make-believe. But that was so good, it was like being a kid again. Although at the time I was just caught up in it, I had no idea what I was doing. But it was like when I was in school and everyone else was playing football and charging about in the yard, all I wanted to do was hide away in

the corner. To have someone else joining me in that corner, it was special.

—*I hate to sour the memory, Anthony, but let's move onto what went wrong between you and Arla.*

—It was my fault really. Like always…

Anthony sighs and there is silence for a while. This particular memory is something we've been skirting around and now it's come down to it, I'm worried he won't want to talk, that it's going to be too much for him. I want to tell him that it's OK, that we can leave it be. But I really feel that it isn't, that there's something in this part of our story that will help us understand at least some of who Arla Macleod was and why she committed the heinous acts of the 21st of November 2014.

—All my life I've been frightened. Of other people, other children – everyone. I've cowered, I've hidden, I've not told, I've kept secrets. Now it's time to start talking.

—*It's up to you if you do. Only you can make that decision.*

—OK. No more fear. I haven't told this story before, not to anyone, not even my family, it's so horrible. After this episode goes out I'll no doubt get my comeuppance and that'll be right – it'll be what I deserve. But I'm going to tell it anyway.

A part of me is begging to stop and ask Anthony what he means here. A part of me wants to know whether he has received the same threats I have. Has Anthony had the same abuse online? Is that why he retreated to the sanctuary of his parents' house, why he never left and took his place in the big, bad world? I want to know if his phone has been plagued by texts, whether it sits, like mine, muted in my pocket, little pulses of hate alighting every few minutes. I hold back though; I let Anthony continue to tell the fifth story.

—So Arla and I had been playing the lift game, Elevator to

Another World. I always got scared when we got onto the part where the woman might enter the lift. When we got to that floor, I could always feel pressure in my bladder, the hairs rising on my arms. What would happen? What would I do if the woman entered the lift? Would I look at her? Would I try and speak to her? Would I piss my pants?

Just to remind you, the Elevator to Another World game Anthony is talking about is supposed to transport the player to another dimension. Elevator buttons are pressed in a certain sequence, and at one point a young woman is supposed to enter the elevator and game players are not permitted to look at her. If the game goes the way it's supposed to, the player will then press the button for the first floor and the lift will instead begin ascending to the tenth.

—I remember we got to the fifth floor and when the doors opened there was someone there and I nearly screamed out. It wasn't a young woman though. It was Alice.

—*Arla's sister?*

—Yeah, and she was as surprised to see us as we were to see her. She was just standing there as the doors opened, looking at us. I saw her do a bit of a double take, look from me to Arla and back again. She cocked her head to one side and this sort of flutter went through me, like, I'd almost forgotten how beautiful she was.

'Mam's looking for you,' was all she said to Arla.

I don't know what I expected right at that point. Maybe more from Arla – like a flash of rebellion; she was the older sister after all. Maybe I thought she would tell Alice to get stuffed or something, but she didn't. I remember it really clearly, Arla just put her head down, nodded like a beaten dog, you know? Compliant.

Alice seemed different then too. She seemed more assertive, clearly the dominant one in the relationship. It was like she was the parent and Arla was the kid. I said nothing, I just kept quiet, let them get on with it. Arla got out the lift and they went off. Arla waved at me without even looking back. I was pretty surprised, disappointed, but I got it – I understood. Of course Alice was the boss; she was the pretty one, she was the one that had been assimilated into normal society. Arla was the outcast, the freak. It made a horrible sort of sense. I could relate, anyway.

But as they walked off, Alice turned round and she gave me this smile, this big, warm smile like everything was OK again between us.

—*What time of day was this?*

—Late morning I think, maybe lunchtime. It's funny, you don't even think about that when you're young – meals and stuff – but when you're an adult it becomes so important. Anyway, I had lunch in the hotel with my mum and dad. It was a buffet style all-inclusive thing. I'm standing there at the hot plate having this internal debate because all I want is the chips and the pizza but I know I should be eating the salad, and suddenly there's someone right next to me. I'm properly scared, really terrified, and can feel myself starting to collapse in on myself.

—*Alice again?*

—'Alright, Anth?' he says. It's Kyle. But, not the Kyle from before, the Kyle who laughed at me and called me 'Empty'. It was the Kyle like he was when I first met him – when he was just a friendly sort of person, before Jack and Greg showed up. It was the Kyle who I'd thought I'd made friends with.

—*I imagine you didn't want to have anything to do with him, though?*

—You'd think that, wouldn't you? But there was still this part of me, this little part, that was so desperate for acceptance. I still cringe thinking about it, the way I was just so eager to welcome him back. I guess because he was speaking to me like a proper person, calling me Anth, not 'Empty'.

So he starts telling me about this party – that him and the others are going to this party in some old, abandoned house up on the cliff. He says they met a guy – some local – and there's going to be booze and girls and DJs and stuff. No parents, nothing like that. He kept going on about the girls, how there'd be loads of them. And underneath it all I realised what he meant. I knew he was saying, 'Even one for you, Empty, even one for you.' That's what seduced me ... Man, I mean, I was only sixteen.

—*Not many sixteen-year-old boys would have turned it down, to be fair.*

—True. But you know the real reason I wanted to go? The thing that swayed me? It's so pathetic. It was the fact that if they were going, then I knew Alice would be there too. If she hadn't given me that smile she gave me as she and Arla walked away ... it was pathetic that I just fell for it.

—*You were only young.*

—I was. And here was Kyle on his own without Jack and Greg, and I just thought that we might all be OK again. I figured that, if things got bad, I could just leave, you know? If they started with that 'Empty' stuff I could just walk away. Maybe being with Arla for those few days helped my confidence a bit?

So I arranged to meet Kyle and the others later. When I told my dad that I was going out with the boys he looked so pleased, so proud. I was almost in tears again, determined not to let him down. I had a shower and got changed. I picked out the most 'normal' clothes I had – just plain T-shirt, jeans, trainers. There was nothing I could do about my weight but at least I wasn't wearing that damn 'Empty' T-shirt.

It was a really warm evening, I remember that. I remember it was six or seven and still boiling. I met Kyle at the mini-golf course round the back of the hotel. Jack and Greg were there. When I saw them all together I nearly turned back, but Kyle was shaking my hand, clapping me on the back, really welcoming me. The others were sort of sheepish, subdued, and I wondered if they were actually sorry, like they regretted what happened?

We walked down that long path, down to the beach and I remember they all got cigarettes out. I didn't ask for one and they were pouring vodka into this two-litre bottle of Coke. They passed it round and I nearly said no but I drank too because, if nothing else, it would give me some courage. All of them seemed tense, their smiles looked painted on and I got this really bad feeling, this sudden longing to just be back with Mum and Dad, to watch one of the cheesy shows or sip one of the silly virgin cocktails in the bar and play Scrabble or dominoes. I guess that was the moment I could have turned back.

'They won't be long,' one of the boys said, and I remember wondering where Alice was. Then Jack pointed and he was, like, 'Oh no!' and the others all started hooting and groaning.

I looked up and I saw Alice walking down the path. The boys were laughing and I swigged more of that Coke and vodka mix. Alice was stunning. She hadn't even got make-up on but she blew everyone away – I could see it in their faces; I could hear it in the hush that fell. When she got there, Alice pulled out another bottle of vodka and waved it at us. I remember laughing along with the boys but I still had this nagging feeling that everything wasn't right.

—*Who else were they waiting for?*

—See, I wasn't really paying much attention. Sounds stupid, doesn't it? We just started walking across the beach for ages and ages, right over to the other side. I could see the top of the cliffs. There were these fields or something on top. It looked like corn, you know when corn is all green? Not ripe? That's where we were making for – those cliffs. The house was up there, some old mansion. Everyone was drinking from the bottles and I could feel myself getting braver and braver, and then suddenly my phone bleeped. I looked down and I've got a text from Arla: I'm doing the Hooded Man. Alone.

That's all it said.

And that's when I felt my heart drop.

Just to reiterate, the Hooded Man Ritual, which was mentioned in episode four by Angel, is like the elevator game. A sequence of numbers are inputted, this time into a rotary telephone and a request for a taxi is spoken into the receiver. Said cab is supposed to turn up, driven by a man in a hood, the suggestion being that this hooded man drives you far from the world as you know it and into another, before bringing you home at your request.

The Hooded Man Ritual is regarded as one of the most dangerous games you can ever play, according to discussions about it on the internet. There are countless Reddit threads, Tumblr posts and blogs on the subject – significantly more now than back when Arla and Anthony met.

A recent development surrounding the Hooded Man comes from accounts by those who claim to have performed the ritual. There are sprawling subreddits claiming that the hooded man has introduced himself to his passengers, referring to himself as 'father'. Speculation abounds online about this entity being some sort of demon, or archangel – perhaps Lucifer himself, or Haniel – an angel from Jewish lore. There are accounts of those who have felt a sense of loss in the presence of the hooded man. There are also those who proclaim to have found some sort of solace in their 'father' entity when speaking to it, feeling mesmerised, hypnotised or soothed by his presence. There are also numerous accounts of 'shadows' following people back into this world – sightings of figures, spectres at the corner of the vision. As I've said before, much is made of the dangers of the Hooded Man Ritual.

For what it's worth, I'm agnostic about all this. Discussions surrounding the 'father' entity have only sprung up in the last few months. Anthony himself has never heard of this aspect of the game, which goes to show that these games have a certain fluidity to them; they are internet creatures that are ever changing, morphing and shifting – the folktales and songs of an older, oral tradition now told and sung by people online.

What also strikes me, though, is the sincerity with which people speak of their experiences of these 'games' and their outcomes. There are heart-felt, well-written accounts of those that have performed these rituals. And, as I have said several times the Hooded Man comes with by far the most warnings.

The same warnings that concern inviting the black-eyed kids into your home.

—*Was it the danger presented by the Hooded Man Ritual that scared you at that point?*

—Yes and no. I sort-of did, sort-of didn't believe in it. But I'd spent loads of time online reading about it. It was fresh in my imagination. I guess I hadn't had time to look at it rationally.

—*So what happened next?*

—This was when it became my fault, all of it. You see, a part of me wanted the game to be real and a part of me knew that it wasn't. And I wanted to go to the party with Alice but I also had this brain wave, this stupid ruse. I thought that, if it worked, I would get the best of both worlds ... excuse the pun.

—*Go on...*

—So I made up this lie. I told the others that my parents just texted, that they needed me to come back and do something. Kyle comes over to me and he's all concerned about how I'm going to get to the party. He seemed like he genuinely wanted me to be there. He kept saying, 'Everyone wants you to come, Anth...' And I didn't even stop and wonder why he was suddenly so desperate for my company. He writes down the address on the back of my hand and a taxi phone number and tells me to book one as soon as I get back. I tell him that's not going to happen, that I can't just book a taxi – the staff on reception are going to notice a teenager heading out at midnight. What if they called my parents? I also felt a bit of relief because there was still that part of me that remembered them calling me 'Empty'. What if that happened in front of Alice? How would I get away? What if my parents woke up and couldn't find me? But Kyle was, like, insisting. So I said, yeah, OK. I'd find some way.

—*How did it go down? The ritual, in the end? I'm assuming you performed it.*

—Man, I remember coming back to the hotel, out of breath and sweating. Lucky I'd put on so much deodorant for the party. I was a bit giddy and excited so I went and splashed cold water on my face in the toilets. I took a few deep breaths and then went down to the games room to see if Arla was there. She was there with that other girl, and when she turned around and saw me, I saw this unbridled happiness on her face. In that moment she was beautiful, you know?

So we start talking about the ritual – the rules – and Arla turns to that other girl and asks her if she's coming along with us. I remember wanting to scream, *What? What are you doing? This is our thing!* I didn't even know who this other girl was, she just sort of followed us about. Another little lost soul. I remember willing the girl to say no, and when she shrugged, I started telling Arla about the rules again. The girl just flounced off, barged right past us and I remember having a really horrible thought – I remember hoping she'd just fuck off; that she'd huff off outside and run into Kyle and Jack and Greg. She was welcome to them.

Just to note, I explained to Anthony, after this interview, Angel's side of this particular event.

—So that was another thing that was my fault. Maybe if I'd been kinder, more inclusive, more accepting. Maybe none of this would have happened?

—*Maybe? Maybe not. I think, in this case, the wheels were already in motion. I doubt there was much you could have done to stop it.*

—Yeah, you can't change the past. That's what therapy's taught me – rumination on the past is only productive if you are seeking ways to make things right. By talking to you, I believe I'm doing something.

—*I do too. Now, the ritual…*

—Yeah. So we sneaked out of our rooms and met by the lift. Even though it was before midnight, it felt so surreal in that hotel. Everything was quiet and still. You could hear TVs burbling from behind people's doors, people snoring. We nearly fell at the very first hurdle as well, because when we got down to reception, the receptionist gave us a look. 'Everything OK, you two?' she said and I swear I nearly puked all over myself. I managed to squeak out something and there was a moment when I was sure she was about to ask us what room we were in.

'My brother and I can't sleep,' Arla said to her. 'Mam and Dad said we could come down to sit in the drawing room, so long as we didn't mess about.'

It was brilliant. The receptionist just smiled and nodded us on.

The second hurdle was the room itself. It was huge, with great big lamps and a pretend fireplace. There was chess and draughts and stuff down there, as well as this old black rotary phone – either an antique or an ornament I guess. Because it was so hot, the curtains were open and you could see the night sky outside. If there'd been anyone there, they'd almost certainly have asked what we were doing, but most of the guests were families so by then everyone was in bed.

That old phone was in the corner so we walked over, dead quiet. Arla got out the chess set and I remember giggling, maybe she didn't want to do it after all. She told me it was in case anyone came in. It was cover. I had the rope and a lighter I'd nicked off Jack in my pocket and I was getting them out and tying the rope to the phone's handset when I remembered the taxi.

—*The taxi?*

—Yeah. To get back to the party. I told you, Kyle gave me the address. So I picked up the handset of that old black phone to call one but there was no dial tone. It was just for show. A little hole opened inside me then as I had no idea how I was going to see Alice. That was when I realised I had no choice but to tell Arla about the party. She and Alice shared a mobile – this old Nokia thing. The only way I was going to get a taxi was if we rang one from that. We couldn't ask reception. The thing was the taxi number Kyle gave me didn't work. And neither of us knew any other numbers. In the end we sat and hoped that Alice or one of the others would ring Arla's phone. Someone did, I don't know who it was but they told us someone would come to pick us up.

By then though it was nearly midnight and we didn't have time to perform the cleansing ritual.

—*Cleansing ritual?*

—Yeah. You have to do it before the Hooded Man.

—*Why?*

—The Hooded Man is dangerous. If it works, you're actually going to another place. Using sage or salt stops certain *things* from coming back with you. It's important.

We couldn't burn sage in the living room but I'd sneaked a few packets of salt from breakfast and we were supposed to spread it around the drawing-room door. But there wasn't time. We just had to start.

So we turned off the lights and sat there in the dark looking at the clock on Arla's phone. When midnight hit, we sat opposite each other on those big, soft chairs, on either side of that phone with all the chess pieces laid out and counted to thirteen. Then we just looked at that antique rotary telephone. I swear to you, even now, there was something in the air, some *charge*. I remember the windows behind us, all the hotel gardens were lit with these soft lights, hedges and walls and stuff. I remember having this horrible sensation that there was something out there. Something looking in. I almost couldn't look. Arla must have felt it too because she pulled the curtains closed. Then we counted to thirteen, and began the ritual. First, we dialled that number. It seemed to take ages and the clicking and whirring of that phone seemed deafening. The handset was still on the hook. I could feel myself sweating and I knew, I just *knew*, that if that curtain opened, that something outside would be right there pressed up against the glass, staring in.

I was shaking, I remember. Arla was holding the black cord and the phone dangled from it like the broken wing of a bird. We dialled the next number two, five, five, one … I can't even say it … and the air became even more charged – it was like the room was getting bigger, smaller. I could hear my heart throbbing in my head. Arla laid the handset back on the table and looked at me.

We counted to thirteen together, my words came out in little terrified breaths then Arla looked at me.

'Your turn,' she said.

I remember bending my head down towards that handset. The

earpiece looked like the eye of a squid glaring back at me. I bent over
without touching it and I whispered into it.

'Hello, I need a cab please.'

I was shaking, I was shaking so hard that when I began to untie
the cord from the handset I dropped it and it clattered on the table,
knocking the chess pieces over. I remember Arla nearly screamed
and we sat with our hands over our mouths for ages, praying that
no one had heard us. I put the cord back in my pocket – we'd have
to burn it when we got to the party; we couldn't do it there in the
drawing room.

'We have to open the curtains,' Arla said, and we both looked at
each other. Neither of us wanted to say but I knew she was thinking
the same as me.

What if there was something there?

—And was there?

—I remember when that car pulled up outside the hotel, man,
I nearly shat myself. I was so scared, but I was laughing, giggling –
almost delirious, you know? Arla though, she got suddenly really
serious. She was adamant it was the taxi from the game; that it *had* to
be. I remember pulling back the curtain, looking out the window and
the relief when it was just a hatchback, an Astra I think. I remember
turning to Arla and she looked crushed. I got the feeling she'd been
waiting for this her whole life. She almost dragged me outside into
the car park, head down. It was still really warm, really still – you
could hear the sea whispering and everything smelled green, tropical.
It felt like something out of a dream.

—The car…

—It was just sitting there and we were hiding behind the palm
trees outside the hotel. Then the doors opened. I can't remember if
it was relief or disappointment that filled me.

—Who was it?

—Kyle and some older guy.

—So what did you do when you saw them?

—I could have stayed hidden and then sneaked back in with Arla

– she had realised by now that this wasn't the Hooded Man, that the ritual hadn't worked … After all, we hadn't done it properly – we hadn't attached the second cord. To be honest, I felt like I was in way over my head.

—*You mean in the ritual? Or was it the sight of Kyle and the older guy that made you feel that way?*

—Both equally. I just wanted to go back upstairs and see my mum and dad. I just wanted to run away from it all, like a coward. A wuss. But then someone else got out the passenger door and all my brain and heart turned to mush. All the game stuff just vanished.

—*I'm guessing it was Alice?*

—It was and she was standing there, framed by the car head-lamps, a half-empty bottle of Coke dangling from one hand. I was a moth to a flame, I could just feel myself being drawn to her. Arla was straight over, snatching at the bottle and chugging loads of it at once. I saw the older guy raise his eyebrows and look at Kyle. Kyle made some gesture and the older guy, he just sort of shrugged and nodded at us to get in. Arla and me, we got in the back with Kyle, and Alice got in the front with the guy and we were away.

—*Did it not seem odd that they had come back to get you at the precise time when the car was supposed to show up for the Hooded Man Ritual?*

—It should have done I guess; it should have raised so many red flags, but in that car, with that bottle being passed about, and ciga-rettes and the music blasting, the car racing through these empty, winding roads – all the worry, all the doubt just evaporated.

—*You had that feeling of acceptance again?*

—Totally.

—*How was Arla on that trip?*

—Just the same as the rest of us; drinking, smoking, laughing, singing along. She had this fury to her, though – this anger. I never even gave that a second thought. I was just glad – glad that we were having fun, that no one was calling me 'Empty'. That I'd been accepted back into the fold.

It's hard to be sure about the facts around this part of the story. It is entirely possible that the arrival of the car at that precise time was a freak coincidence. But there's also the possibility it was coordinated by Alice and Kyle – some kind of conspiracy. Also, I recall Angel's words from the previous episode:

'This sounds just so stupid but I just started telling them about Arla and Anthony and the stupid baby games they were playing. They were all laughing and it felt good, man. Like, it was suddenly funny; like, it felt OK again.'

Back to Anthony.

—So we seem to be driving for ages and that feeling of elation began to dim. It began to feel wrong to be there, we were too young. We were in way over our heads and we knew it. We weren't like Kyle and the others. I was terrified my parents were going to find out, but all I could think about was seeing Alice again. And I remember saying stuff, making jokes, my confidence swelled by the booze. I remember Alice laughing and I just felt that rush again and that was stronger than the doubt so I just kept drinking that fear away.

We got there about 12.30. The house was in the middle of what looked like a cornfield, all this grass stuff round it. At first glance you would say it was a barn rather than a house. But we could see flashing lights in the windows and hear the sound of music.

When we got out of the car I remember being much more drunk than I thought I was. Arla and I had been necking the vodka so everything was fuzzy, like a dream. Everyone's voices sort of floated around me and I remember suddenly worrying again about my parents, that I hadn't even left them a note. What if they sent the police to look for me, got the party shut down, and it was my fault? I remember panicking and saying something to Kyle, something babyish about what would happen if *he* got caught? He put his arm round me and just sort of led me on, through that field of corn or whatever. He said his dad didn't know he was out either and he didn't care, that his dad would bail us out if we got in trouble. He was laughing and I was too. Alice was ahead of us. I remember her turning around and just being filled with this sense of … I mean it was just stupid teenage puppy love – drunken foolishness – but it felt so good then; right at that moment I was in love with her.

—*Where was Arla at this point?*

—You see, this is where it gets hazy. And I feel terrible. Just so guilty. And I want to stop now – everything inside me is telling me to stop talking to you – questioning why, *why* am I telling you all this? Then I remember that it's for *her*.

—*Alice?*

—No. It's for Arla. It's for what happened to her.

—*What happened to Arla, Anthony?*

—We'd been separated. Arla was behind me with Jack and Greg, I could hear them laughing and I knew the tone of it – I knew that something wasn't right. Arla was too loud – she was shouting and slurred. Every time I heard her voice I felt this sense of responsibility for her. I'd dragged her there. She didn't know Kyle or Jack or anyone. And yeah, her sister was there too, but Alice wasn't even interested, she was off.

—*What happened when you got to the house?*

—This is where things get really blurry. The alcohol was really starting to have an effect now and there was this music coming from the place. It was deafening: *dumf-dumf-dumf* – this bass blasting out. Inside it was huge; there was a hay-store or something – like, a mezzanine with a ladder. It was full of people and there were these flashing lights. Everyone was dancing. I'll be honest, I was really scared, I didn't like it at all. But Kyle and the rest of them were all jostling me along and passing cans of beer around, cigarettes. They started dancing and I just sort of got caught up in things … got carried away…

—*And Arla?*

—It must have been about an hour in when I thought of her

again. How horrible is that? And this is not an excuse, far from it, but Alice was dancing with me. Once you got used to the blasting music, it was kind of ... you got lost in it a bit. And, like I say, Alice was there and we were dancing. You know, I didn't even *think* of Arla. How awful is that? I'm ... I'm so ashamed of myself...

Anthony sits and stares for a long time, lost in memory. He cries silently, tears sliding slowly down his cheeks. I find it hard to feel any-thing but sorry for him. Perhaps there'll be some who won't. There'll be some people who think that Anthony is, if not completely, then sig-nificantly culpable for what happened to Arla Macleod that night, and therefore, in some way culpable for what happened in November 2014. All I know is that right now I feel sorry for a man who is clearly full of regret for something that happened a long time ago.

—I did see Arla, yes. I saw her briefly. She was dancing with Kyle and Jack and Greg. She was out of it and they kept looking at each other and laughing. They were pushing her about, but sort of sneakily, pretending not to, you know? They were catching her as she staggered and I could see their hands all over her. It was horrible and I couldn't turn away.

—*That sounds awful.*

—It got worse. She was all over the place and they were round her like a pack of wolves. They were taking it in turns snogging her, they had their hands up under her clothes, all of them. I saw it, but somehow it was like it wasn't real – like it wasn't really hap-pening. It was hard to see through the lights and the people but I saw them leading her off somewhere, off into a corner, and then through a door. There was this little voice inside me that was scream-ing – *screaming* – at me to say something, to tell someone she was in danger, that it looked all wrong, that it looked terrible. Yes, that she was in *danger*. I kept remembering Kyle and the rest of them in the swimming pool, 'scouting out the talent'. It fucking chills me to my core even now.

But then this other voice inside me started speaking. This was the voice that was watching Alice dancing; cos by then, it was just me and her and I couldn't turn away from that, I just couldn't. And if I told Alice what was happening to her sister, that would have spoiled everything. So that other voice just told me everything would be fine, that Kyle and them weren't much older than me or Arla, so she would be OK – they would look after her. Oh God … what was I thinking?

—*Anthony, you were only a child. This doesn't rest on your shoulders.*

—We both know that some of it does. We both know that.

—*Did you see Arla again after that?*

—Yes, thank Christ. It must have been about two or three in the morning. Kyle and Jack had found me and Alice and we were going to walk back to the hotel along the beach. I was tired, the high of the alcohol had worn off and those worries were back again tenfold. What if we got back and our parents were all there looking for us – police helicopters and stuff? Ironically, I heard that the party got raided after we left.

—*Was Arla with you by then?*

—Yeah. It's hard to remember the details but she was with us, I'm sure of it. We were all flat, bedraggled, tired – probably all a little bit worried to be honest. Kyle and the others were still trying to sound cocky, confident. They were seventeen or eighteen – not much older than us, really – but they seemed a million miles away, like adults. It was so surreal walking along that beach, our feet sinking into the sand. I was walking on my own, and I remember the feeling – this confusion and guilt nestling like a fur ball in my belly. I couldn't turn round and look at the others. It was horrible. I feel like I've blanked it all out until now.

—*What about the next day?*

—None of our parents realised what we'd done. It was amazing really if you think about it. I must have got back at about four am and just passed out. But I was still up in the morning for breakfast with my parents. I remember seeing Alice and Arla in the breakfast room too. Arla just kept her head down but Alice did look at me.

This time, though, her gaze was like a laser across that room; I'll never forget it.

—*Do you think Arla told Alice what had happened to her?*

—I reckon so. This is the thing as well: the next day, the Macleods left, they went home. Alice never even said goodbye. It was clear that she blamed me.

—*Did you ever find out exactly what happened to Arla that night?*

—I didn't. Not at first. Alice just told me that she'd changed, that something had changed her.

—*You were still in touch with Alice after Cornwall?*

—Yeah ... sorry, it's complicated. Alice gave me her phone number at some point that night. I was just so overwhelmed that I totally forgot about Arla.

—*So did Alice ever mention what happened that night? She must have seen what happened too, right?*

—No. I could never bring it up. I didn't have the words, not then. I never even had the balls to text her afterwards – it was her who got in touch with me! It must have been a fortnight or so after the holiday; I was back at college and I got a text out of the blue. Just, like, 'What's up?' – something innocuous like that – and we just started chatting. We moved onto MSN messenger after that. Alice had her own computer in her bedroom by then.

—*And she told you about Arla?*

—Yeah, eventually. It was a few months after we'd started talking. We'd been telling each other about our lives and stuff. That awkwardness wasn't there when we were online. We didn't really mention Cornwall. Alice was telling me about things at home. It sounded pretty bad. Arla had gone off the rails a bit, was kicking off, going out and not coming back, coming home drunk. Their parents were losing their shit over it. Then Alice just came out with it, just said offhand something along the lines of, 'Arla's never been the same since she let those lads have their way with her in Cornwall.'

I remember it hit me like a fist. I had no idea what to say back. I remember this guilt filling me like a balloon – it consumed me. I begged Alice to tell her parents, to tell the police, to tell anyone, she *had* to. But she was just so blasé about it. Whenever I mentioned it, she would just go offline, vanish.

I didn't sleep after she told me that. I was just *obsessed* with it, constantly messaging and texting Alice to get her to tell her parents – to make sure someone knew. That's when she just broke off contact with me. Just stopped replying to my texts, blocked me online. I guess it made sense. But you know what the last thing she said to me was? After I'd begged her again and again to tell her family? All she wrote was, 'They know.'

⁂

A few things link up here: Arla's wayward behaviour; Alice's 'boyfriend' who Paulette mentioned, sending the 'zillion' messages – presumably Anthony urging Alice to tell her family about what happened to Arla. This final message from Alice is what chills me, though, and finally suggests a shred of a motive for Arla's acts against her family in 2014. Did Lucy and Stan Macleod find out what had happened to Arla and do nothing? Was Arla even blamed? From what I know of the way Lucy Macleod treated her daughters, the latter doesn't seem too farfetched. Also, we must note that this traumatic event in Arla's life could have been the trigger, or even perhaps the cause, of her alleged psychosis. I'm no psychologist, I cannot make these judgements, I don't know enough about the mind to do anything but speculate.

I have two questions – one for us and one for Anthony. The first is why, if Arla wanted to exact revenge on her family for knowing about what had happened to her and doing nothing about it, did it take until 2014 for her to act? Why not earlier? Is there some significance to be found in this lapse of time, or was it just that Arla's psychosis had become all-consuming by then? We may never know the answer. The Macleods are all dead, save for Arla, and my interview with her has taken place. I won't be allowed to speak to her again.

The second question I ask Anthony.

—Why did you not say anything? Why did you not tell the police?

For a long time Anthony will not meet my eye. He shakes his head a couple of times and finally looks up.

—I'm presuming something.
—What?
—I'm presuming they've made contact with you by now.
—What? Who?
—Yeah. They have then.
—You can tell me, Anthony.
—I'm not saying. There's no way. I'm not risking my safety, my parents' safety. You saw the video of that old guy, Marsh, right? That wasn't them but they arranged it. It was them who hacked him, doxxed him – sent that hunter group after him.
—What do you know about him?
—All I know is that the guy was linked to Arla Macleod somehow, and I know that you'll be next. So will I. The difference is, I deserve it. You, perhaps, don't.
—Who are they, Anthony?
—I'm going now, Scott. I've done the right thing – I've said what I needed to say. Now I'm going to let them come. They'll find me. They'll find you.
—We can shut this down. You can tell me who they are and I won't broadcast it, I promise. All I need is a name. I can work from there.
—OK, no. I want to do it in the open. I want to show them I'm not scared anymore. Show *him* I'm not scared. Broadcast what you like. I'll give you his name.

He does. The reason I'm not broadcasting it in this episode is my choice, not Anthony's. It's for a good reason. I will reveal in the next episode who has been pursuing me for the last few months.
And why.
You see, during the interviews and editing process of this series, ever

since episode one was released, I have been under attack. I am lucky in that I have always kept my identity quiet, my online presence minimal – because Six Stories *has never been about me; it is always about the cases. Listeners of the show, though, will have seen the flurry of negative traffic that has now more or less consumed the* Six Stories *social-media platforms. There are posts calling for my head. I am described as a ghoul, among other, less eloquent, things. I can handle this, though; it's not pleasant but it's bearable. What has been unnerving me is the barrage of text messages and emails that have been arriving. They have all been from burner phones and public IP addresses. However, these are just the foot soldiers, the grunts. I am looking for the general. Thanks to Anthony, I have found him.*

So here it is, the gauntlet, officially laid down.

You have my number, you have my email address, you probably know everything about me, just like you know everything about everyone you've destroyed online before.

But this is different because I also know who you are.

And I also know why you do what you do.

So get in touch and let's make episode six.

This has been our fifth.

Until next time…

TorrentWraith – Audio (Music & Sounds)

Type	Name
Audio	**Arla Macleod Rec006 [320KBPS]** Uploaded **1 week** ago, Size 60.2 MiB. ULed by JBazzzzz666

I'm sorry.

This isn't proper. It's not, like, a report. It's just … I don't know what else to do.

They just won't stop. Nothing makes them stop. It's like pain, hearing them. Have you ever had a toothache? It's worse than that.

Has your eardrum ever burst? That's pain. That's the worst pain ever. It doesn't stop. It's in your head, just this never-ending throbbing. You can hear it, you can hear the infection. It's this terrible heartbeat – beating and beating and pouring pain into you with every beat.

I turned off the radio and went to get one of my CDs, but I forgot they didn't let me have them here – *you* don't let me have them; you said they would trigger too many memories. But that's what I wanted them for. He was my only escape and you took him away. Why? I can't listen to the radio. Their crying and their begging to come in, it's louder than anything on the radio.

I wanted my CDs so I could show them that I understood, that I knew a way back into their world.

But now all I've got is a screaming black emptiness.

That's what it's like.

That's why I have to do this.

Tonight I'm going to let them in.

Again.

You told me what you used to say to your son when he was little: you used to tell him that, whatever happened, whatever he'd done in his life, you would protect him.

※※

I can't take it. I can't stand it anymore. I can't fight it anymore. It can't be done. No one can protect me.

I'm sorry, I know you've tried. I know that this therapy – this recording – should have found the triggers. It should have given some ideas about what's made me this way, and how to help me.

I know you've tried to protect me.

I feel like I've let you down.

I feel like I've let everyone down.

I should have been more careful. I opened doors I should never have opened. I let ghosts in – ghosts that follow, ghosts that never leave. All I wanted to do was vanish. I only ever wanted to disappear.

We never closed the ritual, you know. We were supposed to burn the rope; we were supposed to dial a number and say, 'Thank you for the ride.'

But we didn't.

Then *they* came.

※※

I keep hearing them. I can't stop hearing them – their crying, over and over and over, wailing and wailing to come in.

Shadows and eyes all over, all around me, pushing me, begging me to let them in. And I'm all on my own. I know … I *know* you've said that I'm not, but I am … I am. And I can't do this anymore.

I can hear them now. You said to make a recording whenever I saw and heard things, well I hear them now, I can hear them now. I can hear their hands on my windows. I hear those hands every night – that pale, faultless skin squeaking against the windows, the shape of them behind the curtains.

※※

I'll tell you about my dream, last night.

Cos I had a dream, right, a dream that confirmed it, that let me know what I have to do.

It were a sign or whatever – a metaphor or something.

I'll tell you about it.

I was back at the house – the house in the field. The house on the cliff. It were dark this time, like it were night, and I had a feeling in my belly. It was like a rock, like I'd swallowed a big black rock. There were loads of movements in the grass – it were swishing back and forth, back and forth, and I just wanted to scream. I were screaming but my mouth were all dry, my teeth all sticky and no noise was coming out. I were the crow but I couldn't fly no more. I were caught on something. I kept trying to flap my wings and they just … I could feel the feathers just falling out. I could feel the roots of them just pulling out of my skin, like I were a dead thing.

I tried to call again and this sort of ragged sound came out, ripped my throat. I could feel it all the way down, harsh and nasty, a dead-cry. Then I were laying in the grass again, all curled up, me again.

But they heard me, cos the grass round the house went suddenly still. Then there was this sound, this hissing sound. And all at once, they began to rise up. There were loads of them, all rising up like snakes – kids, all turned to face me. It should have been funny, like one of those whack-a-mole machines. I remember feeling like I'd pissed myself – I could feel it warm, running down my legs as they rose up, heads and shoulders – little boys and girls with, like, old-fashioned haircuts, and shirts, like formal dress and that. They had pale skin, like them porcelain dolls Mam used to keep on the windowsill, with that sort of blueish skin. These had black hair, though, and … and they … they all looked at me at once with their black eyes. Like bullet holes in their faces.

I should … I should say something to me mam, me dad, me sister, but what? What do I say? How do I put it into words? It just sounds … It's not like they can even hear me. But I want to tell them it was what I had to do.

I'm feeling that same feeling now. All the hairs on my arms go up. It's warm but I'm freezing.

I can't go on. I can't keep feeling so scared like this all the time. It's like torture. I can't sleep. They're crying and I'm so scared…

They all started coming towards me in the dream, but at the same time, all moving in, getting closer like a swarm and behind them I could see the lights in the windows of the house have all gone out. I'm back at Redstart Road. I'm back in the garden.

The kids with the black eyes, they're close and they're silent, still moving … and, you know how dreams are. My crow body's fallen away, bones all skittering like kindling, and I'm me again. I'm me and I'm twenty-one again. I can feel this … this *ball* of anger inside me. You know like you do when you're young, when you don't fit nowhere, when no one wants you?

I can hear their feet, crunching and crackling up the path in the back garden. I can see them creeping, and I can hear them giggling.

I can hear Dad shouting, waving with that big wooden cross that leaves you black and bruised like a banana. He's screaming words from the Bible and I can hear them giggling.

I've got something in my hand. I can't see it but I know it's a hammer. I can … I can still feel it in my hand … the wood. They get closer, the kids. They're spilling into the garden, slithering like snakes. Dad's screaming and I'm still screaming and I swing the hammer, and I … I can feel that still too, all the way through my body. I hear the *snap* of bone and a sort of *squish* and one of the heads come off. It's too easy. Bones and skin too brittle and soft like rotten fruit. And then I'm stood there watching it. All the other kids they're just still, like statues, poking out of that long grass stuff. Then they all turn their heads at the same time and look at the one I chopped down. It's just a little boy and … oh God, there's this slippery sound as something starts to rise up out of the place where the kid's head has been. I'm frozen still, I can't breathe – hands in my lungs, two cold, stone hands squeezing them tight.

I'm looking at this kid, this headless kid. I can't look away and this white thing starts flowering from the mess of red, rising up all slick and bloody from its neck. It's like this two-pronged wishbone shape, and it starts swelling. Two pale prongs that start blowing up and … Oh my God I can see faces swimming in the swellings, two little faces with black eyes and they're making a tiny screaming noise. The other kids they all turn back to me and I swear … I swear they're grinning. When I look back, there's two heads now … two heads with faces straining from that whiteness, their hair all slick. And they've stopped screaming now and they're just looking at me. I can feel my brain slide, like something's come loose. It's like I can feel my sanity coming undone.

So I just start swinging that hammer, swinging it at anything, at all of them, and I can hear bones cracking and feel the blows going through my arms. It's a blur – you know, like dreams are? I can feel liquid spattering my face. I can feel it running down my arms, over my hands, flecks of rotten bone spattering my clothes. I can hear more of that squealing as more of those heads start rising through the bodies. Like that monster – that snake thing – what's it called? A hydra? And, like, even when I chopped off the two heads, two more came out of each … each branch…

A fucking hydra. Cut off its head and two more grow in its place.

Then I'm above it all – you know how dreams are – like I'm a bird or something.

Oh Jesus, it were horrible. Because it were me, but it weren't me … I was the crow.

I can't … I can't get the feeling out of me. I can still feel the hammer against them … against their heads … that crunching sound…

They cry when I try to sleep. There's thousands of them – thousands more of them now. Heads like a fucking hydra.

I just can't do this no more…

I just can't…

§§

I'm sorry. That's what I want to say. To you for trying to help me; to everyone here who's been kind to me; just to everyone. I'm sorry…

But I'm going to let them in again…

Because if I don't….

§§

Extract from the Stanwel Examiner:
'Macleod Killer Dead at 23'

Arla Macleod, the Stanwel woman who bludgeoned her entire family to death with a hammer has been found dead in the secure hospital where she had been detained since her manslaughter conviction in 2014.

The twenty-three-year-old committed suicide at Elmtree Manor, the medium-level secure unit where she had been sentenced to spend the rest of her adult life.

A spokesman for the hospital today spoke only to confirm the death of a patient some time on the night of the 27th or in the early morning of the 28th July 2017.

Macleod, who was born in Saltcoats, Ayrshire, and moved to Stanwel as a young child, was undergoing pioneering new therapy at Elmtree Manor to treat the complex mental illness deemed by a judge in a court of law to have diminished her responsibility in the killing of her mother, stepfather and younger sister.

This conviction has not sat well with the general public, especially the residents of Stanwel, many of whom believe that Arla Macleod's notoriety has brought a degree of shame and unwanted attention to the town.

However, Arla Macleod's death has been seen by some in Stanwel as a relief. A resident who lives on the same street as the Macleod family home – the site of the massacre – which has remained unoccupied since the incident in 2014, told the *Examiner*, 'It's finally the end of what's been a terrible few years, what with the press attention on the town. Most of us think it's what she deserved.'

Another recent suicide has added to increasing spec-ulation that Arla Macleod was sexually assaulted as

a teenager. Ex-caretaker at Saint Theresa's Catholic
School in Stanwel, Mr Albert Marsh, killed himself
after an exposé by a vigilante paedophile hunting
group, raising questions about whether or not he was
involved in the Macleod case.

Saint Theresa's has dismissed these claims and reit-
erated that it has always conducted rigorous background
checks into all members of staff.

An anonymous associate of Macleod recently told the
Examiner that Albert Marsh's death was a 'distraction
from the truth' and that 'people should be looking past
what is on the surface'.

Coroner Alan Peterson heard, during the inquest into
the suicide, how Macleod had managed to break off a
loose section of the reinforced plastic that covered
her window in her private room in Elmtree Manor and
use it to cut her wrists.

Nursing staff at the hospital had apparently not
noticed the fault in Arla Macleod's room. Macleod had
shown no suicidal tendencies and was 'responding' to
therapy and treatment from renowned medical professionals, the inquest heard.

Patients at Elmtree Manor are not so rigorously
monitored as they would be at higher-level secure
hospitals such as Broadmoor or Rampton – places where
many believe Macleod should have been sent. It has been
speculated that this relaxed attitude to the killer
may have led to the oversight and, ultimately, to her
death.

The coroner also heard that there was no reason for
Ms Macleod to have been placed into the secure isolation room, which is standard practice at Elmtree Manor
for those patients who are not responsive to treatment
or are showing signs of suicidal or extreme behaviour.

Macleod's psychiatrist, Dr Barrington, a senior member of staff at Elmtree Manor, described Macleod's death as 'deeply unfortunate and unprecedented'. Barrington would not give any further details of Macleod's state of mind, due to patient confidentiality.

The spokesman for Elmtree Manor, speaking after the inquest, described the death of Arla Macleod as 'deeply regrettable' and explained that there has been a swift review of inspection standards at the hospital.

News of Macleod's death has been the talk of social media, and the interest after the inquest has shone unwanted light, yet again on Stanwel.

Another unnamed local resident told the *Examiner*: 'It was just disgusting how easily she got off. That hospital she managed to get put in was nothing more than a glorified holiday camp. It's us who still live in Stanwel that have to cope with the scar she left behind. I don't feel sorry for her one bit.'

Episode 6: Troll Hunter

—It changed my life. You hear most people say that phrase in a positive context don't you? But yeah, it umm … it totally wiped me out, totally shifted my entire … It … it made me different. It changed me inside. It changed the way I see the world.

I remember the day. I'll never forget it. I remember coming home. Of course I still had that big house, the 'Cursed Manor'. I remember pulling up in the cab, looking out the window at this hokey ruin, this fucking parody – with all the security gates, the barbed wire and the like. Inside, of course, it's as lavish as you fucking want: thick carpets and dimmer switches; the little studio that looks over the cliff on the far side.

When we came home that night, I was embarrassed by the place. I handed a wad of notes to the driver, couldn't even look at him. The press were already there – only one or two, and the fact that I was disappointed there weren't more made me want to fucking slash my own throat right there and then. I would bleed to death in the flashbulb light. But that would have made it all about me, wouldn't it?

When the gates were closed, when we got inside that house that was so full of … shit … just nonsense – all those old sculptures, the taxidermy, the voodoo dolls, the shelves of plastic Halloween *junk*, I wanted to tear it all down, to burn it. I wanted to sit out in my studio and watch it crumble to ashes. I wanted to watch that empire I'd created, that my ego had fashioned, the fucking palace of narcissism I'd raised – I wanted to see it turn to a mound of blackened ash. Then I wanted to blow it all away, leave a stain on the earth that I could curl up on and die.

That's what I wanted when we came home that night.

Oblivion.

The voice you're hearing – the Mersey-American drawl; a Scouser who's been dragged face first by his hair through the Deep South – is not instantly recognisable. I certainly did not expect such softness to come from such a striking figure. But I am star-struck, yes. The man I'm talking to, despite his almost-whisper, the rasp in his voice, is enigmatic; he wields his personality like a scythe. Maybe that's in poor taste. But I think Skexxixx would probably be on board with that description of him.

§§

Welcome to Six Stories.

I'm Scott King.

In this, our final episode of this series, there is much to discuss. I am fully aware of the death of Arla Macleod, so it is with great care and precision that I've edited this episode.

I won't say much more. All I will say is that hackneyed phrase: it's been a journey – a journey whose end is upon us.

But there's still so much to tell.

I start this episode with a man whose influence has run like a black vein through the story of Arla Macleod. It will not surprise you that when I began to research this case, the artist known as Skexxixx was one of the first people I wanted to talk to. Having been relegated almost to obscurity after his second album, Through the Mocking Glass, *was released in 2007, and not appearing in person, or recording any musical follow-ups, in the wake of the Macleod Massacre in 2014, his profile rose slightly. Skexxixx has taken a lot of flak from the press, being cited as a 'reason' why Arla Macleod killed her family. Of course, more cases of Skexxixx's supposed influence have subsequently been dredged up – mostly from his halcyon days, or his 'hell-cyon', as he calls them with a smile so brief I almost miss it.*

The fundamentalist Christian Joseph Randolf, who attempted to blow up a shopping mall in Canton, Ohio, told police he had been 'possessed' by subliminal messages in Skexxixx's music – a claim so ludicrous it was resoundingly dismissed by the rest of the world. Yet these persistent accusations did not stop, reaching their peak just before the release of Through the Mocking Glass *in 2007.*

When I got in touch with Skexxixx's representatives in my research for this series, I was told firmly – and rather stroppily – that he would neither discuss nor comment on 'an individual case, which bears no personal relevance to Skexxixx whatsoever'. However, his agent then contacted me again and told me Skexxixx was going to be in the UK for a short time and would be willing to discuss things 'on his terms'. I didn't reply to this in the end, feeling that I would not be able to get the answers I wanted if I had to compromise my questions, so I simply left the invitation hanging.

I was therefore fully prepared to be ignored or told where to go when I approached Skexxixx's representatives again. I already knew Skexxixx had made no attempts to resurrect his career – he parted company with his record label long ago and paid them off in a brief legal wrangle about undelivered albums. I was also aware he had no interest in any other kind of publicity. So I spelled out in detail what I wanted to discuss and, to my great surprise, I was granted an interview, which we conducted in a day-room suite at a London hotel.

Before the interview, Skexxixx's UK publicist told me in no uncertain terms that any mention of Arla Macleod had been vetoed – that Skexxixx would walk if I even went near that subject. And so it was with a degree of trepidation that I sat down opposite the Lord of Nothing himself.

Skexxixx's real name is Leonard Myers. He's originally from Aigburth in Merseyside and now a long-term resident of LA. He's in his forties but looks much older – something I was not expecting. Skexxixx is a far cry from the insectile, painted dervish from the early noughties. There's a hint of smudged eyeliner on his lower lids and his gait is a shuffle; an ill-fitting jacket fails to hide the paunch that presses at the waistband of his jeans. His teeth bear no trace of the trademark blackener that his fans used to emulate – made infamous by Arla Macleod. All of these features point to an eccentric, washed-up rock star – a figure far removed from Skexxixx's earlier incarnation as the scourge of the Christian West.

Oddly enough, how everything went wrong for Skexxixx is little documented – mainly because the attempted press coverage at the time of the Macleod Massacre was threatened with lawsuit after lawsuit. Ultimately, Skexxixx won a huge, undisclosed sum from an unnamed tabloid, thus allowing him to vanish into a more-than-comfortable obscurity.

Why is any of this relevant, though, if I'm not allowed to discuss with him the late Arla Macleod?

That will become clear.

—His name was Olli. He never even opened his eyes. They let us hold him, let us say goodbye. I can't ever rid myself of those fleeting moments – those last hours when my life ended…

Have you seen the press lately? Jumping all over everything. Those fucking news websites – shit rags putting up 'instant-reaction' photos of celebrities who've just suffered a bereavement. Scum, all of them. If that had happened to us, I don't know what I would have done. I'd have been locked up for it, I know that.

Skexxixx leaves that threat hanging and stares straight ahead, past me, into the middle distance. As I've mentioned, the coverage of the stillbirth of Skexxixx's child with then partner, actress Sonia Dawlish, was fortunately kept to a minimum. It probably helped that Skexxixx the musician was falling into obscurity. His second album had not done well and the man was already refusing interviews; he even walked offstage after two songs when he received a hostile reception at the Reading Festival in 2007.

Now the man directs his cold stare at his publicist, who scuttles out of the room and comes back with a carafe of water, twists of cucumber floating inside like snake specimens in formaldehyde.

There is something that Skexxixx wants to talk to me about. He says that no one has 'bothered' asking his opinion on the subject before. He was made aware of Six Stories *before our meeting and says he has listened to some of the series so far. He describes it as 'a hard listen'.*

—Imagine me having feelings?

He says this with a rattling laugh. His eyes are blank.

—I can't tell you when it all started. I don't even know for sure. I have someone taking care of all the Facebook and whatever. I was against all of that at first. Then I just thought of it as a little place for fans to go and chat or whatever. I was made aware of it but I didn't really give a fuck about it. It never felt like any of that – the messages and posts and stuff – was really coming at *me*. I spent most of my time in my studio.

It was only when I set up the Twitter account back in 2010 that it all began to get to me. I had some new songs. I had been through some shit, had some therapy, and I felt like it was time to start giving something back. I had no idea of the reaction – the furore – this would create.

Around 2010, Skexxixx began emerging from his grief. It was a tentative thing – a far cry from the king of controversy he'd previously been. He was not so much embracing nothing; perhaps he was making a small attempt to become something instead? He began tweeting snippets of lyrics and a few promo pictures. Gone was the sneering defiance of before; instead these showed a new seriousness, a focus.

—At first, the overall reaction was pretty good, man. I mean there's always people who send you weird shit, send you abuse. But it wasn't *bad*. I could ignore it, let it go.

But then … Look, this is an exclusive, man. I've never spoken properly about this before; no one's even been interested. Aren't you the lucky boy? So, anyway, there's a few organisations out there for people in a similar situation to mine. They help out, provide counselling and care for those who've been bereaved. I figured I wanted to help. I'd been personally affected. It felt right. Not for me, but for Olli.

Contrary to what was claimed online by the vast majority of both Skexxixx and non-Skexxixx fans, none of this was for publicity. Skexxixx made that very clear. Using his name would be the decision of the organisations themselves.

—They all got back to me, those organisations. I'll not name them – I'll not name any of them. I feel bad even saying this to you, as I kind of get what they meant – I understand where they were coming from. And I'm not looking for revenge. But it shocked me. Because you know what they said, every single one of them? Something along the lines of, 'It would not be appropriate at this time for an artist with such a controversial image to become a patron of our organisation. It would send out a confused message.'

I remember just feeling numb, all the life drained out of me. It was like I'd been stabbed. I would know, because I *have* been stabbed. It was unexpected. It was shocking and – ironically, I suppose – more controversial than anything I'd ever done onstage.

I could have shamed all of them, exposed their hypocrisy. But I didn't. I thought that was a good decision.

Then things got bad.

—*Can you tell me the first time you remember it happening? Or, a better way of putting it, the first time you remember it getting to you?*

—That's a good fucking way of putting it, yeah. So I was prepared for the onslaught as soon as I hit Twitter with my new stuff, man. I had the usual right-wing Christians who seem to spend most of their time arguing online with atheists, using very un-Christian language towards me. It always makes me think, if their God is so powerful, so omnipotent, so divine, why do they feel the need to defend him over a dude sending out a few tweets? I mean, surely God doesn't give a shit, right?

But it wasn't them, though. I mean, they did keep telling me I'm going to hell and I'm just, like, 'Prove it.' But then some of them they started talking shit about Olli, telling me it was my fault. Man, how can you call yourself Christian and talk shit about someone's dead kid?

I take a deep breath before asking my next question. I have to ask it but I know he's not going to be happy.

—*Do you think you might have provoked some of that at all?*
—Are you fucking serious? Provoked people into telling me that it was my fault my kid was dead? Provoked people into telling me that their fucking God struck him down to punish me because I wrote a fucking song? Bullshit. Did you know that that very famous and very controversial church group – more controversial than I've ever been, by the way – made a parody of one of my songs? It's called 'The Folly of Hell' and they called their version 'Olli in Hell'. They made a fucking video with a baby dancing in some flames. And they call themselves Christians!
—*My God! No, I didn't know that.*
—And you know why you've not heard about it? Because if it goes online again I'll fucking bankrupt them and they know it. I'm now a bigger threat to them than Satan. But it wasn't even them. It wasn't the fundamentalists that got to me in the end. It was...

Skexxixx gives an almost whispered command and his publicist scurries over with a folder. Skexxixx opens the plastic wallet and holds out the pages to show me, his long fingers still tattooed with occult symbols. He wears only one ring – a single silver band on the middle finger of his left hand. Olli's name is engraved on its surface.

The folder is filled with printouts – newspaper articles that document Skexxixx's disappearance, and the trolling he received. Their tone is faintly accusatory. As if he almost deserved what happened to him.

—But this is the sort of thing that upset me. It still does...

He holds out more printouts, filled with tweets and Facebook and Instagram posts. I am amazed at the hundreds, if not thousands of horrible messages that I see, all directed at Skexxixx himself or else mentioning him:

'Would love to attack that fag Skexxixx with a claw-hammer'; 'Watch it you cunt, you're FUCKIN DEAD'.

I ask what it was, if anything, he thinks sparked these comments. Skexxixx looks irritated and I fear he might be about to walk out. I need to be a little more careful.

—This. Something like this was what 'sparked' all that hate.

His hands are shaking as he shows me his own tweet asking people to donate money to a bereavement charity.

—See, you're making out like I provoked these people, like, I said something to upset them. It's not the fucking case. And these messages come whether I tweet something or not now. They're relentless. And you know what, there's only a small number of them out there – one or two who make it their fucking life's work to try and get to me. And it's working. Because every time they tell me I'm shit, a little bit of me believes it. You're probably thinking, 'Oh, poor baby', but it's true man, it's fucking true. Every time they tell me I should die, that little black place inside me tells me that yes, it was my fault Olli died; it tells me I should die. Sometimes I don't have the will to rise above it.

OK, you really want to know why I think it happens? My theory is because it doesn't fit the story, does it? It doesn't slot into the narrative – Mr 'Embrace Your Nothing' wanting to help. That's why I tried to disappear again. I thought fuck the music, man, fuck it all. People don't deserve it. People are just going to see me as this animal.

—*Have you ever tried reporting them? Finding out who they are? Getting the law involved?*

—But then they win. That's *how* they win – they get you to react. That's a victory for them.

—*And you? What do you do with it all?*

—I'm the fucking king Satan, aren't I? I deserve it, right?

The man is visibly rattled. It seems like all this has aged him, even in the last few minutes of our interview. He's breathing hard, and I hate to say it, but I feel a little nervous in front of him. I'm sat here seeing some of that old persona straining to come out – the media's devil-man. I am not sure what to say. I think changing the subject might be the best plan. But I'm flustered and blurt out something that I've been planning to build to.

—*Can I ask you something about* Through the Mocking Glass?
—Sure, go ahead.
—*Who are the black-eyed boys and girls in 'Dead-Eyed March'?*

There is a long and terrible silence. It goes on for one whole minute plus eight seconds; I know because I've checked the audio. It feels like a lot longer. In that time, Skexxixx glares at me, unblinking. I remember dropping my eyes and flushing with guilt, with shame. What did I expect him to say? To expand on the rumours that circulated about his own experiences with the black-eyed kids? These stories are the subject of online debate and theory the world over. As if he's just going to tell all to me, here and now ... And in that minute, a crushing voice inside me tells me that what I'm asking is simply stupid; that we all have our demons, our ghosts who follow us throughout our lives. Sometimes we can shake them, scatter them behind us like leaves, and sometimes we just have to endure them, allow them to stay attached to us like shadows on a dying day.
I wish I could eat my words. I wish I could take them back.
At last he looks up and speaks.

—I think you're asking the wrong kind of questions...

After this exchange, Skexxixx's UK publicist informs us our time is up. The man himself gets up and shuffles away, a single hand raised in farewell. He doesn't even look back.
I am left to return home and mull over what Skexxixx has told me.

I have sympathy for the man. I can't imagine what it's like to suffer the death of a child and then to have that used as ammunition to bait you; to be blamed and punished simply because you are in the public eye. I can, however, empathise with his experience of online abuse. After episode five went out, the abuse I received on social media became impossible to control, and that's why the Six Stories *Twitter account has been shut down and I no longer administrate the Facebook page. Like Skexxixx says, when they tell you that you deserve to die, a little part of you believes it.*

As a result, a rather large part of me now understands why someone like Arla might have felt such an affinity with an artist like Skexxixx. We often forget that a singer, a writer, a celebrity, is a person too. Buried beneath the image is a person who feels the same rejection as the rest of us. I wonder if Skexxixx knows how much solace, how much comfort, his music must have provided to Arla, how it must have made her feel. I hope he hears this and I hope I can assure him that, while listening to his music, Arla Macleod and many others felt that perhaps they were not so alone in the world. I wonder how knowing this would make him feel.

§§

So far this series, we have been looking at the case of Arla Macleod – the Macleod Massacre of 2014. As I mentioned at the beginning of this episode, I am fully aware of the reports concerning Arla's suicide in Elmtree Manor. It is not my place to discuss the perceived failings of the system, or of Arla's doctors, therapists and the other staff who were responsible for her. The inquest about her death is ongoing, as far as I'm aware. But I'm also aware of the new pressure that this has placed on me in my reporting of the case. Because her death begs a number of questions; why did Arla agree to talk to me in the first place? Was Arla allowed access to this podcast? And if so, why? From what I can gather, Elmtree Manor is careful about what kinds of media it allows its patients to have. For example, any news reports are used only to stimulate discussion, not just piped in to fill the silence. And patients' therapists work with their families and use their discretion to decide what media they can be exposed to.

Doctor-patient confidentiality means it has proved impossible to find out whether it was deemed appropriate for her to listen to Six Stories. If she was, maybe it was part of her therapy? We'll never know.

There's a lot of speculation around this issue. I have made myself available to the police, should they want to discuss anything they deem relevant to the case.

But we must move on. We must conclude this sorry tale. For this, the final episode of the series, will attempt to tie up at least some of the loose ends and give us a degree of closure in the case of Arla Macleod.

If that's possible.

※※

I talked to Skexxixx at the start of the episode about what's known as 'trolling'.

Trolls often like to stress that the reasons behind their taunting and harassment of people online is simply about humour. However, in recent times, the rise of the troll's darker purposes – such as those described by Skexxixx and countless other people in the public eye – has become more prominent.

An academic study in Canada surveyed a group of people who fit the troll archetype – male with an average age of twenty-nine – about their online behaviour. The study showed that, of the fifty-nine percent of these men who actively comment on websites, a tenth said that 'trolling' other users was their preferred behaviour. The study also found that enjoyment of trolling is associated with sadism – the pleasure taken in causing pain to others, which is often seen in sex offenders and serial killers. For me, this finding makes a degree of sense.

Common advice online is 'Don't feed the trolls'. Like with playground bullies such a tactic denies trolls the reaction they're looking for. And so far, that has been working for me – online at least. However, the vicious text messages and threats I have been receiving go way beyond simple trolling, making me wonder what exactly it is that my personal troll wants.

I have asked several times on this show for an open dialogue with the troll who was threatening me, but my efforts have been to no avail. I thought that the interview with Skexxixx might offer me some sort of motive for their continued harassment, but it didn't. However, I have recently begun to empathise with Skexxixx – meaning I understand his desire to disappear. With Arla Macleod's suicide, publicity around this series has been kicked up a big notch. However, like Skexxixx I have turned down all media interviews, trying to keep myself as far as possible from the public eye.

In fact, out of respect for her dead family, for everyone affected by the actions of Arla Macleod, and because the harassment I was receiving was getting ever more vicious, I nearly decided to cut this season short – to apologise and vanish for a while. Leave the end of this series splintered like the edge of a broken stick. Or a bone.

But then I got a phone call.

And everything changed.

§§

The following interview took a little while to edit.

The following interview did not take place on my terms.

I'll be honest and tell you I was in two minds whether to put it out at all. But, as Six Stories' *focus must always remain on the case at hand, I have decided that I will air it.*

As I've said many times before, Six Stories *is not about me. My interviewee, however, has made it that way – making this particular series more about me than I am, or ever would be, comfortable with.*

By contrast, I am not allowed to identify my interviewee. Apparently he's a big deal in the dark recesses of the internet, but I haven't heard of him. I guess that shows how much I know. Maybe it also shows my age.

If I were to reveal the name of this person, I will apparently be 'doxxed'. This means that my personal details, address, phone number – everything about me – will be shared online. It is not for egotistical reasons that I don't want this to happen. It is simply that, if just anyone can find me, I will be exposed to significant personal risk. I have been

shown that this person somehow really does know everything about me.
So it is on his terms that our interview progresses.
   Yet I cannot and will not hide my disgust. The 'free speech' that my
interviewee waxes lyrical about gives me that right. So I will refer to him
henceforth as only what he is: a troll. Nothing more.

   —Our first … sorry, *my* first trophy was the king of self-pitying
narcissism himself. The man who names himself, aptly, after a
puppet in a film – Skexxixx.
   —*What do you mean by 'trophy'?*
   —It made the news. So…
   —*So?*
   —So I won a prize.
   —*Which was?*
   —Which was none of your business.
   —*I spoke to Skexxixx personally, in the flesh. I know the effect that it*
had on him, what you and your followers did. How heroic and coura-
geous of you.
   —My heart bleeds for the little snowflake. I hope he took a long,
relaxing soak in a bath of fifty-pound notes. I'm sure he's devas-
tated. The guy's made ridiculous money – from suing newspapers
and churches, I may add, rather than his vapid attempt at music.
   —*You were making jokes about his stillborn baby. You – and whoever*
your harem was – were relentlessly attacking him for no reason. I've seen
the things you all wrote.
   —Oh Christ, open your eyes, sheeple, the grief-hungry media are
desperate to promote people like him to propel awful examples of
humanity to some sort of god-like status. It's pathetic.
   —*I'm sorry, what? This was about his child.*
   —It wasn't though. It was about the media portraying him as a
victim. He was an advocate of being 'broken' wasn't he? – 'Embrace your
nothing', being 'empty', that was his whole aesthetic, right? But only
when it suited him. Only to get more publicity. I'm glad he wasn't able
to have a child to be honest. What would that kid have grown up like?

—*Why Skexxixx though?*

—It was easy, to be fair. People like him are asking for it. A washed-up rock star who's supposed to be controversial now doing good in a vain attempt to raise his shattered profile. I had to show his deluded 'fans' that he was actually 'nothing'. His charity world, it was all a sham.

—*But what did any of it have to do with you?*

—I was tired of him, tired of arguing with his devotees. They all thought he was some sort of deity from another dimension. It was pathetic. Don't get me wrong, he highlighted issues. But someone like him was not the right messenger. Someone else should have done it. The thing with people like him is that he liked to promote mental illness as somehow fashionable. Look at all the forums dedicated to discussing his puerile lyrics, his second-rate Alice Cooper image. His whole message was that a broken person is far more interesting than someone who's getting help. People like him use their influence to perpetuate people's problems. It's sick. There are vulnerable people out there who believed the rubbish he wrote about things from other worlds.

Leave people's brains to the professionals.

—*You mean people like you?*

—I didn't say that. You said that.

—*Would you agree though?*

—It's not for me to say. I'm not a rockstar, I'm just a voice for those who feel underrepresented.

—*OK, if that's what you proclaim, why not express it in a constructive way instead of trolling people? That just seems a little vulgar, a little immature.*

—I'll express myself in whichever way I see fit. Sometimes you have to lower yourself to someone else's level in order to have a proper discussion with them.

—*It sounds like you engaged a lot with Skexxixx's own fans. Why even bother?*

—My point exactly. Free speech allows me to say whatever I like on whatever platform I choose.

—So you felt that you needed to 'shut down' someone like Skexxixx?

—Not someone like him; him. Entirely. And I did. We did. The more of those type of agendas we can shut down the better. That's the media; that's celebrities, musicians. All of them are obsessed with their own image, with how they come across to everyone else. Skexxixx thought he was controversial. Honestly, I've seen more controversy in a dishrag. He invited me and my followers to listen to him. He invited his own 'dead-eyed march'. And then he learned a lesson.

—Yes. I know. But you and your followers also got a man killed.

—Whoa, whoa there. Hold up. No. Show me the evidence for that. Show me the evidence that I got someone killed.

—You sent the details of a man to a paedophile hunting group who then wrongly accused him of chatting online to children. He subsequently commi—

—Stop right there. I didn't do a thing … personally. And I asked you to show me the evidence.

—Why Albert Marsh though? Why him? What did he do that you know and I don't?

—I have no idea.

—You sent me a text telling me that this is what you are capable of. You don't possibly mean you did that solely to taunt me.

—If I did it at all … You see, you don't have any evidence whatsoever to connect me to that.

—I have the text messages.

—That someone sent you from a number that isn't this one. That wasn't me. I'll tell you something for nothing, and that's that you're starting to piss me off.

—My heart bleeds.

—Don't get cocky with me. I promise you, if you keep going, you won't enjoy the consequences. The problem is, I know everything about you, but you know only what I choose to tell you about me.

—It doesn't take a genius to work out who you are. Your on-screen alias isn't foolproof.

—True, but the thing is, I can make your life incredibly difficult. If someone was to doxx you, Scott, it's like a plague – like fleas or bedbugs. If the internet turns on you, it's impossible to escape. You don't want that to happen. You don't want to suffer what is called, I believe, a 'consciousness mob' like our friend Skexxixx, do you?

—*What on earth is that supposed to mean?*

—Allegedly it's an organisation of like-minded people who like to subvert – to make people think.

—*Like a flash mob? Controversial.*

—No, idiot. Like people who are sick of being served up the same old bullshit actually fighting back.

—*For example?*

—For example, you remember the 'killer clown' thing a couple years back – people dressing up as clowns and scaring the fuck out of the general public? It was worldwide, it was organised, it was orchestrated. That, my friend, was a 'consciousness mob'.

—*And what, pray tell, was the point of that exactly? A vulgar display of power?*

—I wonder how you would cope if it was happening to you? If the world as you know it began to close in around you and there was nothing you could do? What do you think might be the next one Scott – the next 'consciousness mob'?

—*How about BEKs – black-eyed kids? Your followers would only need some novelty contact lenses. Some masks. Some clothes from the dress-up box.*

—You said it Scott, not me.

—*Why did you call me? Why did you want to appear on* Six Stories?

—Think of it as a favour. What exactly were you going to put in this final episode? Whose story were you going to tell? You had nothing and I stepped in to save you. You should be thanking me.

—*What do you have to do with Arla Macleod?*

—I'm talking about you.

—*Me?*

—The thing is, with these sorts of stories, the sheep don't make the news, the wolves do.

—*Is that what you're after? Fame? This seems like a pretty messed-up way to get it.*

—The thing is, I know they'll probably catch me – the authorities, whatever. Like you say, it doesn't take a genius to track me down. But whatever happens, even if they do find evidence they can pin on me, at least I'll be remembered. I am only one head of the monster.

—*That's a very interesting thing to say.*

—I'm an interesting guy.

—*Can I ask you some more questions?*

—If you must.

—*I am fully aware of what you are capable of. But what I'd like to do is get a bit more insight into you.*

—Oh, really? Do you want to see if I was raped as a kid? Bullied? That sort of thing? That would fit your agenda, wouldn't it?

—*I don't have an agenda. I want to know more about the … What is it, the thing that you do?*

—You mean enlightening people online. OK…

—*How did it … I mean how did you start? I'm just asking for a little bit of history. Like you say, who else am I going to get on the show? So this is your moment, why not take it?*

—Oh, that's easy. I started out of boredom really. Remember bad dial-up internet in the nineties? There. I started going into chat rooms – you remember those, right? Full of stupid children. Anonymous, no real security. I just used to mess with people for sport. Like hunting. I'd start out by logging in with a girl's name. If you did that, you'd get a shitload of messages from lonely old perverts. 'ASL?' – remember that? I always said I was seventeen, something like that. I used to string them along until, inevitably, they'd ask to 'cyber', which back then meant badly spelled sexual fantasies. I used to wait till they'd told me they'd come and then tell them I was a guy. It was hilarious. They used to get so angry, so upset. Those were my first trophies. So, it was either that or just 'pwning noobs' as the kids used to say – picking a target and going for them. Pretty soon I had loads of trophies. I had people who looked up to me on there, who emulated me. But I was always the best. It wasn't even difficult to be good at it. You just needed a bit of something about you. Most people online actually don't have that. I found that I could use this influence on other people, start waking people up.

—*You spent a lot of time online in your formative years?*

—Yeah. Yeah, I did. I was smart enough to see that the internet was a massive fucking thing, that it would begin consuming people's lives. Does that make me a social retard like them? No. Look at kids today – look at their fucking parents. How many times do you see little Jimmy shouting, 'Play with me, Mum. Play with me, Dad.' And what are Mum and Dad doing? Staring at their phones. You know what message that sends? Do you have any idea? That message is that this – this Facebook post, this tweet, this careful way I'm sculpting myself online; this precise fucking picture of a happy family I'm painting to get one up on my other parent followers – all of this, little Jimmy, is more important than you. So what happens? What happens to little Jimmy? Mum and Dad don't want to play, so they shove a tablet or a phone in front of little Jimmy and it becomes a pseudo-parent. Do you think that a fucking tablet can stand in for parental love? What sort of a kid does that turn out? Just today, this very morning, I passed a woman walking along, pushing a buggy – one kid in there, the other one she had by the hand; he couldn't keep up with her. He was stumbling, tripping. And you know what she was doing? You guessed it – staring at her phone. I saw him drop his toy – some sort of teddy or something. Mum didn't even see it, and they just carried on. The kid's face – he was destroyed, utterly destroyed. And she's just pulling him along, no doubt posting shit about what a good fucking mother she is on Facebook.

I watched for a bit. I watched the kid. He went from upset and crying to a sort of … blankness, like he knew that nothing or no one was going to come to his aid. He must have only been about three. That kid's growing up messed-up. Angry. I can guarantee it.

—Do you have children? You sound old enough.

—Let me think about that for a second. Oh yeah, none of your fucking business.

—Fine. It's just either you had a terrible time as a kid, or you have kids yourself. That's how it sounds.

—We're talking about terrible parents whose kids grow up numb, blank. Not mine.

—All of this, it makes me think of attachment theory – of Harlow's monkey experiments. Was that what it was like for you? Taunting defenceless animals to earn your 'trophies'?

—Maybe you're not as stupid as I thought. A-level psychology at least. There was a similar experiment; have you heard of the 'still-face' study? That was Edward Tronick in the seventies. Basically, within three minutes of a mother not moving her face, not responding to her baby, the baby starts getting distressed. Three fucking minutes! I think that's very fucking relevant these days, don't you? Mum or Dad staring at their phone – that's a blank face. Even at kids' concerts, football matches, that sort of thing. Imagine looking up to see if Mum or Dad is watching you and all you see is a phone; how's that encouragement? You should do anything for your fucking kids, *any-thing*. No matter what. You should protect them by whatever means.

I'll summarise the 'monkey experiments' I mention for you. Harry Harlow, a psychologist studying attachment theory, conducted experiments on rhesus monkeys in the 1950s, taking them from their mothers at birth and placing them in a cage with only a food-dispensing wire mesh figure. The effects of this were horrific, leaving the monkeys psychologically and developmentally damaged. When the wire-mesh 'mothers' were coated in terry cloth but did not supply food, the monkeys clung to them and cuddled them, particularly when they were frightened, suggesting the need for affection was deeper than the need for food.

Tronick's 'still-face' experiment is used these days to test degrees of attachment in infants. What I am interested in is why the troll seems to be so agitated, so knowledgeable about such things.

—You know quite a bit about this subject.

—It's called not being a fucking moron. Next.

—It makes me wonder if your mission, as it were – your whole moti-
vation for this … this 'waking up' of people by trolling them – comes
from somewhere personal.

—You've tried this angle. It didn't work. Put it this way: vegans
are pretty easy to troll – throw an 'mmm, bacon' gif up after some
video about the meat industry then sit back and watch the butthurt
in all its glory. Does that mean I have some unresolved issue about
animals?

—I don't know, do you?

—This is getting tiresome.

—Where would you like to go then?

—Well, you asked where this came from; you asked where it
started, so I've told you. So after my first successes, I started trolling
forums. The best ones were mums' groups, 'concerned parents', that
sort of thing. It was fun for a while, until they kicked me off.

—Wow. Big of you.

—In your words, Scott, those years were formative. I had followers by then. I'd realised how simple it was to exert influence. We
swamped those Skexxixx forums – filled them will all sorts of nonsense. People believed it though; those blind idiots fell for it hook,
line and sinker. All I was trying to do was show them how simple-
minded they were, how easily led.

—Is that the point then? Change? You want to make people be …
what? More aware?

—Are you happy with the way the world is? Would you want it
this way for your kids?

—My opinion doesn't matter right now…

—To be fair, that's true.

I have searched and found particular examples of Mr Troll's early
work that google has archived, and he's right, it's pretty juvenile stuff.
But there's a lot of it and reading for long enough, you can see why

people flock to him. He's certainly a little more intelligent, a little more charismatic than the others. I get the feeling he's older than he makes out. Yet, as you have seen, it does make me think about the BEKs – Arla's black-eyed kids. Was this something cooked up by our troll on the Skexxixx message boards? It's impossible to tell. I've heard of other people being terrorised in similar ways to how she claims she was throughout her life. I also think about Skexxixx. I wonder if one of these 'mobs' was sent after him? For now, I let Mr Troll carry on.

—You won't believe me, but at the heart of it, I was trying to help people, make the world better for the next generation. But it was futile. No one wanted hope, they all wanted to be 'broken' somehow. All of them desperate to be more fucked-up than the others. Pathetic.

Now that all the kids are off Facebook, it's a lot more fun on there. Facebook is now a mass grave for old profiles, with elderly relatives who've only just discovered the site is all shouting about politics. And no one's listening ... except us. We're doing something about it.

—*And Twitter?*

—Twitter's good for celebrities – the ones that run their own accounts. You can tell who they are because they're so fucking vain they end up constantly searching their own names. I remember in the early days tweeting that I'd like to kill [*celebrity name bleeped out*] and he retweeted me. I hadn't even tagged him so he must have been searching for his own name. When I pointed this out, he deleted the tweet and blocked me, the fucking sap. They're so fucking precious about their image, their PR, it's infuriating. I mean they usually just block you, but when we mobbed Skexxixx, he went down like a fucking torpedoed battleship! That even made the news!

—*I guess I'm still wondering why you make so much effort. Aren't there better things to do with your time? You sound like an intelligent person. All this seems beneath you.*

—It teaches people a lesson, wakes them up. They'll laugh and then they'll think. Skexxixx certainly did. Look at him now, exposed and broken as the sad sack he now is. Now more and more will wake up to the fact that being depressed, being ill, isn't cool.

—*Sending vigilante paedophile hunters to someone's house is more than a prank. It's just … for me there's more to it than just a laugh. That's not just words on a screen. That's not awakening anyone.*

—They didn't kill him though, did they? He did it himself. Ask yourself why.

—*Because being publicly accused of something like that to millions of people online would have ruined his life?*

—The thing is, he didn't matter. A friendless, lonely old man. He gave himself as a sacrifice for the greater good.

—*Jesus Christ.*

—Not quite.

—*Another question then.*

—Fire away.

—*Why Arla Macleod?*

—Arla Macleod killed her family with a hammer in 2014. That wasn't me either. Arla Macleod was a spoiled, whining brat who killed her family, for fuck's sake. She should have been publicly crucified, yet she became a sort of sick hero, the face of a broken generation. She was fed and washed and medicated up to her fucking eyeballs, and you're saying the most important thing is my online behaviour? Arla Macleod deserved to rot for what she did. But instead a whole group of idiots aspired to be like her.

—*I'm calling bullshit. You're not that stupid.*

—Call what you want. And you're right, I'm not stupid. You have no idea what my position allows me to do. I can work where I like, with whom I like. It's called an education, a reputation – it opens doors. If I decide I want … access … to somewhere, to someone I can get it. No problem…

I've been interviewing people for long enough to note changes in the voice and pauses when things touch nerves, when something grinds an emotional gear. Maybe it's just me but with the mention of Arla

Macleod, the troll's voice speeds up just ever so slightly. His arrogance is tempered by a little ember of sourness. I know, though, that if I piss him off he'll vanish back under his rock at the dark bottom of the internet, so I am careful around this subject.

—So next question, then: Why have you and your … associates been hassling me ever since I started this series about the Macleod Massacre?

—Are you really that stupid? None of this has anything to do with Arla Macleod. It's all about you. The fact that you took on this case shoved you into the spotlight, moved you into our sights as it were. You're turning over stones that are better left alone. The thing is, Scott, you accuse me of rabble-rousing, but there are people you've mentioned on your podcast who have lives, careers – they've moved on, away from all that. But you're bringing it all up again. So aren't you exactly the same as me in the end?

—What do you get? What's your pay-off? Is it cash? I've heard that there's big money in trolling.

—Maybe so. Maybe it's more than money…

—Like what?

—Like influence. I've been trying to explain this to you this whole time. The more that people see what we're capable of, the more people will listen to us. It's about waking the world up. You're providing me with a platform and that simply spreads my influence. It's not just me. I am just the commander. We are legion.

And there follows an interminable diatribe about 'awakening' people, about the narcissism of the millennial generation, et cetera, et cetera.

However, I have a theory that sounds almost as conspiratorial. The troll's had his say – lots of say – so I want to have mine.

There was something I noticed while editing this interview. In fact I noticed it while it was going on, and you may have too. While my troll likes to pontificate on the stupidity of people generally, he has a particular vitriol reserved for parents and anyone who, in his eyes, promotes mental illness. Now, I'm no detective, no psychiatrist – pop psychology is about my level and is a criticism often levelled at my show. However, I've covered plenty of killers and I've read a lot of books so I know that there has to be a driving force, a reason behind doing what my troll is doing. It's more than just 'fun'. In particular I feel this whole idea of 'awakening' the world is a cheap concealer. It has to be.

So for what it's worth, here's my theory…

No. Actually, I'm going to let you hear how I described my theory during my interview with Mr Troll. See what you think.

—So, let's get this straight – your whole reason for contacting me was to get on this show and help build your media presence, correct? To perhaps recruit? Although why you chose me is a mystery. I'm small fry in terms of true-crime podcasting. But that follows your MO, I suppose: pick on the smaller people?

—Correct. Yes, it must be hard to swallow, but you matter very little in all this.

—And what happens if I decide to not add the audio of this interview at all to the podcast and instead turn you over to the police?

—We've been through this.

—I want you to say it again.

—Oh, for the recording? OK. So if the last episode of this series doesn't go out by the date I've specified, or you somehow manage to reveal my identity, then I have it on good authority you are to be doxxed. For the record, I don't want this to happen; I have not asked for it to happen; and if I find out who wants to commit such an act, I will beg them to stop.

—Bullshit. You know fine well who—

—I have shown you a screen grab from someone online who has your full name, address, place of work and family details on it.

—What if I say do it? Go on, doxx me.

—Then you'd be very stupid indeed. I've seen what happens to people who've been doxxed. You don't want that, Scott. Especially not you. Because you don't just deal in true crime – you talk to people involved; you create ripples. Remember the last series? It was a good one but I know as well as you do that there are people out there who'd love to know where you live. Or where your family live. Don't be stupid.

—*Fine. Can I ask you something else?*

—You can. But try and make it interesting this time.

—*Will you answer me honestly? Remember you get to decide which bits of this I broadcast.*

—Like I said. You can ask.

—*OK. So the Macleod Massacre – you knew that it's a controversial case that would thrust me into the limelight, but you also knew that Arla Macleod would speak to me. Why do you think she did?*

—I have no idea. And FYI, I didn't know she would. That just made it more convenient.

—*Here's what I think. I think you had access to Arla. I think you reached out to her and didn't get what you wanted – whatever twisted thing that was. I believe you helped her make contact with me. I think you planned this for a long time. This wasn't as opportunistic as you make out.*

—Think what you like.

—*I also think that you're responsible for her suicide.*

—Oooh – big words, cowboy. How do you get there?

—*It doesn't matter.*

—Tell me.

—*No.*

—Tell me or I'll … You know what'll happen.

—*Have you ever met Arla Macleod in person?*

—Why does that matter?

—*Because I think I know why she killed her family.*

—Yes. So do I. So does everyone: she was fucked up and spoiled and ultimately deserved to rot in jail. She got off lightly. I know how much you want it to be something else. And I know how much your ego was swollen by her request to talk to you.

—*Yes. I believe that too, to a degree. But I also think that something else happened. I believe that someone knew Arla Macleod online from the Skexxixx message boards, they knew enough about her to exert influence over her. I believe that, after she killed her family, someone believed the notoriety and internet fame she received was unjustified. I believe that someone wanted her dead. I believe that person was you. And I believe you did it to hide something. I think you understood that her death would overshadow the terrible thing that happened to Arla Macleod on holiday. I believe that you had something to do with it.*

—And where's your evidence?

—It's a theory.

—It's a good one. Imagine being a mother, a father, and knowing what happened to your daughter and doing nothing about it – or blaming her for it. The question it begs is whether they deserved it? Imagine being a parent and not bothering to protect your daughter. Imagine being a sister and caring so much about what people thought of you, about your outward appearance, that you'd manipulate your own parents and shift their attention onto yourself, for your own ends. Maybe they deserved to die too? Maybe Arla was a bullet through the Macleods' rotten hearts?

—You seem to know a lot about the Macleods. It's almost as if you knew one or more of them personally.

—Oh please, even the papers have speculated on this; it's hardly insider knowledge. And you're responsible for revealing plenty of the same on your show.

—Yes and I believe you used that as a … as a smokescreen to hijack this show and spread your agenda. You've ranted to me on this podcast against bad parenting, people being more interested in how they appear to others. I believe you have a reason for feeling that way. I believe you're carrying shame inside you … or guilt. I believe you were either there in Cornwall, when whatever happened to Arla happened, or you know more about it than you want to admit. I believe you had a closer relationship to Arla Macleod than you make out. Maybe you spoke to her when you were on those Skexxixx message boards all those years ago? Maybe you tried to help a lonely girl, maybe you were rebuffed?

—Oh please. You're full of pretty little theories. You can't prove anything.

—Maybe I can't. But if this isn't true, why don't you deny it? Surely being able to orchestrate something like this is a demonstration of your influence, your power? Surely if you did this you should be revelling in it, not hiding from it like a scared little boy. Because that's who you are inside, isn't it? That's who drives all this? A frightened little boy. I believe you probably did have something happen to you – something that would besmirch your reputation, something that left some emptiness inside you, some whirling, black, empty hole that cries out inside you, that drives you to do this shit. That's why you hated Skexxixx so much; you saw him give hope to empty people like you; you saw his own emptiness and, for whatever reason, you hated it. The same with Arla. For whatever reason, people looked up to her after she did what she did, and you couldn't stand that. Who are you, really?

—That doesn't matter.

—It does matter. Of course it matters. People are dead and I believe their deaths are directly or indirectly your fault. I think you're now after me because I've turned over the stone you hide under. Like all cowards, you're running away.

—You're telling me that I am that influential, that I can cause people to die – that's high praise indeed. But did I cast the fatal blow? I think not.

—I'm also saying it won't be difficult to find you and prove what you've done. Tell me who you are! Tell me here and you'll get your notoriety. You'll get what you want.

—It doesn't matter who I am. You are as stupid as the rest of the sheep. You can put all your effort into finding me, exposing me, then finding the evidence you need to prosecute me; you might even turn the tables and try to doxx me. You can do all of those things but in the end it doesn't matter. None of it. You see, behind me, there are thousands more vying for my position, vying to be top dog. It's like a hydra, Scott; every head you cut off, two more grow in their places. And we're everywhere – hiding, waiting. You'll never ever stop us. If you try, there'll be repercussions and you know it.

—So if it doesn't matter, tell me. Tell me who you are…

—Goodbye Scott.

§§

Cruelly, frustratingly, infuriatingly, our call ended there. He hung up. I tried calling back but I imagine it was another burner phone that he'd immediately thrown away. For all of his cheesy super-villain talk, he's educated, experienced, careful and ultimately a coward.

It's a sorry end to what I thought might just be a breakthrough. I am left with no definitive answer in the case of Arla Macleod – only theories and more questions.

This is not a whodunit – we know who dun it. What we don't know for sure is why. That's why I took on the case of Arla Macleod – to discuss, to theorise, to speculate on what caused a young woman to do what she did, then to reach out to a show like this.

I believe that somehow, Arla's family found out what happened to her in Cornwall and – for the sake of her mother's narcissism, her stepfather's piety and her sister's public reputation – did nothing. I believe all of these elements had their part in the family's decision-making, to whatever end. I also firmly believe that somewhere, some way, our troll had his grimy hand in proceedings.

The official line is that Arla Macleod was suffering from psychosis. She killed her family during a psychotic break. This appears likely, but I believe this psychosis was induced or exacerbated by what happened to her in Cornwall. But who did that terrible thing to her? What exactly happened that night? And why did no one outside the family tell?

I don't know. I don't know if we'll ever know. There are too many loose threads, too many questions…

And now I'm frightened. I don't know how much more I can say, lest I be doxxed.

But what worries me most is that this series becomes a springboard for our troll, sending him to where he wants to be. I don't want him to eclipse the sad tale of Arla Macleod. I don't want his hatred of the enigma she has become to be the main point of this investigation. That's why I will not name him. I will not give him any excuse. Although I don't believe he is a man of his word, so I presume that he will have me doxxed anyway.

So where does this leave us in the sixth episode, on the last inch of our path?

The answer is that I'm not sure. All I know is that, like Skexxixx, I will have to think about vanishing for a little while, disappearing under my rock, working out how to step up my own personal security.

And where does it leave us with the late Arla Macleod? I wonder if, like the troll, Arla used my podcast too. For her, maybe it was a way to reach out and try to explain, one final time why, she did what she did.

All I can say is that here, at the end of episode six, we truly have the essence of what Six Stories *is about.*

And that's not me, not Skexxixx or the troll. It's not even about Arla. It's about you – your thoughts, your theories, your opinion of what happened to Arla Macleod and why she killed her family in 2014.

I hate myself for having to say this, but I feel like I can no longer watch as you discuss, theorise, debate and sway in your various directions around these cases like so much corn beneath the wind.

I will stop speaking now, and leave it up to you. All I can hope is that if anything changes with regards to this case, I can add something, an update of sorts that might feed your discussions. A seventh story, if you like.

Until then though, this has been our last.

And I have been, as always, Scott King.

Farewell.

Six Stories: An Update

Audio extract from a news report on BBC Radio 5 Live
A doctor at a controversial psychiatric unit has today
been arrested.

Dr Jonathan Barrington, former therapist to Arla
Macleod, who killed her family in 2014, has been found
guilty of breaking patient confidentiality laws by publishing audio records of Macleod's therapy sessions
online. Barrington will almost definitely face expul-
sion from the GMC and a hefty jail sentence.

Audio extracts of the sessions were leaked onto several
torrent sites before being deleted. However, they are
now reappearing in the dimmest corners of the dark web as
swiftly as they were taken down. *YouTube*, *Twitter*, *Facebook* and other social media sites say that anyone caught
posting these audio files will be prosecuted and banned
for life. Other, more obscure areas of the internet are
proving more difficult to police, however.

Barrington, when asked why he had released the recordings, an action sure to have ruined his career, answered
only, 'I had to.' He would not elaborate further. Barrington's son, a recent émigré, was unavailable for
comment about his father's crimes.

Among countless malicious communications found on
Barrington's hard drive, the personal details of Scott
King, host of true-crime podcast *Six Stories*, were
also found. Threats to 'doxx' or share online Mr King's
personal details were also recovered. Whether these
details were indeed shared is not yet known.

King was involved in documenting the case of Arla Macleod on his podcast series but has since shunned all media activity and was unavailable for comment on these findings.

The trial continues.

※※

Welcome back to an extra episode of Six Stories, *for a short while, at least.*

I'm Scott King.

The only audio that remains of Dr Jonathan Barrington's sessions is buried deep in a dark place online, shared by a name I will not reveal. By now, you'll all understand why.

What I can say is that Dr Barrington is clearly my troll. And he's clearly worked long and hard to become the focus, the centre of attention in the case of Arla Macleod. He's worked to bring the Macleod Massacre back into the spotlight. And he's used me to do this. But I also think that Barrington's agenda towards Arla Macleod goes beyond simply hijacking the case, and using it as a stepping stone to notoriety. As I told him during our interview in episode six, I think he has something to do with Arla – some personal motive. Some connection that prompted him somehow, through some means, to have himself appointed as Arla's personal therapist. I believe, like I said to him, he's covering for someone.

As I'm sure you do, I have my theories about why Barrington did what he did ... and might have done. All I have to work with, though, is what I know – what I have presented in these six episodes. And from these threads, the frayed edges of this whole mess, I try to build my ideas.

I believe that Barrington, in his quest to turn the 'broken' generation away from Skexxixx's message of embracing emptiness, discovered that he held a lot of sway over these young, lost and impressionable people who spend so much of their time online. I believe he may even have encountered *Arla herself in a chat room or on a forum. Certainly, in those long hours spent alone while her mother and father watched Alice training, Arla was at the mercy of whoever she came across on the internet. And then later, after Arla killed her family, perhaps Barrington saw rearing up, Hydra-like, around her the same sentiment as had surrounded Skexxixx.*

Perhaps I'm in no position to comment. Perhaps I am as guilty as him of using the case of Arla Macleod — of using all of the cases I cover — for my own ends.

But in here lies a paradox — he knew that if Arla died, she would become a martyr. Look online now and those pictures of teenage Arla are everywhere again — her defiant image is, yet again, two fingers to a society of conformity. That's what I don't understand. He has done precisely what he's worked against for all this time.

When I started out I wondered if I was going to get any resolution to the Macleod Massacre. Usually I delve into cold cases, try and get a fresh perspective on something that happened a long time ago, get different perspectives on a long-forgotten death.

I rake over old graves.

This whole series, though, has been opportunistic from the off. I didn't know what I was going to do when I sent that request to Elmtree Manor to see if Arla Macleod wanted to talk. I was just throwing my hat into the ring as I sincerely believe in not passing up opportunities when they present themselves. This was one of those opportunities and, like any case, it leaves us with questions whose answers have been lost, forgotten, carried to whatever place that comes after death.

Only the Macleods will know what really happened that night in 2014 and maybe only one of them will really know why.

But that's reality, unfortunately. That's what happens in most cases. There's no final resolution, no twist, no nice tying together of loose threads. Brutal cases leave gaping, open wounds, some that will never heal. That's how life works. There's a smokescreen that Dr Barrington has brought down entirely on purpose — and it's thick and inpenetrable.

And it's within this fog that we will end.

There's little more I can do here save for re-treading the same roads. I have nothing more I can reveal.

Barrington told me that when one troll vanishes two will sprout up in its place. I find myself accepting this. Accepting that there's no place for me to go anymore where some troll won't follow. All roads lead to me having my pale and vulnerable underbelly exposed by someone who has a vendetta against me, or is, as Barrington told me, using me to gain leverage.

He's certainly done that himself. When this final update airs, it will grant him the notoriety he craves, the profile he desires, the attention that he needs to fill whatever gaping wound is inside him. But hasn't he already achieved that? He's all over the media now, after all. Maybe that's what he wanted, to become a bigger mystery than Skexxixx, than Arla. Maybe he's done just that and this nagging feeling I have that there's something beneath is just me looking too deep.

What I really hope is that one day he finds some peace, that ultimately, he realises that behaving this way only accentuates this emptiness, and that whatever satisfaction he gains will only be fleeting. That he'll never be able to mend the fracture he may have been part of causing.

As for Arla, her story is over. Angel; Tessa; Paulette, Anthony and Skexxixx – their stories will be left in the balance, to be speculated upon.

Mine too.

As I've said before, I will seek to disappear, to take cover from the glare of the internet, the media, even my own fans. This case has rattled me, it has changed me, has made me cautious.

Whether Six Stories *will return is uncertain. If it does, I think my own face is the first thing I will hide.*

But I will remain, for now, Scott King.

This has been our last.

TorrentWraith – Audio (Music & Sounds)

Type	Name
Audio	**Arla Macleod Rec006 [320KBPS]** Uploaded **2 hours** ago, Size 32.4 MiB. ULed by JBazzzzz666

—*What happened when they found out, Arla?*

—It were … it were so hard. Alice had told me that it'd be OK – that they'd understand. She said that I just had to sit them down and tell them … about Cornwall. I were so scared . I was looking at Alice, but she wasn't saying anything. She was just staring at me, blank-faced. So I explained what happened to me that night. I told them what those lads did. I broke down crying. I were sobbing … sobbing so hard. I could feel all the hurt trickling out of me, with my words, my tears. I knew it were a good idea to tell them, and I were starting to feel better. But then, when I looked up, they was all just gone.

—*Gone?*

—They'd all just got up and left the room – even Alice. She said they'd understand, her boyfriend had begged her to say something. He'd said that you shouldn't keep these things bottled up. Families, mams and dads, they'd understand, they'd help. He'd been through bad times and his parents had helped him. They were all disgusted with me. We never talked about it again. They never mentioned it.

—*Did you ever try talking about it with them?*

—No. I knew. I knew how it would make them look, what they would look like to everyone if folk found out. Alice was about to skyrocket with her swimming. If there'd been a fuss, if people found out about what happened to me I would have ruined all that too. Mam said I'd nearly ruined Alice's career when I were a teenager with all my nonsense. So I just shut up and didn't mention it again.

That were the night I heard *them* crying the first time. That's when I saw *them* shuffling down the path at the back of the garden.

–Your parents?

—No. The black-eyed kids. It were like all that hurt, all that pain had drib-
bled out of me and turned into something else.

I thought it would help!

*—I think Alice's boyfriend was right that talking always helps. Why do you
think your family reacted in that way?*

—I don't know, I never felt nothing after that. I never felt nothing.

—What would you tell fifteen-year-old Arla? How would you soothe her?

—I don't know. What did you tell your son when he was fifteen? When he
felt bad? How did you make him feel better?

—Arla. You know we can't be personal here.

—He must be a lucky boy to have you as a dad.

*—You protect your kids, you should protect your children. Whatever mistakes
they make, whatever stupid and terrible things they do … you should … I'm
sorry… [Pause] Let's bring her into the room. That young girl. Let's bring in fifteen-
year-old Arla, shall we?*

—No. I hate doing this, I really hate it.

—Let's imagine fifteen-year-old Arla's here. Sat in the chair over here.

[*Silence*]

—What do you feel towards that young girl?

—Anger. Just … I'm angry with her.

—Why do you think that is? Why are you angry with her?

—[*Indistinguishable – sobbing*] … fucking known better!

—She was fifteen. She was a girl.

—I'd never even had…

—'She'd' never even had…

—Sorry … yes; she'd never even had a boyfriend before. She lived her life
online, talking about Skexxixx for God's sake!

*—So how was she to know, that fifteen-year-old girl? She was naive, she was
young, inexperienced.*

[*Sobbing*]

—*What would older Arla say to her, to that little, naive, inexperienced girl?
What would older Arla say to make her feel better. Not to punish her, she's been
through enough.*

—I don't know.

—*Had young Arla ever known forgiveness?*

—I … sorry, she were always being told she were no good, that she
should be more like Alice.

—*What do you think that did to her?*

—I … it … I know that it … it made her want to be more like her sister –
her prettier, successful sister; her sister who everyone liked more; her sister
who didn't play stupid games. That's all she were doing, that's all. She were
just trying to be like her. So when Alice told her there were a party, that those
lads had invited them, of course she wanted to go! She should have stayed
though. Oh God, she should have stayed and finished it! She should have
stayed and closed it!

—*What do you mean, closed it?*

—The … the ritual. She should have closed it! That's why all this happened … [*Hysterical sobbing*] … That's why they're here. That's why they're
here right now. They're always here!

—*OK, OK. What was it that young Arla did? What is it that she should have
done?*

—The … the ritual. The Hooded Man! You see, when you do that, when
you open up the worlds like that, it lets things in. It lets things in and … Oh
God I…

—*'She'…*

—Yes, sorry, she … When she got back, she felt so dirty, so dirty, she just
lay there in bed – dirty, filthy … just lay there instead of closing the ritual, and
that's why they came. That's why they've been following her…

—*What about Alice? Did she know what had happened to young Arla? Did
she know what they did to her?*

—She knew, but she couldn't tell. She'd never tell. She told young Arla
that night that she'd never tell cos of what Mam would do. Cos Mam would
blame them both and it would only make things worse. Dad would think
they had devils inside them and he'd kick them out the house. She would

ruin it for Alice. Alice was the one doing it right. Alice was taking her chance and Arla … she couldn't ruin that for her. So young Arla, she just held on to it. All this time, she's been holding on to it.

—*Does … does young Arla ever want justice? Does young Arla want those people to pay for what they did?*

—Yes.

—*What about older Arla – Arla who knows that she was taken advantage of? Does she want it made right?*

—I don't know. I can't feel … I can't feel it anymore. I just want them to go away. The dancing boys, the kids, the black-eyed kids. Why can't they just take me? Why?

—*Who are the dancing boys, Arla?*

—They were just dancing with me at first. Then … then they started *doing* things to me. I were screaming at them. Oh God, I were screaming at them to stop. I were begging for them to stop, but they just kept going. They were hurting me! It were hurting so bad and I were screaming and they wouldn't stop! They were laughing and they wouldn't stop…

—*What were their names, Arla? Can you tell me their names?*

—What? It doesn't matter. Why does it matter?

—*Please Arla. Their names, please try.*

—I remember one of them was called Kyle; he was the one. He were dancing. They were all dancing and laughing – even afterwards … like I didn't matter. Like I was nothing.

[*Indistinguishable – sobbing and movement*]

—*Arla, we can make this right. We can make all of this go away.*

—You can't! You can't make it right! No one can! No one can anymore! It's done!

—*I'm sorry Arla.*

[*Long silence, punctuated by faint sobs and heavy breathing*]

—You don't need to be sorry, Doctor. It's not like *you* did anything.

I'm OK. I'm fine. I'll be fine.

—*I'm truly sorry. I'm so sorry.*

—Doctor? What's the matter?

—*I'm going to tell you something, Arla. A long time ago my son came to me, just like you came to your parents and he told me about something he'd done. Something he couldn't keep inside himself any longer. He told me he knew I would understand. Because of what I did for a living, he knew I'd be able to help him.*

—Why did you become a doctor, a therapist, whatever? Why did you want to help people like me? Put broken people back together again?

—*I've always believed, Arla, that people can be put right. My son … let's say he had some problems, began hanging around with bad people, terrible people. Let's say those people got inside his head, made him do bad things, terrible things. Let's say I knew that there was good inside him, despite what he'd done. Let's say I knew I could help him. Give him a new start somewhere else, cover his tracks. You can always try to put wrong things right.*

—Is that what you tell your son, Doctor? Is that what you tell him when he does stupid things? Do you tell him it'll be alright? No one ever told me it'll be alright.

—*I told my son a long time ago that it'd be alright.*

I told him, 'Kyle, I'll do anything to protect you. That if anyone starts digging around, I'll show the world that there are worse things than the things you've done, that there are people out there who've done much, much worse things than you. I'll do anything to show people that. Even if it means the end of me. Anything.'

And that's what I did.

That's what I have done.

THE END

'Bold, clever and genuinely chilling with a terrific twist that provides an explosive final punch' Deidre O'Brien, *Sunday Mirror*

'A genuine genre-bending debut' Carla McKay, *Daily Mail*

'Weolowski evokes the ominous landscape and eerie atmosphere of the area with sharp, direct prose …There is more than a whiff of modern horror here, and *The Blair Witch Project* feels like a touchstone, but the meat of the story is the typically fractious and fraught relationships between the teenagers struggling to find their place in the world and their role within society. Impeccably crafted and gripping from start to finish' Doug Johnstone, *Big Issue*

'With a unique structure, an ingenious plot and so much suspense you can't put it down, this is the very epitome of a must-read' *Heat*

'Wonderfully horrifying … the suspense crackles' James Oswald

'*Six Stories* is a stunning literary thriller with a killer ending. This is going to be in my top ten books of the year, for sure' Liz Loves Books

'Wonderfully atmospheric. Matt Wesolowski is a skilled storyteller with a unique voice. Definitely one to watch' Mari Hannah

'Dark, mysterious and definitely not without elements of horror, I was more than a little unsettled while I read it. A genre-bending book, with some hauntingly threatening prose … I could not put it down. Highly recommended!' Bibliophile Book Club

'A stunning piece of writing – chock full of atmosphere, human insight and beautiful writing. Take a note of this guy's name. He's going to be huge!' Michael J. Malone

'A complex and subtle mystery, unfolding like dark origami to reveal the black heart inside' Michael Marshall Smith

'Original, inventive and brilliantly clever' Fiona Cummins

'For fans of thrills, chills and an up-to-date take on the darker side of society' J.S. Collyer

'A tight, claustrophobic mystery' David F. Ross

'A remarkable debut from a fine new fictional voice' Shelley Day

'Sharp as a butcher's knife, cutting straight through to the nerve of its reader. A read-in-one-sitting experience that will surely inspire many authors to explore new methods of narration' Bleach House Library

'Pulsating with life, with characters who are so incredibly realistic and a plot that is both haunting and terrifying, *Six Stories* is bang up to the minute, relevant and fresh. This is a book that knocks the breath out of the reader … An absolute triumph and highly recommended' Random Things through My Letterbox

'Current, fresh and skillfully delivered … Matt Wesolowski has built up a dark, atmospheric setting with his vivid, descriptive prose. The voices were so distinctive that I felt like I was listening to a podcast rather than simply reading the transcript' Off-the-Shelf Books

'A quirky, but extremely well-written thriller … *Six Stories* scores extremely well in the dialogue and authenticity of the interviews … a very clever concept' Trip Fiction

'The literary equivalent of dark metal – gritty, dark, often shocking, and always exciting. A masterful debut' Kati Hiekkapelto

'Chilling, beautiful, addictive, dark, haunting and utterly magical. There's a constant thread of menace and chill' Louise Beech

'This is one of the best novels I've read this year, perhaps in memory' *Nudge* Books

'Its plotting, pacing and unique content make it one of the most impressive books I've read recently. Wesolowski is a major new talent in crime fiction, and I cannot wait to see what he does next' Crime by the Book

'A new style of mystery, one that encapsulates the twenty-first century, the internet, and social media … a dazzling fictional mystery' Foreword Reviews

Acknowledgements

My gratitude extends to all those who made this book possible – as well as much else beyond: Sarah Farmer; Luke Speed at Curtis Brown; my family; my friends; my fellow Orenda authors, who have welcomed me into the fold; Karen Sullivan, the eternal, unrelenting and gracious heart at the core of the organisation; West Camel, the man of eternal patience and editor extraordinaire; and Mark Swan, the genius of cover design.

Thanks also to Lesley Roll, Helen at Forum Books, and all the other authors, too numerous to mention, who have encouraged and graced me with their wonderful company (on panels as well as beating me at football!).

A special mention must go to the phenomenal book bloggers who bequeath us wings out of their love of literature.

And as always, my boy Harry. It's all for you…
Everything.